Dear Reader,

Arabesque is plea.................................um-
mer series: four rom.............................. of
beach resorts frequen........................ ......lude
Martha's Vineyard, M............. ....land Beach, Maryland; Idlewild Lake in ....igan; and Sag Harbor, New York.
The heroines in each novel are all Howard University alum-
nae who belonged to the same Alpha Delta X sorority in
college.

Each Sizzling Sands novel introduces you to one of the
Alpha Delta X sorors. In the first novel, **Lady in Red**, Scar-
let "Carly" Thompson is a cosmetics company CEO who
finds adventure and romance on Martha's Vineyard. Next, in
Southern Comfort, we meet Rachel Givens, a jewelry designer drawn to Highland Beach where romance and mystery
unfold. In the third novel, **Last Chance at Love**, journalist
Allison Wakefield finds love and passion while visiting
Idlewild Lake. And in **Dare to Dream**, painter Desiree Arm-
strong looks to recuperate in Sag Harbor after a fire destroys
her gallery and her spirit, but instead finds an old flame.

With marquee romance authors **Deirdre Savoy**, **Sandra
Kitt**, **Gwynne Forster** and **Donna Hill** contributing to this
series, we know you'll enjoy the passion and sizzle of this
hot summer series, one of the best in Arabesque's decade of
publishing romances.

We welcome your comments and feedback, and invite you
to send us an e-mail at www.bet.com/books/betbooks.

Enjoy,
Evette Potter
Editor, Arabesque Books

FREDERICK DOUGLASS MUSEUM
& CULTURAL CENTER

**Don't miss this exceptional museum and its wonderful
Douglass collection on your next trip to Maryland!**

Charles Douglass built *Twin Oaks* for his father, famed abolitionist
Frederick Douglass. It was one of the first cottages built in Highland
Beach. *Twin Oaks* now houses the Museum and Cultural Center, which
includes priceless artifacts and memorabilia. The view from the balcony
was specially built at Douglass's request, *"so that I as a free man could
look across the Bay to the Eastern Shore where I was born a slave."*

Highland Beach was founded in 1893 by the Douglass family and char-
tered in 1922 as the first African-American township in the state of
Maryland, and remains as the only other municipality in Anne Arundel
County, Maryland.

Support of this cultural institution is critical to develop new educa-
tional curriculum, as well as preserve *Twin Oaks* and artifacts of the
Douglass family and one of America's most famous sons. This cultural
center welcomes group tours of families, church groups and education
organizations. Open by appointment only.

__Yes, I'd like to support the FREDERICK DOUGLASS MUSEUM &
CULTURAL CENTER. Enclosed is my one-year contribution of
$25.00.

__Contact me about:
   __Corporate Support   __Group tours

Name _____

Address _____

Address _____

City/State/Zip _____

Phone _____ E-Mail _____

3200 Wayman Avenue, Annapolis, MD 21403   (410) 267-6960

Sandra Kitt

Southern Comfort

BET Publications, LLC
http://www.bet.com
http://www.arabesquebooks.com

Southern Comfort is a work of fiction, and is not intended to provide an exact representation of life, or any known persons on the fabled shores of Highland Beach, Maryland. The author has taken creative license in development of the characters and plot of the story, although historical facts and sites referenced may be actual. The cover photography is meant to evoke beach life in Highland Beach, and may not be an exact representation of the shore or evirons. The sorority, Alpha Delta X, is fictitious and does not represent as fact any know woman's service organization. BET Books/ Arabesque develops contemporary works of romance fiction for enterainment purposes only.

ARABESQUE BOOKS are published by

BET Publications, LLC
c/o BET BOOKS
One BET Plaza
1900 W Place NE
Washington, DC 20018-1211

Copyright © 2004 by Sandra Kitt

First Printing: July 2004
10 9 8 7 6 5 4 3 2 1

Printed in the United States of America

To all the intrepid early settlers of Highland Beach, from Charles Douglass, son of Frederick Douglass, to Mrs. Bertha McMurdock, a longtime homeowner, your history inspired me.

ACKNOWLEDGMENTS

Many thanks to all the residents of Highland Beach who graciously hosted my visit while researching *Southern Comfort*. And to my agent Lisa Erbach Vance for her support.

One

It was close to dusk as Lucas maneuvered to the right lane and signaled for the approaching exit from the New Jersey Turnpike. He couldn't help but calculate that, had he continued southbound, he would be in DC in another two hours. Tired from two late performances the night before and a day of business, he was ready to get home. He knew, however, that he couldn't ignore the urgent request in his grandfather's voice when he asked Lucas to stop by their house on his way to DC. His grandfather assured him there was no personal emergency but that there was something important that needed to be discussed.

After paying the toll, Lucas made the rest of the two-mile drive through the Philadelphia suburbs where he'd been raised. He was always surprised by how little they seemed to change. Finally he parked in his grandparent's driveway outside their split-level cape. While he grabbed his duffel bag and saxophone from the trunk, the neighbor's dog, an aging Rottweiler, began to bark loudly as it trotted from the back of the house next door to investigate his arrival. The dog's size and growl made him seem particularly menacing, but Lucas gave a low whistle of greeting to the animal and leaned down to briefly pat its rump. The Rottweiler stopped barking and began to wag the stump of his tail in recognition.

"Good boy, Brody," Lucas said affectionately. "Now go home," he pointed to the neighbor's house.

The dog made another half-hearted bark and then ambled away.

By the time Lucas reached for the front door, it opened and his grandfather stood in the entrance. It struck Lucas as unusual that his grandfather, and not his grandmother, greeted him.

"Granddad," Lucas addressed the older man, shaking his offered hand and affectionately embracing him, towering over the older man by several inches.

Nicholas Scott was nearing eighty-five but was still in remarkably good health. Tall and lean due mostly to the restricted diet because of his diabetes, he shared his grandson's broad shoulders. He had a full head of wavy hair that had yet to go all white. The hazel eyes behind his glasses were only now beginning to show the symptoms of cataracts, but so far Nicholas had refused the surgery to correct the problem.

"Good to see you, son. Glad you made it okay."

Lucas followed him into the house, where a gray long-haired cat approached to rub against his legs, arching its back and purring loudly. Lucas dropped the duffel to the floor, freeing a hand so he could bend to scratch the cat's head.

"It took me longer than I thought. I ran into a little traffic," he explained, leaving his duffel and instrument case in the foyer.

"I figured, but your grandmother and I were anxious. You know how old people get." Nicholas moved into the living room and sat in a worn leather recliner.

Lucas grinned as he followed, taking a seat on the sofa adjacent to his grandfather. "I don't know what old people you're talking about." He glanced toward the kitchen. "Where's Gram?"

"She's upstairs. She'll . . . be down in a minute," Nicholas murmured, running his hands up and down the arms of his chair. "How did everything go last night when you played?"

"It was great. The club was packed for both sets, and the audience really got into the music. The club invited the group back for a jazz weekend in September."

"So all those music lessons we forced you to take are paying off. The question is, are you making any money playing that sax of yours?"

Lucas smiled. "I'm doing okay, Nick. I know you and Gram worry about me becoming a starving artist and all that, but it won't happen. I was a lawyer for almost fifteen years, and I was able to me sock away enough to carry me for quite a while."

"Gram and I were worried that maybe this whole wanting to be a first-class sax player wasn't a good idea. Thirty-eight seemed a little late to be taking chances with your future."

"I can always go back to litigation, but I don't think it'll come to that."

"Glad to hear that," Nicholas said. He crossed and uncrossed his legs, moving about restlessly.

"I'd been thinking about doing this for a while. I had to try to see if I had it in me to be a first-rate musician. Playing the sax gives me something that law didn't."

"But you're a good attorney, Lucas."

Lucas grinned. "Thanks for saying so, but you're a little biased. There's a part of me that needs what performing gives. I don't know if you can understand that."

"I understand that it makes you happy. That's mostly what we care about." Nicholas cleared his throat. "Have you eaten? We're done with dinner, but your grandmother saved you a plate."

"I'm good. Unless Gram has some of her lemon pound cake," Lucas hinted hopefully.

Nick chuckled. "I'm sure you'll find something in the kitchen."

Lucas finally focused on his grandfather's nervous movements. He seemed distracted and ill at ease. That, along with the fact that his grandmother had not yet appeared to greet him, now had his full attention. Something was wrong.

He bent forward and touched his grandfather on the back of his hand. The restless movement stopped, and he was taken by surprise when his grandfather suddenly grasped his hand tightly. Lucas felt the strength in the aging fingers, but also the intuitive love. Touching his grandfather got the older man's attention, and for a long moment Lucas could look directly into his eyes.

"Is everything okay? It's not Gram, is it?" he asked, a thread of apprehension pulled at his heart.

"No, no," Nicholas was quick to assure his grandson.

Finally, Lucas could hear the sound of footsteps coming down the staircase. He stood up. "Gram?"

"Yes, honey. I'm on my way."

Lucas relaxed when his grandmother responded, her voice a bit raspy with age. Nick also stood up, almost in relief, Lucas observed, as Kay Scott appeared in the living-room entrance carrying what looked like a gift box covered in pink moire silk against her chest.

She was only a little shorter than her husband and still carried herself with an erect, elegant grace. Her hair was tastefully colored an ash blond, not out of style with her age, and it was generally agreed that she looked far younger than her eighty years.

"Let me take that," Lucas said, relieving his grandmother of the box and placing it on the coffee table. She held her arms open, and he wrapped her in a hug, kissing the top of her head.

Kay seated herself next to her grandson, patting his arm and exchanging a quick glance with her husband. "I know you're wondering what this is all about," she began.

"I was a little worried," Lucas agreed. "I can't remember you ever calling me on my cell phone before," Lucas said.

"I hate them myself," Kay scoffed. "But this is one of those times when I have to say I'm glad you carry one."

Surprised, Lucas looked closely at his grandfather. He seemed to have withdrawn somewhat into his own thoughts and was content to let his wife explain the summons that had led to this detour.

"Gram," Lucas began, more confused than ever.

She looped her arm through his. It was shaking slightly. "Everyone's fine, Lucas. Your father's okay, and your aunt and uncle and cousins and their kids. Everyone's fine, I promise. It's your mother," Kay said clearly.

Lucas experienced an immediate reaction in his gut, a roiling in his stomach and a tightening of every muscle in his body. He felt his grandmother squeeze his arm protectively as she watched him closely while he, trying to register her ominous opening, turned his attention to the photographs that were carefully arranged on a console table.

The photographs were of himself, his father, his grandparents, his cousins, and his friends. He examined in particular his younger self, aware, as always, of the stark difference between himself and the rest of the family. They had light brown, blond, or in a few cases, auburn hair. They had gray, green, or blue eyes. They all had white skin. But he was different. The color of his eyes were virtually the only thing that marked him as a Scott. Lucas's hair was almost black, coarse but with a slight wave. His nose was long but slightly wider, his lips fuller, and his face more sculptured. More than anything, it was his skin color that set him apart. Light mocha, it was a cross between that of his white father and his black mother. He didn't remember anything about her.

"Julia," Lucas said awkwardly. "What about her?"

His grandfather cleared his throat and sat forward in his chair. "We got a call—"

"From Julia?" Lucas asked, not with surprise but as a point of information.

"From your father," Nicholas corrected.

His grandmother tightened her grasp on his arm. "Brad called to say he'd heard from an attorney down in DC. Lucas, your mother passed away this morning."

Lucas continued to stare at his grandmother because he didn't know what else to do. A shock wave rippled through his body. He felt a tingling in his hands and feet, a ringing sensation in his ears. Then nothing.

He could see his grandmother's eyes begin to fill with tears, and that surprised him more. He accepted that the news was sad, but there was no need for his grandmother to get upset. He wasn't going to. He couldn't.

"Julia died at her home in Highland Beach. I'm so sorry, Lucas," she whispered, her chin trembling.

"I'm alright." Lucas placed his arm around her shoulders.

"We wanted you to hear the news from us or your father, and not your mother's attorney," Nick explained.

Lucas closed his eyes, trying to block out an unexpected looping of images in his head. "Why didn't Dad call me himself?"

"Brad took the news very hard," Kay said softly.

"Did he?" Lucas asked blankly.

"I don't think he ever got over your mother. The breakup . . . and everything that happened after."

Lucas wasn't listening. He was trying to stop the rapid-fire playback of his memories. They were few and very blurred.

"What happened?" he asked.

"Your father would never tell us what caused the split, but I know—"

Lucas shook his head. "No. I mean, what happened to Julia? How did she die?"

Kay look bewildered. "We don't know exactly. We were

only told that she'd been ill for about six months. Brad probably knows but I . . . I don't think I want to ask him just yet."

"The attorney asked that you call him," Nick said.

"Why should I talk with her lawyer?" His sharp tone drew both his grandparents' focus. "What difference is it going to make now?"

"I believe he said there are some legal issues to clear up. Maybe Julia left you a message. Maybe . . . she knew she was dying and didn't want to leave things unsettled," Nick suggested.

"Oh, I hope so," Kay said fervently.

"She's about thirty years too late," Lucas said coldly.

"Lucas, you were a little boy. There's so much that happened, so much you don't know and don't understand about Julia. You have to talk to the lawyer. Please promise that you'll go." Kay asked earnestly.

Lucas stood up abruptly. "I don't know."

His grandfather got up from his recliner to stand next to Lucas. "Son, you need to understand that what happened years ago wasn't only your mother's fault. Things got . . . complicated. All of us were guilty. We all did what we thought was the right thing for you at the time. Brad, me, and your Gram. Even your mother, though you might not believe that.

"Now, I assured the lawyer that you'd get in touch with him tomorrow when you get back to DC," Nicholas said, with a stern directive that had always worked on his grandson when he was a teenager. "Stay here tonight. You can finish your trip home in the morning after you've had some sleep and have had some time to take all this in."

Kay lifted the box she'd brought with her and held it out to Lucas. "I've been saving this for you since you were in high school."

"What's in it?" Lucas asked, staring at the box but not making any move to take it from her.

"Some things that . . . belonged to Julia."

"I don't want it."

She held the box out again. "Please, Lucas."

It was the plaintive tone of her voice that caused him to reluctantly take it, not any curiosity about what was inside.

"And you'll go see the lawyer tomorrow?" his grandfather asked.

Despite his private objections, Lucas nodded. "I'll call him when I get home."

The look of relief on his grandparents' face was palpable. They trusted that he'd keep his word, and now he had to.

"I'm going to take my stuff upstairs," he said quietly, staring at the box in his hand.

"Yes, that's a good idea." Kay reached up to cup her cool hands around Lucas's face. He was forced to bend his 6'1" frame to accommodate her kiss on his cheek. "Come back down when you're ready. I'll make fresh coffee, and you can have some carrot cake. I know it's one of your favorites."

Lucas tried to smile at his grandmother's offer. He said no more as he got his duffel bag, lifted his sax case, and headed up the stairs. His grandparents stood transfixed, listening until they heard the quiet closing of his bedroom door. There were no other sounds to be heard.

Kay started toward the staircase. "I think I'll go and make sure he's okay."

Her husband gently grabbed her arm. "Leave him alone, Kay. It's time to step back and let Lucas get through this by himself. Maybe he's right when he says it's too late."

Her expression was deeply troubled and fearful. "Did we do the right thing?"

He shrugged helplessly. "I don't know."

It was late the following morning when the sudden ringing of his cell phone woke Lucas up from a sound sleep. The regular phone would have been easier to ignore, but his cell phone was meant as a shortcut to reach him when all else failed. He groaned in protest when he looked at the digital clock and noted that he'd only gotten two hours of rest since arriving back in DC. He blindly searched for the phone, checked caller ID, and flipped it open.

"Hello, Jen," he croaked, sounding like he'd been dead to the world just moments before.

"Where are you?"

Lucas closed his eyes but tried to stay awake. "I'm in bed."

"I tried calling you at 7:30 this morning. Why didn't you answer the phone?"

"I only got home a couple of hours ago," Lucas explained. He lay on his back, sprawled in the middle of his bed. "I turned the ringer off so I could sleep." He yawned expansively.

"I thought you were due home last night, Sunday. What happened?"

Lucas's eyes struggled open and he stared at the ceiling. They burned from lack of sleep, but he was awake now. Jennifer Cameron had been one of his best friends since they attended law school together at Yale. But that didn't necessarily mean she had the right to know every single thing about his personal life. He didn't particularly want to reveal the news he'd received about his mother. That would mean having to deal with it himself, and he wasn't ready.

"Nothing happened in New York. The gig was good. I made a stop at my grandparent's house and . . . I decided to stay the night, that's all."

But that wasn't all. He had to call Julia's lawyer. He needed to call his father. He had to find a way to reconcile the fact that his mother was dead with the fact that he didn't know how he felt about it. He rubbed his hand across his rough whiskers, trying to subdue the turmoil in the pit of his stomach.

"What's so urgent that you have to track me down this early, Jen?"

"Only a former attorney would call ten o'clock on a Monday morning early. I've already done half a day's work. One of the partners dumped a case on me. It's not what I usually handle. I think he's trying to get back at me for a complaint I voiced about having to take work home at night—"

Exasperation crept into his voice. "Jen, how many times have I told you you have to pick your battles? Is it worth going to the mat over a few extra hours after five? So you're a little late to dinner or getting to the gym. The partners only remember the people who put in the time and don't complain."

"I know, Lucas, don't get angry with me. It just made me mad that Brian, who's my age and thinks he been personally anointed by God, is the one rubbing this stuff in my face."

Lucas propped his pillows into an elevated position for his head. He tried to listen and follow the urgency of Jennifer Cameron's grievance, but they didn't hold a candle to what he had had to deal with the night before.

"Listen to me. You have to learn how to play this. This Brian guy is just trying to put you in your place. A, you're a woman, so he has to be careful about harassment, and I'm not talking the sexual kind. B, you're white so he can't get you on that bias. He's either threatened by you, or he's trying to embarrass you. You have to figure out which and why, and deal with it. You can get back at the firm by billing for the overtime; that's standard. They're only going to pass the charge along to the client. You know that."

"You make it sound so easy," she complained.

Lucas yawned again, suddenly spotting the pink fabric box which he'd left on his dresser when he'd gotten home earlier. It reminded him of everything that was on his mind. He didn't have time to hold Jennifer's hand. "It *is* easy. You're dealing with civil law, not life-or-death criminal cases," he said a bit

impatiently. "Pace yourself. And lighten up. What you probably need is a date. Someone to take your mind off the office
politics. You take it too seriously."

"I'd love to have a date with you. Are you volunteering?"
she asked, laughing.

"And ruin a great friendship?"

"I don't see why we can't have both. We could be best
friends and lovers," she suggested.

Lucas chuckled silently. "Ain't no such animal."

"I'm betting you'll change your mind one of these days."

"That's a woman's prerogative, not mine," he teased, swing-
ing his long legs out of bed and sitting on the edge of the
mattress. "What's the case about?"

"It looks like a bias issue, and that's your expertise. I really
do want to get some input from you."

"I'm not practicing law right now, remember?"

"I'm not asking you to. I just want the benefit of your
experience. I thought maybe we could meet for lunch today."

"I can't."

"Or maybe later for drinks or dinner?"

"Not today. I . . . I have something personal to take care of."

"Oh? Is it anything I can help you with?"

"Not this time. Thanks for the offer. And now that I'm
awake, thanks to you, I'd better get moving."

"I can take a hint. I'll let you know how things work out
with Brian. Can I still pick your brains if I need to on this
case?" she asked.

"Sure. Give me a call later in the week, okay?"

"Sounds great, thanks. Love ya much. Talk with you soon."

As soon as the call ended, Lucas tossed the cell phone on
the bed and headed for the shower. He instantly turned his attention to the news from the night before. He'd spent a
sleepless night waiting for the usual response: deep sorrow
and pain, maybe a rush of memories and reflections, a surge
of mourning and grief. None of it ever happened. Instead,

he'd wrestled with rage that eventually drained him, leaving only a bone-deep weariness in its place. And he felt empty. Like there was a hole in the center of his life.

When he finished his shower, Lucas called his grandparents to assure them he'd gotten home safely. The second call he made was to the law offices of Whitlock, Lehane and Harris. He made an appointment to go in and discuss his late mother's affairs. But before he did anything else, he felt that he needed to find a resolution to his own conflicting emotions, and relief from the pressing tightness in the middle of his chest. He felt the desire to destroy something. Instead, he channeled that feeling into doing something creative and calming.

He'd laid soundproofing on the walls of the second bedroom in his condominium so that he could close himself in with his music and his practice. Although Jennifer had been trying to talk him into doing yoga or Pilates for years, Lucas had decided that he got similar benefits from playing his sax. He was about eight when he developed an interest in the saxophone. In part, it was an attempt to thwart his grandmother's insistence that he take piano lessons. But mostly he'd been influenced by a musician who'd been a frequent customer in his father's first Manhattan restaurant, called Peacock Alley.

Lucas recalled how, on weekend visits to his father in New York, he'd loved being allowed to stay up late on Friday nights, hanging around the restaurant and being indulged by the staff and guests. It was especially fun, after the restaurant had closed, to observe the special people in his father's inner circle who sat around drinking coffee and playing impromptu sets on thier instruments to entertain each other. He'd liked the shiny horn played by Jones. He'd liked the way Jones played with his eyes closed, and how he seemed to be far away in another world with his music.

Removing his saxophone carefully, Lucas stood in his practice room facing the window. Not so close that he was aware of the neighborhood or people, but back far enough to see nothing but sky. He blew air into the cavity, like deep breathing, and produced sounds to soothe his troubled soul. He improvised and exercised on the buttons in his own unique form of meditation, the resulting music connecting him and keeping him real in ways he hadn't been able to find in law or in friends, or his family . . . or in relationships. In his music Lucas had always found peace, even if he knew it to be only temporary.

Two hours later when he walked into Kenneth Lehane's office, he was composed and focused.

"Lucas Scott," he said, shaking hands with the middle-aged attorney.

"First of all, I want to express my sincere regrets at the passing of your, er, mother," Lehane said, openly studying him.

"Thank you," Lucas responded stiffly. He was completely aware throughout the introductions that Kenneth Lehane had seized on the fact that he did not look like Julia. Even past her death, Julia was keeping secrets.

The two men sat down.

"Once she was diagnosed with cancer and told there was nothing to be done, Ms. Winters contacted me about her estate," the attorney explained.

Lucas wasn't sure which he was reacting to the most—the news that Julia had terminal cancer, or that even though she knew she was dying she'd made no attempt to contact him.

"I know you're an attorney, Mr. Scott, so you understand how these things work. It's all a formality at this point. You've been appointed as your mother's executor and are also named a beneficiary. Ms. Winters left instructions about what she wanted done after her death. A private burial service. No flowers, no viewing, nothing." Lehane glanced at Lucas. "I assume you'll take care of the arrangements?"

Lucas felt his jaw tighten, his body already objecting to all the visceral havoc that he would have to withstand. He silently nodded.

"I've had inquiries from Ms. Winter's friends and professional associates. What would you like me to tell them?"

"I'll get back to you on that," Lucas murmured.

"Fine. I have a folder of information you can take with you to review at your leisure," Lehane said, handing a thick legal envelope to Lucas.

"What kind of information?" Lucas asked, reluctantly taking the papers.

"Oh, insurance policies. Management statements from whatever stocks and bonds Ms. Winters owned. Statements from several bank accounts."

"I don't think she intended for me to have this," Lucas said, handing the folder back.

Lehane ignored him. "I think she did. Ms. Winters was a smart woman, Mr. Scott. She also got wiser as she got older," he said significantly. "You can tell me what you think at the reading of her will. It will be held here in my office. There are only a few other beneficiaries besides yourself. Mrs. Marguerite Santiago, Ms. Winters's caregiver, and Rachel Givens."

"Rachel Givens?" Lucas asked.

"Do you know Ms. Givens?"

"No, never heard of her. Nor Mrs. Santiago. Do you know Ms. Givens's relationship to Julia?"

"In early conversations she mentioned that she was very fond of Ms. Givens and had a special relationship with her. Your mother knew Ms. Givens from her summers on Highland Beach in Maryland. That's where Ms. Winters owned her home."

Lucas felt another stab to his gut. "There's still a probate procedure, correct?"

"That's right. But Ms. Winters was a careful woman about her holdings. She had no intentions of letting the state benefit from her assets," Lehane said dryly. "It's all spelled out in her will. Now, this . . ." He reached over to remove a small black book from a pile of legal documents on his desk. "I was also instructed to give you this."

"Her address book?" Lucas identified it, idly leafing through the pages.

"That's right."

Almost instinctively, Lucas found himself thumbing through to the S section. He stared at his name and current address. Before that was his grandparents' address, and his father's. It was a surprise that Julia had current information on his whereabouts. He continued to flip through the pages. To his surprise, several were well-known people in the entertainment field.

"Shouldn't this stuff go to my father?" Lucas asked, beginning to feel uncomfortable. It was too much, too soon. Or was it too late?

"I'm following her specific instructions," Lehane informed Lucas.

Lucas moistened his lips and shifted uneasily in his chair. The attorney gave him a sympathetic look.

"I know this is a lot to deal with suddenly, especially while you're grieving."

"You don't understand," Lucas said. But he couldn't explain what he was actually feeling.

"This will be over soon. I'll have my secretary confirm the date and time for the reading of the will."

Feeling dazed, Lucas stood, shook hands with Lehane, and left the attorney's office with the manila envelope. He drove aimlessly for more than an hour, processing years of denials and ill will until he was worn out from just thinking. He had no interest in the official policies and certificates and bank books belonging to Julia Winters. He didn't know what he was supposed to do with her personal address book, filled with names of people who knew her, admired her, and probably loved her. He was deeply jealous of all of them.

Lucas remembered what his grandmother Kay had said to him the night before, about how his father had taken the news of Julia's death very hard. His father was so upset that he had recruited his own parents to break the news to Lucas. But when Lucas thought about it, he couldn't recall a single occasion when he and his father had had any discussion about Julia. It was as if they'd entered into a silent agreement not to because she was not a part of their lives. She didn't exist. Lucas had to wonder now how his own feelings about Julia might be different if he and his father had been more open with each other.

On impulse, Lucas looked around for a safe place to pull his car over out of traffic. Then he located his cell phone, dialed a number, and waited for a response.

"Hello."

He was taken aback by the sound of his father's voice. Usually upbeat and easy, his tone was filled with the cadence and weight of despair. "Dad, it's Lucas."

"Lucas," Brad Scott repeated, a catch in his throat.

Lucas heard more than the emotion of loss in the sound of his name, but he couldn't interpret it. Was it relief? Regret?

"I heard the news. I stopped by Nick and Kay's last night on my way home."

"I should have called you myself."

"Dad, it's okay," he assured his father. He found it awkward and painful to listen to his father's grief. He wasn't sure what to say to comfort him.

Brad cleared his throat. "Sorry I missed your gig last night. How did it go?"

"Fine, fine. When you didn't show up like you usually do, I figured you got hung up at work."

"I was there when I got the call from this woman who told

me she took care of your mother while she was sick. Julia left instructions that I was to be notified if . . . if anything happened to her."

Lucas clenched his jaw tightly as he listened helplessly. His father needed empathy, and he wasn't sure he could give it.

"I didn't realize you were still in touch with her."

"I was."

"How long?" He could detect his father's hesitation.

"Always. Lucas, your mother and I didn't hate each other just because we got divorced."

"You never talked about her. I believed otherwise."

"I know, I know," Brad sighed. "I always wanted to say something. Julia wouldn't let me. She felt very strongly about . . . about interfering in your life, especially as you grew older."

"Why?"

"She was afraid. She was sure you hated her."

Lucas swallowed, holding back the infantile rage that would have him say she'd been right. It was true when he was seven, and twelve, and eighteen. Then the feelings had turned to indifference.

"Does that mean you talked about me to her?"

"She always wanted to know how you were doing. How tall you'd grown, how you were doing in school. You know . . . things like that."

"Things a mother would be interested in. She could have called at any time and asked me herself. She could have stayed."

"The story is not that black and white."

"No pun intended," Lucas said sarcastically.

"Absolutely none," Brad said with sudden spirit. "Julia doesn't deserve that."

"Dad, I didn't call to get you upset. I didn't call to talk about Julia—"

"She was your mother, Lucas," Brad interrupted sadly.

"It never felt like I had a mother. I never knew her and now it doesn't matter. Listen, I just wanted to make sure you're okay."

"Yeah, I'll be okay. I appreciate the concern. What about you? How are you doing?" Brad asked.

"I'm good," he said smoothly. "The other reason I'm calling is to let you know I'll take care of the funeral arrangements."

"You . . . You'll do that?"

"I thought this way would make it easier for you."

"But, I know how you feel—"

"What I feel isn't important right now. I'll call when everything's arranged. Come down and stay with me a few days," Lucas said.

"Yeah, that's a good idea. I'd like that. We should spend some time together," Brad said.

"Mind if I ask you a personal question?"

"Of course not. Go ahead."

"You never stopped loving Julia, did you?"

"No. I never did."

Lucas finished the call to his father, but sat for a time. Hearing that his father had continued to love Julia for the past thirty years came as a total surprise. But it was a revelation that provided little balm to years of his own disappointment and anger. He also realized that he might feel cheated of a rightful place in Julia's life, abandoned by her as a child, but the fact still remained that he was her son, and she was his mother. He could either claim that right, or truly lose her forever.

He called Lehane from his cell phone.

"I've decided there needs to be a memorial service for Julia separate from the funeral. I'll return her address book to you. Will you send out the invitations through your office?"

"I'd be happy to," Lehane agreed. "Anything else?"

"I'd also like you to contact the local papers. I want them

to run an obituary. One more thing," Lucas said quietly. "Is it possible for me to get access to her house? I want to see where she lived, and what was so special about Highland Beach."

Two

"Excuse me."

Rachel Givens barely heard the shouted apology from a tall, black CEO type who roughly bumped her shoulder as she tried to squeeze through the tight and noisy crowd pressed together in the small Soho gallery.

The din of conversation was also deafening. No matter which direction Rachel turned, there were people hindering her movement and vision.

It was typical New York City and very exciting, which was why she wanted to live here. Rachel used to love it. After all, gallery opening nights were not about the work. They were about who showed up . . . and with whom. She searched the crowded room hoping to find Malika Mbunta, aka Alicia Glover, a friend, neighbor, and fellow artist who'd invited her to the opening. Rachel had met Malika when she'd first moved to New York nearly eight years ago. Both had been exhibitors at the summer outdoor crafts fair on Columbus Avenue. The fact that Malika got along with one of her best college friends, Desiree, was a plus. She'd studied art with Desiree at Howard University, and Desiree also lived in New York. The three of them sometimes hung out together. Although she was a perpetual graduate student cum painter/dancer/bookstore clerk, Malika's social connections put her on the right A-list of black folks who were invited to artsy professional events in the city. Right now, though, Rachel couldn't see her anywhere in the crowd.

She pushed her way through the throng, hoping to at least get closer to the artwork on display at the exhibition. The artist was certainly talented. One painting in particular caught her attention, and she stopped to examine the composition. It was mounted at eye level on the pristine white wall. Almost six feet long but only sixteen inches high, it was a simple landscape of a barren flatland. A few brush strokes indicated a small cluster of trees at one end of the canvas. A thin strip of blue-green suggested water flowing in front of the trees. The colors were muted and soft. Something about the painting reminded her of Highland Beach, Maryland. Set right on the western shores of the Chesapeake Bay, Highland Beach had been a wonderland of beauty, serenity, and endless days of sunshine. Rachel fondly recalled the many summers her family had spent there, and of course she'd never forgotten Julia Winters, whom she'd met when she was eight.

Rachel liked the painting because it spoke to her of those memories. She knew that the picture was probably expensive, but even if she could afford to buy it Rachel was sure she didn't have a single wall in her apartment that could accommodate the length, nor would anyone be able to stand back far enough in her apartment to appreciate its subtlety.

She turned away, once more looking for Malika, but enjoying people watching as well. As much as Rachel welcomed the opportunity to see fresh and innovative art, she was equally drawn to the variety of people who migrated to the black art scene.

"Rachel! Hey, girl. Come here. Come here. I want you to meet some folks from my printmaking class."

Rachel pivoted to see a short, rotund, dark-skinned black woman beckoning to her.

She tried to move toward Malika, only to nearly collide

with someone gesturing with a filled glass of red wine. Adroitly, Rachel ducked under the outstretched arm, avoiding an accident. Red wine left stains, and she didn't want stains all over her favorite Eileen Fisher off-white sheath.

"Hey, everyone, this is my friend, Rachel Givens," Malika said as Rachel joined them.

Rachel smiled and said a quiet hello through Malika's introductions, then promptly forgot everyone's names. The two women and one man were discussing an artist with whom she wasn't familiar. So instead she admired the middle-aged black man with long iron-gray dreads with cowrie shells attached on the ends. One of the women had dyed her hair platinum blond, which contrasted sharply with her black lipstick. Although Rachel tried to listen and catch up with the discussion, her attention began to wander. Her gaze sought out the painting she'd admired. She was instantly swept up in another recall of Highland Beach. She hadn't been there in years.

"I love that necklace you're wearing," one of the women finally commented, bringing Rachel's attention back to the group.

"Rachel designed it," Malika said. "Earrings, too. You should see her stuff. She's good."

"It's so unusual," the woman continued.

"Thank you," Rachel smiled.

She automatically fingered the necklace, made of multiple strands of same-sized beads in varying shades of orange. The strands were attached at the ends to the clasp mechanism, and she'd then twisted the strands together for effect.

"I wish I could wear things like that," the second woman commented, "You're tall and can carry it off. My neck is short and squat."

"I'm not that tall," Rachel said. "Only 5' 6". And it's not the length of your neck, but the size of what you put around it that makes the difference."

"Is that what do you do for a living?" the lone man in the gathering asked.

"Yes, I'm an artist. I design jewelry."

He pointed to her necklace. "Is it possible to make real money with handmade work?"

"I do okay," Rachel said. "I make special one-of-a-kind high-end pieces. I also have a costume line that I contract out to a consortium of women in South Carolina. They mass-produce some of my designs for the larger retail chains."

The conversation then turned to the merits of the work by the artist whose show opening they were all attending. Malika pulled Rachel aside.

"I thought maybe you weren't going to show up after all," Malika said to Rachel. "Where's Desiree? Did you invite her to come to the show?"

"I did, but she couldn't make it. She's busy trying to get her own gallery opened before the end of the summer, and she's running into a lot of problems."

"Soho could use more black-owned galleries. Anyway, I'm glad you didn't stand me up," Malika said.

"Actually, I've been here about twenty minutes. I didn't see you when I came in, so I walked through the exhibit, just in case I met the artist and he asked me questions about his work."

The dreadlocks gathered at the top of Malika's head shook as she chuckled, her mouth with its blackberry lip gloss twisting into a knowing grin.

"I can arrange that. I'll introduce you, but Reid Dixon's more likely to ask you out. That's why I wanted you to come tonight. He's cool and he's your type. I told him all about you."

"I'm seeing someone. And I don't have a type. That's like saying *I'm* a type," Rachel said, accepting a glass of wine from a passing waiter.

Malika looked at Rachel over the top of her black-framed glasses. "You are. I call it the talented-and-smart-and-knows-what-she's-doing-who-doesn't-have-time-for-games type."

Rachel grinned. "Okay, I like that."

"Anyway, that guy you know in Italy doesn't count. When was the last time you saw him? You *know* he's got something else going on."

Rachel shrugged. "I like Claudio. He's sweet and fun, and I know he's got women on the side. When he's with me he treats me like I'm the greatest thing since chocolate milk."

"Exactly," Malika began dryly. "I know it's the chocolate part that got his attention. He sees this fine, brown-skinned girl from the US of A with her booty shake and wild-child hair . . . I mean, how many tall, attractive black women are there in Italy? You're exotic."

"Thanks. Anyway, it's not like the black men here are falling all over themselves to beat a path to my door. Let's just say I have less competition in Italy, and that's okay for now. So, which one is Reid?" Rachel asked, sipping from her glass and looking around.

Malika didn't even have to search the room. She turned in the direction of a small cluster of people standing near the door. "Over there," she nodded. "He's the one all in black."

Rachel shifted to give her attention to the man Malika had indicated. She silently observed Reid.

"Isn't he serious?" Malika remarked, admiringly.

"Hmmmm."

"And the guy next to him, the one with the bald head, that's Ken. He owns the gallery around the corner. He's not bad either, right?"

Rachel considered both men. After a minute she was forced to agree with Malika after all. Maybe she *did* have a type. If asked, she would have to confess that she was not attracted to men who had pierced ears, or who shaved their heads or had tattoos. She'd never been into fads. Anyway, Julia Winters once told her that being different from everyone else was more interesting. It made her stand out.

She was saved from further comment by Malika's urging that they join the two men. She hoped that Reid wasn't going to be encouraged to think this could be the start of something new. She had this infallible fifteen-minute rule. That's how long it took for her to know if something had clicked.

Once Malika made introductions, she gave her undivided attention to Ken the gallery owner, leaving Rachel with Reid.

"Welcome to my show," he said. He was nearly shouting in order to be heard over the din of the small space. "What do you think?"

Rachel laughed. "Is this a test? What do I get if I answer correctly?"

Reid pressed his hand dramatically to his chest. "I can offer gratitude and another glass of wine."

"I like your work."

"That was quick. Is this all about that glass of wine?" he teased her.

Reid looked directly at her, but Rachel knew he was also scoping her out. She was flattered. And she forgave Malika for trying to play matchmaker.

"No, I mean it. Your paintings are powerful because they're simple. Very . . . minimal. You don't overwork your paint or the composition. Less is more . . . something like that."

"You actually did go through the exhibit. I'm impressed," Reid murmured. "So, you're not just here to work the room or to see if Naomi Campbell is going to show up."

"I didn't know she was expected."

"She's not. I just wanted to see your reaction. You're a cool lady."

"I'll take that as a compliment," Rachel said, raising one eyebrow in a practiced way and taking another sip of her wine.

A grin formed on Reid's lips. "Malika was also right about the dimple in your chin."

Rachel forced herself not to self-consciously touch the the cleft inherited from her father. "Malika calls it a dent."

Reid crossed his arms over his chest and raised a hand to stroke his jaw and chin. "Do you have a favorite painting? A best of show, so to speak?"

"Actually, I do." She turned to point briefly to a corner of the gallery. "The long one over there."

He lightly touched her arm. "Come and show me."

He smoothly guided Rachel through the crowd and stopped in front of the painting, entitled "Long Day's Journey."

"You don't think it looks too stark?" Reid asked her.

"That's what I like about it. It reminds me of a place I used to go for the summer when I was growing up. Highland Beach in Maryland. I loved it there."

"Isn't that some sort of black resort? I can't recall the history."

"I haven't been there since I was about thirteen, but I read many years after I last visited that what's now known as Highland Beach was land purchased and settled by one of Frederick Douglass's sons after he and his wife were turned away by a white resort near Annapolis. Sorry. You should have stopped me from boring you with a black history lesson."

"I don't mind. You make it sound like an interesting place."

"Oh, yes. It's a very special place for me."

"So, why haven't you been back?"

Rachel shrugged, her eyes wistful with the idea. "I don't know. It just never happened. I always thought that one day maybe I could afford to buy a house and live there all the time. I became very close to a woman who lives there. I'd like to be able to see her again. And the beach." She pointed to Reid's painting. "When I look at this I get the same feeling I used to get from visiting that little community on the Chesapeake Bay."

"And it doesn't bother you that my paintings don't have a clear Afrocentric theme?" he asked

"Do you feel you need one?"

Reid looked around the crowded room. "There are people here who will be happy to tell you that this is not black art. A lot of my work will probably sell to white collectors."

"Do you care as long as whoever buys your work loves it?"

"I like to think my own people appreciate my view of life," Reid said. "Like the artist Richard Mayhew."

"I sometimes get the same comments about my work," Rachel admitted.

"Malika said you're a designer. Jewelry and other accessories."

Rachel laughed. "I'm going to have to pay her a commission."

"Tell you what. Let's make a deal," Reid said suddenly.

"A deal? What kind of deal?"

"My mother's sixtieth birthday is coming up at the end of the summer. I can only give her so many of my paintings, and she's running out of wall space. Malika said your things are very popular and in demand. I'd like to give my mother something of yours that's original. Like what you're wearing."

"If you're serious about buying something I'll be happy to show you more of my—"

Reid was shaking his head. "No, no, I don't want to buy anything."

"Excuse me?" Rachel asked.

"I'll give you this painting if you're willing to give me one of your designs for my mom."

"I think your painting is worth much more than anything I could make," she said to him.

"It's only worth what someone is willing to pay for it. Or if it has a special meaning, like it has for you." Reid held out his hand to her. "So, do we have a deal?"

She looked at his hand and finally took it. "Okay, if you're serious. Deal."

"I'll hold the painting for you until after the show closes." Reid was still holding her hand.

Rachel gently pulled it free under the guise of searching for a business card in her shoulder bag. "You can call me when you're ready to see some of my work," she said, handing him the card. "I'm leaving on a business trip in a few days, so why don't you call me sometime in August?"

Reid absently looked at the card before slipping it into his wallet and giving Rachel one of his own. "Malika said you're originally from Maryland."

Rachel smiled. "I'm *still* from Maryland. I only decided to move to New York because it's easier for me to get established as a designer here."

"Rachel hates New York," Malika said, overhearing part of the conversation as she and Ken rejoined them.

"I don't hate New York," Rachel objected. "I just don't want to spend the rest of my life here."

"Look, it's getting too hot in here with all these people. I'm ready to cut out and go find some place to eat," Malika announced, looking to Ken for confirmation.

Reid checked the time. "I've got to hang around here for another thirty minutes until the opening wraps up. It's my show, after all."

"Okay with me. Why don't we all go together when this is over?" Ken suggested.

The group got bigger, however, when Malika also included the three people she was with when Rachel arrived at the gallery. They all stood around exchanging ideas on where they should eat. When Rachel's cell phone rang, she stepped away from the group to take the call.

"Hi, it's Rachel."

"Where are you?" her brother Ross asked as an opening.

"At an exhibit opening in the Village."

"It's noisy."

"Yeah, I know. I'm going to step outside so we can hear each other better. Hang on." She signaled to Malika and walked outside the gallery and away from the door. It was after eight, and the July sun had begun to set. Rachel stood so that she could watch the changing twilight colors as she put the phone back to her ear. "What's going on? How are Jill and the boys?"

"Everyone's great. The boys want to know when you're coming down to visit again. I'm supposed to remind you that you promised them a trip to the zoo."

"I haven't forgotten, but I've been so busy."

"Jill wants you to bring some of your things to her next book club meeting. Those woman love to spend money."

"When I get back from Europe."

"Business or pleasure?"

"Both. I have friends I'll be seeing," she explained.

"Okay. The question is still when are we going to see you?"

"Maybe in August before the kids go back to school."

"I'll let them know." There was an awkward pause, then he said, " Listen, Rae. The real reason why I'm calling is because—"

"Rachel, we're ready to go," Malika interrupted as she and the others exited the gallery.

"Give me a minute," Rachel said before addressing Ross once more. "Okay, what were you saying?"

"Look, why don't I call you when you get home? Maybe that would be better," he offered.

Rachel frowned at his hesitancy. "Ross, is anything wrong? Tell me now."

He paused again before he finally spoke.

"I saw something in the paper that I thought might interest you."

"Yeah?" Rachel coaxed. "Oh, I bet I know what it is. That interview I did a few weeks back when I sold some bracelets to Neiman Marcus—"

"No, Rae. That's not what this is about."

"Okay, sorry. What?"

"It's about Julia Winters," Ross said. "Do you remember her?"

"Of course I remember her. I was just talking about Highland Beach and the last time we went there. I haven't see Julia since I was thirteen."

"Yeah, but you talked about her for years afterward. Julia could do this, and Julia told you that."

"I liked her. She was good to me. So, what's this about her in the paper?"

"Rae, it's not good news. What I read was an obituary. Julia's dead."

Rachel heard the words, but for some reason couldn't immediately process them. What Ross said didn't make any sense. And then it did. "Julia's dead." Gone. Gone home.

She struggled with the very idea. That couldn't be. The last time she'd seen Julia, she was smiling and waving at her from beneath an umbrella. She'd been wearing the earrings Rachel had made for her from beads and wire. That was the image Rachel had kept alive in her mind for all those years since. Julia was too young to be dead. Too beautiful and interesting.

"Rae . . . you still there?"

"Could you say that again? About Julia."

"It says she passed away last weekend after a brief illness. She was sixty-one years old. There's also some stuff about when she was a singer and actress, and it mentions some of the shows she was in. Man, I remember I used to think that was bullshit."

Rachel withdrew into a small space where she was alone with memories but surrounded by the outrageous noise and chaos of New York. All these people walking past her were going places, not realizing what had happened. People who never even knew Julia. Rachel could never understand how someone could be alive and laughing, then literally in a heartbeat they were gone. And life just went right on without them.

"Rachel?"

She always believed that one day she'd see Julia Winters again. They'd spoken often over the years, and Rachel had always sent postcards from her travels to show that she'd done just as Julia had urged her to do. *Be curious about everything. See the world and meet new people.*

"Rae?"

"Wait . . . Ross, wait a minute." She turned to the small group waiting impatiently.

"Come on. We're ready to leave," Malika said, beckoning to her.

"We decided on Zoe." Reid said. "You want to meet us there?" he asked her.

Rachel blinked away the images of Julia. "No. I . . . can't make it. Go on without me. I'm sorry I held you up."

"How come you changed your mind? Is it bad news?" Malika wanted to know.

"Yes, it is. Someone I know passed away. My brother just told me. Look, I'm not up to dinner, okay? I think I'll catch a cab and go on home."

"You sure? I can come with you if you want," Malika offered.

"You don't need to do that." Rachel tried a feeble smile. She felt strangely isolated. "It was nice meeting you all. Enjoy your dinner."

"You sure you'll be alright?" Reid asked solicitously.

"Yes, thank you."

"I've got your number. I'll be calling you," he promised.

"I'll talk to you tomorrow," Malika called out as the group left.

Rachel watched them leave, laughing and lively, before she spoke into the cell phone. "Ross, you still there?"

"Yeah, I'm here. I'm sorry about this."

"I just can't . . . can't believe it." But it was sinking in, and her voice trembled as she talked.

"I had a feeling you were going to take the news hard. I remember how much you liked Julia."

"What about the funeral service?"

"It's over. It was held two days ago at a small church in Prince George's County."

"Oh. Does the obit say anything about family? I can't remember Julia ever talking about her family."

"Well," Ross hesitated. "I'm sure she had someone. You know, cousins or aunts and uncles. It's not a big write-up, Rae."

"Do me a favor and save it for me?"

"Sure, if you want. What are you going to do?" he asked.

"Right now? I don't know. I need to be alone for a while to deal with this. I always thought I'd see her again. I wanted to show her that I'd really become everything she said I could."

"I never realized that Julia Winters made such a huge impact on you," Ross said. "You were only a kid when you first met her.

Rachel felt the tears begin to well up in her eyes, to blur her vision until the background of the city street was awash in light and colors. There were a lot of things Julia had said to her. Taught her. Showed her. But the only one Rachel could recall in that moment of realizing her loss was the very one she wasn't sure she'd ever understood.

"She told me . . . don't be afraid to close my eyes, and leap."

Three days later, as Rachel entered her apartment with two bags of groceries and her portfolio, she heard Claudio Vitali's voice leaving a message on her answering machine. Rachel didn't rush to answer. She knew that Claudio, both her sometime lover and business associate, was calling from Rome to make sure of her expected arrival there the following week. It was late and she was tired. She had no intention of calling anyone.

She leaned her display folio against the wall just inside the entrance and stepped out of her backless sandals. The smoothness of the parquet floors cooled her feet. Almost immediately the phone rang again. Rachel ignored it. *Let the machine get it,* she thought, and headed for the kitchen.

She'd spent most of the day with buyers picking through her sample case while she tried to persuade them to place orders of her work for their shops. She'd had her third interview with Henri Bendel, and she'd also managed to get some of her pieces selected for a spread in *ESSENCE*. Then she'd spent another few hours at her supplier in midtown Manhattan, looking for unique beads and stones to use in her designs. At the end of the day, she'd met with her accountant about the tax implications of selling her work overseas. Her designs were becoming popular in London and Milan. The bad news was the incredible hassle of dealing with customs. And the IRS.

The phone rang again.

"Oh, shut up, " Rachel muttered. She began putting her groceries away and then poured a glass of lemonade from the pitcher she'd made that morning. She was hot and bothered, and not interested in talking to vendors, promoters, licensing firms, or customers. She was especially not in the mood to chat and gossip, or listen to anyone else's problems.

She opened the refrigerator and took out a handful of seedless green grapes from a container, popping several into her mouth. Rachel half listened to and monitored the newest message as it was left on her machine.

"Hello, Ms. Givens. My name is Kenneth Lehane. I'm an

attorney in Washington, DC. I'm calling regarding the estate of Julia Winters. I'd like to—"

Rachel gasped and reached for the cordless extension on the counter. "Hello, hello, this is Rachel Givens."

"Is this a bad time? I tried calling earlier—"

"I just got in," Rachel explained. "I haven't had time to listen to my messages yet. You said you're calling from DC. . . . about Julia Winters?"

"That's right. Unfortunately, Ms. Winters—"

"Yes, I know. I heard that she'd passed away," Rachel said. She still felt a terrible emptiness at the news.

"My law firm represents Ms. Winters' estate. I'm calling to advise you that there will be a memorial service for her on Saturday. You're on the guest list."

"I am? How did you manage to find me? I mean, it's been years since I've seen Julia." She heard the lawyer chuckle quietly.

"It's not that difficult to find out about people, Ms. Givens. I spoke with the folks at Howard University, where you graduated. You're on the alumni roster, and it went from there."

Rachel walked with the phone into her living room and settled into a corner of a plush black leather loveseat.

"You said something about a service?"

"Yes, that's correct. Two PM on Saturday, if you can make it."

"I very much want to attend. But I'm leaving Friday for a business trip. I'll be in Europe for at least two weeks."

"That's unfortunate. I'm sorry you'll miss the memorial. However, I'm also calling for another reason. You're named as a beneficiary in Ms. Winters' will. My office has scheduled a reading and execution of the terms of the will sometime after the memorial. Although it's not absolutely necessary, you really should try to be there."

"I'm in Julia's will?" Rachel asked. "But . . . I don't understand why. I'm not family or anything."

"Was she a good friend?" Lehane asked.

"I always thought of her as my friend but—"

"Would you say that she left some sort of impression on you?"

"I think she did," Rachel said, reflecting.

"And you obviously also left an impression on Ms. Winters. Enough for her to want to provide for you, anyway."

"I was a kid the last time I saw Julia, Mr. Lehane. All those years I knew her, I was just a little girl."

Rachel heard Kenneth Lehane chuckle again.

"Well, here's where I invoke the name of Tina Turner," he said.

"Excuse me? What do you mean?"

"What's age got to do with it?" he asked.

Apparently nothing, Rachel decided after the call. But that wasn't the point.

What she remembered of Julia was fixed in her mind, along with the rest of her childhood experiences. Now those memories were unlikely to ever change because she would have no other image with which to compare them. Had Julia also thought of her for all these years as a little girl, or as the woman she'd become?

To find out that she had left some sort of mark on Julia's life made Rachel feel not only bewildered, but also sad. Because when all was said and done, there was the reality that she was never going to see Julia again.

By the next evening, Rachel's living room had been taken over by small piles of clothing, cosmetics, toiletries, shoes, bags, and other necessities. She stood and looked around at the chaos. There wasn't a single thing she could leave behind. Yet, despite the stuff spread out all over the place, she had the feeling she was forgetting something.

The doorbell rang.

"Coming," Rachel called out, carefully stepping over her

sample portfolio, her digital camera, a sketchbook and case with drawing accoutrement, and heading for the door. She peered through the peephole. Malika was standing in the hall.

"It's almost nine o'clock. How come you didn't call me?" Malika asked, walking past her to look around the cluttered living room.

"This is why. I've got to finish packing. I'm going to be crazed tomorrow before leaving for the airport," Rachel said.

She got down on her knees and reached for a neatly folded stack of tops and skirts to go into her suitcase. But she changed her mind, put them down, and reached for something else.

Malika unceremoniously shoved aside an open toiletry bag and sat on the sofa, watching Rachel pack. "Looks like you're trying to take everything in your closet, girl."

"It's hard to know what the weather is going to be like. That's the problem. It could be rainy in London, but hot, hot, hot in Italy. Pass me that dress, please."

Malika held up the dress, turning it back and forth to examine it. "You're taking this? It's velvet."

"Is it?" Rachel questioned absently. "Oh. Forget it then. Give me those scarves."

Malika handed a wad of silky fabric to Rachel. One scarf got tangled in her bracelets, and she fiddled to release it without getting a run in the delicate material.

"Pretty."

Rachel took the scarf and sat back on her heels to gently examine it. "I'm not big on hats," she began quietly, "but when I was younger, this woman I used to know showed me how to wear a scarf."

"Is that the one you told me about? She died recently?" Malika asked.

Rachel nodded. "Julia gave me this scarf. She told me a pretty scarf could disguise a multitude of bad-hair days. She used to tie it around my head like this," she demonstrated, holding the scarf in place and pivoting her head back and forth for Malika to see.

"I don't even bother," Malika said with a dismissive wave of her hand. "I started my locks because I was tired of killing my hair with chemicals. I keep telling you, you'd look *fabu* with your hair like this."

"I like mine the way it is," Rachel said, touching her relaxed hair, cut to shoulder length but currently twisted and held in place with a claw clasp.

"You're the only black person I know whose skin, hair, and eyes are the same color. That is so weird," Malika commented.

Rachel smiled, acknowledging the fact. "My friend Julia called me Honey Child. She said that was the color I looked like . . ."

Her voice trailed off as she continued to finger the scarf. Ever since she'd gotten the word about Julia's death and spoken to Kenneth Lehane, all Rachel had been thinking about was Julia. It did no good to wish continually she'd made the effort to get in touch with Julia as she'd planned on doing this summer.

"You're not going to be finished for hours. Why don't we just order in?" Malika suggested. She didn't wait for Rachel to respond, but got up and headed into the kitchen to look for the take-out menus. "Chinese okay, or you want to try that new Indian place?"

"Whatever," Rachel sighed.

She paid no attention as Malika made the call and placed the order. It didn't matter to her what they had for dinner. She looked at the mess in her living room. It didn't even matter what she was packing for her trip. Because . . . suddenly, at that instant, Rachel knew she couldn't go.

That was it! Of course she couldn't go. Now she knew why it was so difficult to concentrate, to make plans, to get anything done. That's why she'd been so distracted and unsettled. The business trip would have to be postponed.

"They'll be here in a half hour. Ever notice that no matter what you order for take out, it *always* takes half an hour?" Malika asked dryly, returning to her place on the sofa.

"I changed my mind," Rachel murmured, more to herself than to Malika.

"What? Rachel, I've already placed the order. You can't just—"

"I mean, I changed my mind about the trip."

"What does that mean?"

Rachel got up from the floor. She was still holding the length of scarf, and it flowed out behind her as she hurried to get the phone from the kitchen. She returned and retrieved her packet of travel documents from the coffee table.

"It means this trip doesn't have to happen tomorrow. It can wait. I'm going to call and reschedule my flight. There are a couple of appointments I had for next week that I need to change." Rachel looked at her watch. "In the morning. It's the middle of the night in London."

"Where is this coming from? I thought this trip was important. Claudio's been asking you to come for weeks," Malika reminded Rachel.

But Rachel was already punching in numbers on her phone. "I'm not going to lose any business by waiting another week or so. And Claudio will just have to be patient. I'm sorry, but there's something I have to do that's more important right now."

Three

"Hi, Mom. It's me," Rachel called after unlocking the door to her mother's house. Behind her the cab that had brought her from the Baltimore-Washington Amtrak station pulled away.

"Me, who?" came back the distant inquiry.

Rachel left her bags by the door and followed the voice to the back of the house.

"Me, me," Rachel responded, reaching the kitchen.

Her mother, Lydia Givens, stood at the sink. Rachel kissed her on her cheek.

"Sorry I didn't come and get you from the station. My car is acting up again," Lydia explained.

"Don't worry about it," Rachel said, taking a seat at the table.

She observed her mother, a petite woman with smooth, light brown skin and a youthful face. Recently turned sixty, her figure was no longer as tiny as her wedding picture indicated. Rachel had suggested for years that her mother color her hair to hide her premature gray, and she'd done so with medium ash brown to dramatic effect. The difference easily took fifteen years off her age, Rachel thought.

"Whatever you're cooking smells good," Rachel commented.

"It's a pork loin for my book club meeting Sunday after church. It's my turn to host this month."

"I thought maybe we could go out somewhere for dinner later on."

"You paying?" Lydia asked, peering over the rim of her half frame glasses at Rachel. " 'Cause I don't like wasting my money when there's plenty of food here."

"Mom, it's my treat."

There was an open carpetbag on another kitchen chair overflowing with yarn and her mother's latest knitting project. Rachel lifted the needles to see a child's sweater in progress.

"What book is your club reading?"

"The last one by Toni Morrison."

"My all time favorite is *The Bluest Eye,*" Rachel volunteered. "I read it when I was twelve or thirteen, I think. It made me cry."

"You read that for school?" Lydia asked, drying her hands and turning to her daughter.

Rachel hesitated before responding. "No, it wasn't in school. I saw the book at Julia Winters' house one summer. She let me read it."

"Did she? If I'd known about you reading that book, I would have put a stop to it."

"Mom, I was thirteen. I couldn't keep reading kid's books forever," Rachel said.

"Sorry to hear about Julia passing. It was a shock when you called me from New York with the news. Did she have any family? We never saw any during those summers on Highland Beach."

"I don't know. It will be interesting to see who shows up at the memorial service tomorrow."

"Where is it being held?"

"At a church somewhere on Embassy Row." Rachel looked at her mother. "Would you like to come with me?"

Lydia shook her head. "I have things to do. I have an appointment to have my hair done, and I have plans for the evening so you're on your own anyway."

"You didn't tell me you were going out tomorrow night."

"I don't have to tell you everything I do, do I?" Lydia asked.

Rachel gave her mother a look of exasperation. "I wasn't trying to pry."

"Gordon said he might stop by, but I'm not holding my breath. Your brother forgets half the things he says he's going to do, and then does the other half poorly."

"So I guess I'm going to be the only one from the family at the service," Rachel said.

"I guess so. You're the only one who thought Julia Winters was so special, Rae, not that I'm speaking ill of the dead."

"She was special to me." She spotted the knitting bag again and used it to switch subjects.

"What are you making?"

"Oh, a sweater for Chas," Lydia said, referring to her six-year-old grandson by her older son, Ross. She took the chair adjacent to her daughter and picked up the knitting to show her. "He saw the one I made for his brother and said I had to make one for him, too."

Rachel fingered the half-finished garment. She carefully phrased her next comment. "I can't remember when you last made me a sweater."

Lydia looked pointedly at her. "Rae, the last sweater I made you you never wore. You said it didn't go with any of your clothes, and that it looked homemade. Remember that?"

"Did I?" she asked meekly.

"You were too busy being impressed by whatever Julia Winters told you. How she dressed and what she did."

"I guess I didn't appreciate how talented you are, and how much work goes into knitting something," Rachel said.

Lydia sighed. "Well, I guess you didn't think I was as glamorous or as much fun as Julia. That's what kids do with their parents: take them for granted, and then they grow up and forget that it ever happened. Anyway, it's too bad about her. I know how much you admired her."

"You do?"

"Why are you so surprised? I could see plain enough that you liked being around her."

"Julia was a lot of fun. I know you didn't like her very much—"

"Is that what you believed?"

"Well, you always acted angry whenever I wanted to spend any time at her house."

"I was angry because your friendship with Julia Winters interfered with my authority as your mother. What you wanted to do with her was always more important than what I wanted you to do. And your father was just as bad, always defending you, always saying 'What harm is there?' As if he didn't know."

"What?" Rachel questioned, confused.

Lydia waved the question aside. "Yes, it aggravated me. But there was too much going on that summer. Gordon was two and into everything. Ross was getting on my nerves 'cause he didn't even want to be at Highland Beach. As for me and your father . . . you're the only one who had a great summer, Rachel."

"Is that why we didn't go back the next year?" she asked.

Her mother sighed deeply. She seemed tense and annoyed by the subject. "Ross was starting college at Morehouse that next fall. We couldn't afford both tuition and the expense of a summer rental. After your father and I separated, it was out of the question."

"Yeah, but you didn't know that was going to happen when we left Highland Beach that last time," Rachel reminded her mother. "When we were driving home I remember you telling me we weren't coming back."

Her mother shook her head, pensive. "I didn't want to go back there. And despite what you believe, it wasn't about you always being with Julia Winters."

Rachel tried to process the facts of the past and meld it with the revelations of the moment. It had taken a long time for her to accept that her family would not be returning to the rented house on the Chesapeake Bay. It took a long time for her to stop resenting her mother's decision not to go back, and to stop resenting her parent's separation the following winter. She tried forcing away another feeling as well. The one that had stayed stubbornly and guiltily with her. The one where for years, until she was almost out of high school, she'd wished that Julia was her mother.

Rachel found that for that moment she didn't dare look her own mother in the face, afraid that Lydia could see the lingering childhood desire and be hurt by her betrayal.

"Well, it was all a long time ago, right? You can't always get what you want," Lydia said dryly.

Rachel was sure she detected a note of regret behind her mother's flippant remark. Once again she studied the half-finished sweater her mother was knitting.

"You do beautiful work. You could sell your things in a store, you know."

"I thought about it, but I don't think I'm organized enough to make it work," Lydia admitted, getting up to check on her pots.

The phone rang behind Rachel where it hung on the wall. She reached to answer. "Hello?"

"Hey. I just got home. What's going on?"

She listened to the male voice, which didn't belong to either of her brothers. She fumbled for a response even as she realized that this was not a wrong-number call. The caller spoke with a certain familiarity. "Just a minute," Rachel said, handing the phone to her mother.

"Hello?" Lydia spoke to the caller. "Oh, hi. That's my daughter, Rae. . . . yeah, I know." Lydia chuckled at the caller's response.

After her initial surprise, Rachel left the kitchen, retrieved her bags, and carried them upstairs. Her old bedroom had long ago been converted into a generic guest room, making Rachel feel less like a returning daughter than just a weekend visitor to her childhood home in Baltimore.

As she unpacked, she had the astonishing thought that her mother might have a boyfriend. She realized that her mother was a woman with a life outside of her children and grandchildren. That men might find her attractive and interesting, and even sexy. Rachel had to accept that there was a lot about her mother that she didn't know.

When she thought enough time had passed, Rachel returned to the kitchen. Her mother was still quietly engaged in conversation on the phone, so she occupied herself with tidying up the kitchen. Her mother was a wonderful but messy cook, and Rachel regretted not taking the time to learn what her mother would have been willing to teach her.

"You staying the whole weekend?" Lydia asked Rachel when she'd finished her call.

"Until Tuesday or Wednesday. Did I tell you that Julia put me in her will? I have to go to the lawyer's office on Monday afternoon for the reading."

"That's interesting. Why would she do that?" her mother asked. "She hadn't seen you in God knows how long."

"Why did you want to know when I'm leaving? Are you trying to tell me something?" Rachel joked.

"I just want to know what your plans are so they don't interfere with mine, that's all."

"Oh," Rachel said, unprepared for her mother's blunt reasoning. "You have a better social life than I do."

"You think so?" her mother asked airily.

Rachel felt like she was being baited, but she finally gave in to her curiosity. "Who was that?"

"Where?"

"The man you were talking to on the phone."

Lydia turned to give her daughter a grin. "None of your business."

* * *

Rachel was glad that during the next afternoon, the afternoon of the memorial service for Julia Winters, the weather was spectacular. It was as perfect a day as she could have hoped for. As she approached the small, white stone church, she had a true sense that she'd come to celebrate a life, not mourn its passing.

Right inside the dim, cool entrance the first thing she encountered was an enlarged black-and-white professional photograph of Julia displayed on an easel with an elegant arrangement of flowers positioned around it. She felt a rush of emotions as she stood staring at the smiling picture, deeply regretting that this was would be the final image she would be left with of a woman she'd cared so much about. Other visitors entered and walked by her, but Rachel remained riveted to this evidence that Julia was indeed gone.

She stood there for quite a long time. This captured image was polished and posed, showing a woman much younger than she had ever known. The hairdo was sleek, and Julia's makeup, professionally applied. She wore an expensive gown and jewels. She was presented as stunning, but cool and businesslike. This was a Julia who was unknown to her. As beautiful as the photograph was, Rachel knew she would always prefer her own memories of the woman who'd influenced her life. Her vision blurred with tears at the thought of never seeing Julia again.

Rachel moved on finally, until she reached the podium that held the guest book. She lifted the pen with an unsteady hand, and it slipped through her fingers to the carpeted floor. Almost at once, someone reached down to retrieve it for her. Embarrassed that she couldn't control her tears, she barely glanced up at the man dressed in casual black as he held the pen out to her.

"Thank you," she whispered.

He said nothing in return, which drew her attention to his face. She had only a moment to register a tall, lean, and fair-skinned man whose expression seemed completely without emotion. His long face was sculpted with high cheekbones. His brows were dark and matched his hair, cut short to tamp down the waves. But it was his eyes that grabbed her. Beautiful gray-green, but distant and somber.

"Lucas?" A blond woman near Rachel's own age stood in the entrance of the salon and beckoned him. "It's almost time."

Still without a word to her, the man walked away to join the other woman. Together they disappeared through the door. Rachel proceeded to sign her name to the guest book and, helping herself to a Kleenex from the box thoughtfully at hand, followed several other arrivals into a beige-and rose-colored salon where the service was to be held. The room was arranged appropriately with theater seating to accommodate about one hundred fifty people. The room was already nearly full. The gathering of people was as varied and eclectic a group as she'd ever seen. Some dressed in Afrocentric garb, some overdressed in hats and chandelier earrings. Several underdressed in denim or khaki. The races represented were black, white, and others.

Rachel didn't see anyone she recognized. She hadn't expected to. But she also didn't expect to feel like such an outsider in a group where everyone in attendance seemed to know one another. She was instantly stripped of the notion that she'd somehow had an exclusive knowledge of and access to Julia Winters. Belatedly, she wished she'd asked Ross to attend with her.

Rachel took a seat alone three rows back from the front of the room. A program had been placed on each chair. There were more displayed photographs of Julia on either side of a piano at the front of the salon. She almost began crying again when she recognized one of the pictures. It was one of Julia as Rachel last remembered seeing her. She was wearing a big straw hat and sunglasses, smiling broadly into the camera.

She also had on a pair of earrings Rachel had made for her that last summer. Rachel smiled faintly. It was a sign, the assurance she needed that they had shared a unique relationship and it was right for her to be here.

Her attention was caught just then by the approach of an older man with a graying goatee and receding hairline as he seated himself behind the keyboard of the baby-grand piano. Without introduction or prelude he began to play, not a classic piece or a funeral dirge, but a soft melodic arrangement with a jazz tempo. As if this were a signal, the room grew quiet. The lights dimmed until most of the illumination came from the candles placed around the room, and from one spotlight in the foreground of the piano. Then another man, tall and slender, walked out of the shadows to stand in the light. It was the same man she'd first seen in the outer reception area. He stood erect, dressed in a black silk collarless shirt tucked into black slacks. He carried a saxophone.

He took his time placing the support cord over his shoulder, making adjustments in the instrument's position before settling his long, strong fingers on the buttons. He stood facing the mourners, his light-skinned features sharpened under the beam of the spotlight. With his legs slightly apart, he waited for his cue.

Rachel noticed that he kept his eyes downcast. Although he seemed calm, centered with his emotions out of sight and private, a muscle repeatedly flexed in his jaw. She wondered if he was a mourner or had been hired only to perform for the service.

When the pianist segued into a slow phrase, the younger man finally took the reed between his lips, slowly moistening it with his tongue. Rachel found the gesture both tender and erotic. The pianist sounded a chord. In one smooth, graceful motion, the saxophonist lifted his horn and blew a long, searing note that literally made Rachel catch her breath. It sounded like the most plaintive cry, and it rippled through her chest. The wail and long, drawn-out chords reminded her of someone weeping, a heart utterly broken. She knew that in his own way the sax player was also mourning Julia's loss.

The duet was a poignant and riveting musical lamentation, painful to listen to, but beautiful in its effectiveness. Around her Rachel could hear crying, sniffling, and discreet blowing of noses. She rested her hand against her collarbone, squeezing her eyes shut and trying to hold on to her control. She didn't want to publicly share her grief with anyone.

When the music ended, the musicians left their instruments and took seats in the first row, the saxophonist sitting next to the blonde. A minister stood behind a podium and said a prayer, followed by a short program of reflections. But in Rachel's mind, none was as powerful as the testimony performed by the sax player. He remained seated next to the blonde until the service ended.

Rachel saw the two musicians, surrounded by admirers, head into the adjoining room where a reception was to be held. She joined the line of people as conversation resumed and everyone served themselves from the buffet.

"I know you."

Rachel, whose gaze had been following the sax player, turned.

A small, elderly woman stood peering at her through the thick lenses of her glasses. Her bony, brown face was over-rouged. Her hair, or wig, was an improbable shade of auburn, sticking out from beneath a hat and veil not in fashion for some sixty or seventy years. Rachel smiled.

"Excuse me?"

"Aren't you that girl who used hang around with Julia all the time? You weren't from the Beach, but you came with your family. Five of you."

Rachel raised her brows. "Yes, that's right. How did you remember? That was almost twenty years ago."

The woman waved a dismissive hand. "Oh, I never forget

a thing. You're all grown up, but I remember your face. You got pretty, too."

Rachel chuckled. "Thank you."

"I have to sit down 'fore my legs give out. What's that they're serving to drink?"

"Iced tea."

"Good. I'll have some. Don't put any sugar in it, dear. Sugar is bad for you. It'll kill you."

Somewhat dumbfounded, Rachel watched the woman totter to a chair to sit and wait for her. Pouring a glass of tea as ordered, she turned to join the one person who'd spoken to her since arriving. She caught a glimpse of the sax player deep in conversation with the minister. The attractive blonde stood by, protectively, it seemed to Rachel.

"Wasn't that a nice service? I'm glad Pastor Fletcher didn't go on and on."

"Yes, it was lovely. Excuse me but, I'm sorry, I don't remember your name," Rachel said.

The woman looked genuinely surprised, blinking at Rachel through her glasses. "Why, I'm Harrietta Cousins. I was Julia's closest friend on the Beach. She used to shorten it and call me Etta, but . . . oh, never mind that. I used to see you and Julia together all the time. Sometimes I'd see you on the beach with your baby brother. Julia told me all about your family. You were renters."

"That's right."

Harrietta shook her head. "Poor Julia. She had a hard time. Made a lot of mistakes, you understand, but she had a good heart."

"I thought so. She was very kind to me. I used to love to hear her laugh," Rachel said.

She glanced over her shoulder at the sax player. Rachel thought that he had a quiet command and poise about himself. The blonde was saying goodbye, and Rachel watched as she and the musician embraced warmly before she left the room. He didn't show much interest in mingling with the other guests.

"You know why some folks didn't like her, don't you?"

"Excuse me?" Rachel brought her attention back to her gregarious companion.

"So many people made Julia feel unwelcome. They should be ashamed of themselves. It wasn't a Christian thing to do. But I know why. It was the house."

"The house?" Rachel took a sip of the tea.

"Folks on the Beach are particular 'bout who buys there. There's some that feel Julia tricked old Mr. Baskin into selling her his home. Think maybe she wrapped him around her little finger, if you know what I mean."

Rachel, while utterly surprised by this unsolicited gossip, hid her smile at Harrietta's arch revelations. "Ummmm," she murmured, uninterested in old disputes and community intrigue.

Harrietta finished her tea and unceremoniously handed Rachel the empty glass. "I have to go. You know, I didn't have my nap this afternoon because of the service. My granddaughter drove me in. See if you can find her for me, dear."

Rachel smiled kindly. "Who is your granddaughter?"

Harrietta peered around briefly and pointed to a woman, attractive but slightly overweight, in conversation with several people. "There she is. She's talking to Flo. You remember Flo."

"No, I don't," Rachel said patiently.

"Flo is a good woman, but she gossips, you know."

"Let me get your granddaughter," Rachel said, finally slipping away to get the young woman's attention. She introduced herself and led her back to Harrietta.

"Will you be coming to the Beach this summer?" Harrietta asked, standing and letting her granddaughter take her arm for support.

"I doubt it. My parents haven't been there for years. Julia's gone. There's no reason for me to come."

"Well, you can always stay with me. I have three extra rooms and my grandkids don't like spending time on the Chesapeake. Say there's nothing to do," Harrietta explained.

Rachel caught the granddaughter indulgently rolling her eyes at this pronouncement.

Finally, goodbyes were said, and the two women left. Rachel decided she should be leaving as well. Her mother hadn't said if she'd need her car for the evening, but Rachel felt she should return it sooner rather than later. She was turning toward the exit when she spotted the sax player sitting alone on the side of the room. He held a glass in his hand and appeared to be deeply in thought. Impulsively she quietly approached him.

"Sorry if I'm interrupting," she opened, coming to a stop near his chair.

He rose to his feet. Rachel blinked as she watched some deep emotion fade from his features, leaving an expression that was closed and unreadable. Startling gray-green eyes fixed on her.

"Not at all," he said.

"I just wanted to say how much I enjoyed the musical prelude to the service."

"Thank you," he said graciously.

"Your horn playing . . ." She struggled to express herself. "It was very beautiful, very moving. I didn't know a sax was capable of that."

He raised a brow. "I'm glad I did justice to what it's capable of. I tried to bring out some emotion in what people heard."

"Well, it worked for me."

"Glad you enjoyed it." He placed his glass on a service table and rubbed his large hands together drying the condensation. "Are you friend or family?"

"I'm not family, although I always think of Julia as being like family to me. My name's Rachel Givens."

She held out her hand.

"Lucas Scott," he introduced himself, shaking her hand.

The handshake was a quick and polite gesture, but in that brief touch Rachel was aware of more than just the texture of his warm skin, or the sure strength in his fingers. She unconsciously closed her hand as if to capture the feeling.

"My family used to vacation on Highland Beach when I was a little girl. I always looked forward to seeing Julia. I was very upset when I heard about her death."

He nodded, watching her closely. "Then you haven't seen her recently?"

"No," Rachel said regretfully. "But we did talk by phone whenever she and I could catch up with each other. I didn't know she was ill. What about you? Friend or family?"

She waited, looking into his face, aware of the telltale muscle flexing as it had earlier. His eyes seemed not only distant, but also cautious.

"I'm Julia's son."

From the shocked look on Rachel Given's face, he could tell she hadn't even known he existed.

In another life, Lucas might have found her reaction funny. But the truth of it was it annoyed the hell out of him. The blank and stunned look on her face told him that he might have to do the one thing he'd been hoping to avoid. Explain himself. Offer up history. Make up something. Deal with Julia's version of her life, complete with omissions.

The thought occurred to him that he could just blow Rachel Givens off. He didn't owe her anything, least of all a baring of his soul. Let her find out on her own why Julia kept him a secret, or had left out some minor details about her life. But what made Lucas hold back from excusing himself and walking away was less Rachel Given's inability to say a single word than it was the look in her pale brown eyes. Not horrified but bewildered. Hurt, even.

What, in God's name, did *she* have to be hurt about?

Lucas made a silent, ironic chuckle. "You didn't even know about me, did you? How did Julia manage that, I wonder?"

He watched as, finally, she blinked rapidly. He had to admit he hadn't expected to see tears, there and gone in a flash. He found himself wanting to end the encounter, fast. He hadn't expected to be confronted with this kind of response from someone he'd never met before.

"No. She . . . she told me nothing," Rachel confirmed faintly.

Lucas twisted his mouth. "Surprise, surprise," he said quietly, watching as she tried to regain some composure. "Look, maybe you should sit down."

His brief touch on her elbow stirred her into movement. She sank into a nearby chair. Aware of her distress, Lucas reluctantly sat next to her. He could see she was still openly staring. Maybe Rachel Givens thought he was some sort of apparition, and if she just waited, he'd disappear.

"Oh, my God. I'm being such a jerk," she said, shaking her head. "I'm sorry. I just stood there . . . staring at you."

"It's alright," Lucas said stiffly.

"No. No, it's not. I just . . . I just—"

"Find it hard to believe, and you can't get over that you didn't know," Lucas recited, sarcastically. He could see the barb hit home.

"That's fair to say."

She was finally regaining her ability to speak intelligently, but Lucas was aware that she still studied his face intently.

"I can't explain why Julia didn't tell you about me. I guess she had her reasons."

"I can't imagine what," Rachel confessed.

Lucas didn't respond to that. The less said the better.

"Julia always seemed so open and friendly," Rachel continued. "She told me all about her acting and singing career. She used to teach dancing and acting during the summer to the kids at Highland Beach. We'd get dressed in costumes and she'd have props, and at the end of the summer we'd put on a play for the whole neighborhood."

Lucas watched as her face changed with whatever memories she was reviewing in her head. He was involuntarily fascinated by her recall of her summer vacations on the Chesapeake. Yet he didn't particularly want to hear about her relationship to Julia.

"There was so much that happened during my vacations on Highland Beach," Rachel said, sounding almost breathless, like she couldn't say enough about her time there. Or about Julia.

"Clearly," Lucas said.

"Did you spend a lot of time on the Beach? Did you go to school in the area? Julia's death must be a great loss to you."

Lucas leaned forward to brace his elbows on his knees. He rubbed his hands together. "No, I did not spend time on the Beach. No, I did not go to school there, or live there with her. I can't say if Julia's death is a loss since I wasn't really a part of her life. When I come right down to it, you seem to have known much more about her than I do. I would even say that she probably liked you better."

She didn't say anything, and Lucas was forced to sit back again to see her expression. Her face was tight, her eyes narrowed suddenly with anger. She stood up abruptly.

"Look . . . I don't know what to say to you. Julia *never* told me she had a son. She never mentioned that she'd even been married. Whatever your relationship was or wasn't, isn't my fault."

Lucas was taken aback by her sudden outburst, but he did nothing to either stop Rachel or to defend himself. Dispassionately, he let her vent.

"I can't speak for you, but I'm so sorry she's gone. I'm not ashamed to admit I loved her. Julia was . . . she was like a surrogate mother to me."

Lucas slowly stood up and glared at her. "You're lucky. You

got more of her time and attention than I ever did. I'm glad she was a mother to someone."

He walked briskly away, not waiting to hear if Rachel Givens had a counterattack.

"Wait a minute," she called out behind him.

Lucas came to a stop, but only because her tone was anguished rather than accusatory. He turned to face her. "What is it?" he asked impatiently.

Rachel took a few steps toward him. Once again her eyes and her voice were filled with regret. "What was wrong with Julia? What did she die of?"

The question swept through Lucas like a wave of hot air. It reminded him fully of his loss and the end of any possibility for resolution and closure. Rachel Givens and her inquiry made him feel tired and full of overwhelming defeat.

"She had ovarian cancer," he responded.

With that he walked out of the salon, leaving her standing alone in the now-empty room.

Lucas headed for the exit of the church, fleeing the somber and claustrophobic atmosphere. He was enraged after meeting Rachel Givens, enraged by hearing about her relationship with Julia. He couldn't even begin to identify all the things he himself felt about Julia. He'd been trying all his life to figure that out.

He spotted a maintenance worker beginning to remove the vases of flowers from the inside foyer. Lucas called out.

"Excuse me, can I bum a smoke?"

The older man silently walked over, taking a pack of cigarettes from his shirt pocket and holding them out. While Lucas shook one from the pack, the man offered a book of matches. "Keep it," he said.

"Thanks," Lucas murmured, accepting the light.

The man silently nodded and went back to his work.

Lucas walked out of the building. He paused to light the cigarette, inhaling and exhaling deeply. He paced as if the activity of smoking would calm him down and exorcize his demons. He stopped to lean against one of the doors, reviewing the service and every moment of his conversation with Rachel Givens. She'd made him angry, and he knew she wasn't at fault. One thing was clear. He realized that his resolve to pay his respects to Julia and move on had been destroyed in those ten minutes.

Out of the corner of his eye he saw her leaving the building. Silently he stood watching her, his emotions still running high. She stopped, pensively stared onto the street, and then she appeared to closely examine Julia's picture on the front of the memorial program she held in her hand.

Rachel had admitted to him that she'd not seen Julia in years, but she'd come to the service nonetheless. He knew from having just listened to her that her memories and feelings for his mother were still fresh. As much as anything, Lucas was amazed at the apparent effect Julia had had on Rachel Givens's life. Unlike his own.

As if aware that she was being watched, Rachel finally turned and focused her gaze on him. Lucas stared back, totally unrepentant. Neither spoke, though they squared off like they were long-standing enemies. It lasted a long time, and it was Rachel who backed off first. With a deep sorrow reflected in her gaze, she hurried down the steps and headed for the parking lot at the side of the building.

Lucas took one more drag on the cigarette before flicking it away in disgust. It was proof of how worked up he'd gotten that, after more than ten years, he'd needed to have a smoke. Worse, he was about to leave without his sax. Cursing under his breath, he retraced his steps into the building. He saw the same maintenance worker carrying his saxophone, headed toward him.

"You forgot your horn, man."

Lucas took the instrument. "Thanks."

"You play good, man. I was standing outside the salon listening. I hope you do more than funerals. You know that lady who died?"

Lucas took his time removing the neck cord from the sax and putting it into his pocket. "Not very well."

"She sure was beautiful. I seen her once. Years ago. She had a nice voice," he said. "What you want to do with the pictures?"

"What?"

The maintenance man pointed to the picture of Julia mounted on the easel. "There's more inside."

He had no idea. For that matter, he didn't really care. He wanted to put the service behind him. He needed to deal with the unexpected resurrection of his pain, and meeting Rachel Givens.

"Do me a favor and wrap them all up together," he instructed the man. "I'll take them with me."

Rachel waited until her mother's car disappeared down the block before stepping back inside the house and closing the door. She hadn't asked her mother where she was going for the evening, and Lydia hadn't volunteered. It seemed to Rachel that her mother was getting perverse pleasure out of keeping her in the dark. As she got into the driver's seat her mother had even said carelessly, "Don't wait up for me." The fact that Rachel had no plans for Saturday night prompted only a murmur of sympathy from Lydia.

Her only mistake, Rachel realized now that she was alone in the old house, was that she was likely to spend the whole evening rehashing that embarrassing face-off with Lucas Scott just hours earlier. She might have saved herself the humiliation if she'd taken the time to read the program before the memorial service began. Right there in the last paragraph it was printed that Julia Winters was survived by an elderly uncle, several cousins, and her son, Lucas Monroe Scott.

Her son!

"Incredible," Rachel muttered to herself.

She'd spent the better part of the afternoon trying to recall if Julia had even hinted at having a child. Had there been photographs in Julia's house that she'd never questioned, never seen? Nothing. There had been absolutely *nothing* said about a son.

She sat in the living room and reached for the remote, clicking on the TV. Rachel surfed through all three hundred stations in record time, and then clicked the set off again. Too late she realized it had been a mistake to sequester herself in her mother's house, of all places, by herself. Because what Rachel quickly found happening was that her mind repeatedly invoked images of Lucas Scott—complete with his handsome, albeit scowling, face.

She hadn't seen anything of Julia in Lucas's features, and she'd looked. Maybe because he was so cold and unsmiling. His skin was much lighter in color than hers, his eyes an extraordinary gray green. Sea foam, in artist talk. Julia had had delicate features, fine and lovely.

Feeling like she was driving herself crazy with speculation, she called her brother Ross.

"Mom left me home alone," she joked. "I was hoping I could come over to your place and visit with the family, spend time with Chas and Trey."

"I wish you'd told me sooner, Rae, that you wanted to come over this weekend. Jill and I have plans for tonight."

"I know it's last minute. I didn't think of it until this afternoon," she said, hiding her disappointment.

"Normally I'd say come along with us, but the National Association of Black Journalists is having a little gig at the

Smithsonian Exposition Building tonight. For Jill, it's business. She's a member, but she's doing an article about the event for the association bulletin. I'm just going along for a free meal."

"What about tomorrow?" Rachel asked, hoping she didn't sound as pathetic as she felt.

"Yeah, that will work. Trey and Chas have a swim meet sponsored by their summer day camp. Mom's coming so she can cheer on her little brown waterbugs, as she calls them. We'll probably go out somewhere for dinner," Ross added.

"Mom never said anything to me about tomorrow," Rachel responded, feeling a twinge of rejection.

"Probably didn't even think about it. She usually comes to our place on Sunday unless she has other plans or we do."

"Do you know if she's seeing someone?" Rachel asked.

"*Mom*?" Ross asked, incredulous. Then he started laughing. "I'm sorry, it's not funny but . . . I just can't see it. I mean, after all these years? Seemed to me that after what happened between her and Daddy, she kind of swore off the opposite sex. She was really hurt, you know."

"By what?" Rachel asked.

"By what happened."

"Oh, you mean the divorce," Rachel assumed.

"Well, that too. What made you ask about whether she was seeing anyone?"

"An unidentified male caller last night. Mysterious evening plans. Coy smiles."

"I don't know anything, Rae. Maybe I'll try to feel her out about it tomorrow. So, do you think you'll come?"

"Probably. I have nothing else to do until Monday afternoon."

"What's happening on Monday? I thought you only came down for Julia's memorial service. How was it, by the way?"

She hesitated. "Fine. You could have come, you know. A lot of people showed up. And I got the surprise of my life."

"Really? What happened?"

"I met Julia's son. His name is Lucas Monroe Scott," Rachel made a grand statement of the facts. She expected a surprised reaction from her brother, similar to what she'd experienced. Instead, there was total silence on the other end.

"Ross, did you hear me?"

"Yeah, I heard you."

"Well, aren't you stunned, shocked, and weirded out?" She asked flippantly.

"Rae, I knew about Lucas."

"You . . . What do you mean, you knew about Lucas? How? When?" she asked.

"Since that last time we went to Highland Beach," Ross confessed.

"Was I comatose or what?" she asked, annoyed by the aura of secrecy surrounding Lucas's existence.

In the ensuing silence Rachel detected Ross's reluctance to supply details. She was having a hard time accepting that Julia had not shared with her any revelations about having a son. Ross's inside knowledge seemed even more galling because he'd have known about Lucus since they were teenagers.

"Ross, I can't believe you knew something like that and didn't say a word. Not even to me! You knew how I felt about Julia. You knew how close we were—"

Ross sighed. "Look, I don't think it had anything to do with you or me or how much she liked you. It was only by accident that I found out about her son."

"Okay, so tell me. How did it happen?" Rachel demanded.

"Rae, I don't know if I should—"

"It doesn't matter. You're not violating any sacred trust. Julia is gone. You have no idea what I went through when this man introduced himself and told me who he was. I made such a fool of myself, Ross. I just stared and stared, with my mouth hanging open catching flies!"

"Yeah, I guess it did kind of kick the wind out of you," he said. "Well, I was passing her house one day. I think I was headed toward Walnut Creek. She was sitting on her porch, and I remember she was crying."

"Crying," Rachel repeated, as if it wasn't possible.

"That's right. I also think she'd been drinking. I know I saw a bottle of wine on that wicker table she left outside all the time. Anyway, Julia saw me and she called me over. She asked how old I was. So I told her and the next thing she said was, 'I have a son just about your age.' Just like that. But I don't think she meant to tell me."

"What did you do after that?" Rachel asked softly.

"At first I didn't believe her. I thought the woman was high on something. But then she told me to wait there and she went into the house. I was going to leave. I mean, the whole scene made me nervous, know what I'm saying? Then she came back with a photograph album. That's when she showed me the picture of Lucas. He looked like he could be a year or two older than me. And he looked pretty white to me," Ross chuckled, as if it was still hard to believe.

"No, he doesn't," Rachel scoffed at the idea. "He couldn't pass. I don't even think he'd try."

"How do you know?"

"Because of the way he plays the saxophone," she murmured.

"The man plays the sax, so that makes him black?" Ross questioned sarcastically.

"If you'd seen him and heard him, you'd know what I mean. Didn't Julia tell you anything about Lucas? Why we'd never seen or met him, or where he was?"

"Not a word. I certainly wasn't going to ask her about him. It got embarrassing after a while because she started crying again. I just wanted to get the hell out of there. I told her I had to go, and that's when she made me promise, made me swear, that I wouldn't tell *anybody*. I mean, not anybody. So, I didn't."

Rachel said nothing for a long moment. She was thankful

that Ross patiently waited her out, perhaps knowing that he'd dropped a bomb with shattering effectiveness.

"Well," she began. "I guess I didn't know Julia Winters as well as I thought I did."

"She probably had reasons why she didn't want you to know," Ross suggested.

"What reasons?" Rachel asked, helplessly.

"You got me, Rae," Ross replied. "By the way, what did you think of him?"

"Lucas? I only spoke with him a few minutes. I was so shocked to find out who he was I couldn't even think of what to say, what questions to ask. I can tell you that he came off a little arrogant, defensive, and not very friendly."

"Sounds like a nice guy," Ross chortled.

"Maybe I'll find out more on Monday."

"What happens on Monday?"

"Didn't I mention that Julia named me in her will?"

"She did? That's great. I should have been nicer to her," Ross chuckled. "Just don't forget I'm your favorite brother."

"It's probably nothing important," Rachel surmised. "Julia had a pair of diamond earrings that I loved. There was a lace fan she said was given to her by some famous French actress once when she performed in Paris. I also remember a painting of Highland Beach that hung in her living room that I liked looking at. It showed these two little black kids playing in the sand. I loved that painting."

"Did you tell mom about meeting Julia's son?" Ross asked.

"No."

"Why not?"

"I don't know. I just didn't," Rachel said.

It was on the tip of her tongue to mention it when she'd arrived back at her mother's house, but she wouldn't have been able to give any more information. She would have been left making up a story or second-guessing the real story. Somehow it seemed unfair to Julia, and to Lucas Monroe

Scott. As much as Rachel felt slighted by Julia's omission about having a child, as much as Lucas came across as cold and rude, it wasn't her place to out Julia, to expose her to speculation, to give up long-held secrets without knowing why they were secrets in the first place.

Four

"Hi, Jen. Sorry I'm late," Lucas said as he kissed her cheek and slid into the chair.

He removed his sunglasses, hooking an arm into the open neckline of his sweater. Immediately a waitress appeared at his side and took his order for a Bloody Mary.

The pretty blonde seated opposite Lucas smiled her forgiveness with a playful pout. "As long as you didn't stand me up. If you're feeling guilty, I'll let you pay for brunch."

"You know I'm going to pay," Lucas said without rancor. He adjusted his chair, casually glancing around at the other occupants of the popular DC café. He would not have chosen the heavily trafficked Connecticut Avenue as a venue to eat, but Lucas knew this was one of Jennifer Cameron's favorite haunts for people watching and for being seen.

He also didn't think it necessary to tell her that he'd come close to backing out of getting together. That was before he'd realized that lunch out with Jennifer was probably a lot better than indulging in a funk about the past and situations he couldn't change. And he was tired of rehashing how badly he'd behaved with Rachel Givens the day before. For whatever reason, meeting her had set him off.

He became aware that Jennifer was studying him closely, with empathy reflected in her blue eyes. He made an effort to focus his attention solely on her.

"Thanks for coming yesterday," he grinned, infusing his gratitude with warmth.

"Oh, come on. I don't need thanks. I know how hard this whole thing has been for you, Lucas. How are you feeling today?"

"Pretty good." The lie rolled easily from his lips.

"I'm sorry I had to take off like that, but there was this other thing I had to—"

"Hey, you don't have to explain. You have a life. Anyway, I had some things to take care of myself after the service. I wasn't much in the mood for company, so I made it an early night."

Jennifer squeezed his hand briefly, leaning toward him over the table. "You don't look like you had a restful night. I should have insisted on staying with you," she apologized. She was forced back when Lucas's drink was delivered.

Lucas stirred it before taking a sip. "I was fine. Really."

The waitress stood waiting to take their order. Lucas indicated that Jennifer should go first. He was only a little surprised when she then proceeded to select for him as well. When the waitress left, Jennifer leaned in closer again.

"I know you've told me you didn't have much of a relationship with your mother, but she must have been pretty popular. That was quite a turnout yesterday. Did you know any of those people?"

"Only a handful. A lot of people introduced themselves but I hadn't a clue. I know that several had traveled to DC from Highland Beach. There was this one person . . ." He stopped. Lucas decided he didn't want to get into the subject of Rachel Givens. Jen would ask a lot of questions he couldn't and didn't want to answer.

"Who? Was it someone famous your mother performed with?" Jennifer asked.

"No, nothing like that. She was someone who seems to have known Julia most of her life. Apparently, she and Julia were very close," Lucas said stiffly. "I'd never seen or met her before, but her name sounded familiar."

"What's her name?"

Lucas pulled back from pursuing the issue. "It's not important. It's not like I'm ever going to see her again."

Lunch was served, and several moments were spent commenting on their selection.

"Is the omelet the way you like it?" Jennifer asked. "Loose and kind of soft in the center?"

"It's close enough," Lucas mused, glancing at her as he applied salt. "But not what I would have ordered."

Jennifer smiled guilelessly at Lucas. "I was just trying to be thoughtful. You're always so strong and independent and on top of things. Isn't it nice to have someone else take care of you?"

With a nod Lucas conceded her point. "Thanks."

"I know you aren't really annoyed about the omelet," she said confidently.

"Do you?" he asked, curious.

"Look, the last few weeks have been hell for you. Your firm wants you to come back and give up what they call this nonsense about becoming a sax player, your ex-wife calls out of the blue to find out if you're still interested, and your mother dies. Give yourself a break."

"You're right," Lucas said quietly, finishing only half the omelet and then pushing his plate away.

He grinned affectionately at Jen's demonstration of proprietary rights toward him. She wasn't always subtle, but she was sincere. He supposed the same thing could be said about Rachel Givens, and he conjured up an image of her in his mind. The way she'd looked thanking him for his music, and praising Julia. The indescribable look in her eyes when she learned he was Julia's son. The way she looked when she finally pulled it together and was ready to go for his throat because he was rude. Lucas had a feeling that with Rachel you always knew exactly where you stood with her. She wouldn't see the need to camouflage her feelings. And he was sure he knew exactly how she felt having met him.

"I have a question maybe you can answer. Why did the minister refer to the service for your mother as a homecoming? I found that so confusing, like she was a homecoming queen or something," Jen confessed.

Lucas let his gaze wander past her as he carefully considered not only the question but also his answer. "It refers to the spiritual belief by many black folks that the soul of someone who has died is going home to God, the Father. They see that as something to celebrate, rather than mourning death as a sad end to life."

Jen was studying him, paying close attention as she finished the last of her chopped salad. Lucas ordered a second Bloody Mary.

"What a beautiful way of looking at death," she murmured. "I have to admit I'm a little surprised that you can explain."

He was instantly alert. "What do you mean by that?"

She laughed lightly, playing with the ends of her hair before brushing it behind her ears.

"Lucas," Jen began, using a tone to suggest he knew perfectly well what she meant. "It's not like you grew up among black people your whole life, or spent a lot of Sundays going to a black church, is what I mean. Your father's parents practically raised you, and they're white. But I think it's great that you know all of that, and I'm impressed."

"I don't think knowing about the tradition has anything to do with being black. But of course I'm black. How else did you imagine I'd identify?" he asked, puzzled.

"I know that," she said, appearing slightly flustered. "But—"

"There is no but, Jen. There is no other option just because my father is white and Julia was black," Lucas said smoothly. "Are you telling me that for all the years we've known each other and been good friends that you didn't see me as a black man?"

Jen calmly took a deep breath, trying to redeem herself. "I've always seen you as a wonderful, brilliant man who is very special to me."

He watched her. "You didn't answer my question."

"I'm not going to," she said, suddenly stubborn. "It simply isn't important. I judge you by the content of your character."

"Nice comeback, but that line has already been made famous by someone black. You know what I'm talking about. And you're still skirting the issue."

"It's a nonissue, that's why. What about your mother's personal things?" Jen asked, deftly changing the subject.

"I have to go to the lawyer's office tomorrow for . . ." Lucas paused. For a moment his gaze was vacant. "That's it! That's where I heard her name before. Rachel Givens."

"What are you talking about?"

"The woman I met yesterday. She's named in Julia's will."

"Is she a relative?"

"No, but she knew Julia a long time. Since she was child, she told me."

"How old is she?" Jen asked smoothly.

He'd tried guessing that the night before when he'd spent time recalling the encounter with Rachel. "Around thirty. A little younger than you are, I'd say."

Jen played with her knife, frowning. "What do you think your mother left her?"

"I don't know. I can't even guess," Lucas said, suddenly realizing that he'd actually have to see Rachel Givens again.

"It's probably nothing much. After all, you were Julia's son," Jen reasoned.

"Right. For whatever that's worth," he murmured.

Rachel was glad she didn't allow her mother to talk her into wearing stockings to her appointment for the reading of Julia Winters' will. DC in July could be miserable enough, with high temperatures and humidity, without adding the encumbrance of sticky nylons covering her legs. She liked the feel of her black nylon skirt brushing against her bare legs. Worn with an ecru sleeveless tunic tank and a slim belt at her waist, she knew that she was appropriately dressed for the meeting. Simple, tasteful, and cool. Entering the building, she couldn't resist a sigh of gratitude that Kenneth Lehane's firm had chosen a modern, perfectly air-conditioned building. It helped to cool not only her damp skin, but her nerve ends.

After signing the guest book and asking for directions from the security desk, she boarded an elevator for the fifteenth floor. Rachel used the short trip to compose herself. She had also been preparing, since she'd last seen him, for the inevitable meeting again with Lucas Monroe Scott. Recalling his incredible revelation that he was Julia's son, coupled with their hostile conversation after the memorial service, Rachel was expecting Lucas to object to her very presence. But that was his problem.

After announcing herself at the reception desk of the law offices, she remained standing while the attorney was paged. In less than a minute Kenneth Lehane appeared. He was a stocky, middle-aged man with graying curly hair and a closely trimmed beard. He looked more like a professor than an estate lawyer.

"Ms. Givens. A pleasure." Lehane offered Rachel his hand to shake, and a friendly smile that immediately put her at ease.

"I'm sorry if I'm a few minutes late," Rachel apologized.

"Not at all. You probably ran into traffic."

"Actually, the problem was my mother's car. The engine was slow to turn over this morning."

"But you made it. You're the second person to arrive. I'll just take you to the conference room where we'll be getting started in just a few minutes."

"Thank you," Rachel said.

"Did you make it to the service on Saturday?" he asked as she accompanied him beyond the reception area and down a corridor. He stopped at the end in front of a pair of frosted glass doors.

"Yes, I did. It was nicely done, and a wonderful tribute to Julia."

"Good, good. Lucas told me it went well," Lehane said. He opened one of the doors and stood back to let Rachel precede him inside.

Rachel felt her stomach roiling as she entered the room. But the sole occupant was an older woman, sitting quietly and staring into space. The attorney introduced the two women.

"Mrs. Marguerite Santiago, this is Rachel Givens. Mrs. Santiago took care of Julia in the final months before her death. And Ms. Givens has known Julia since she was a child."

Rachel smiled and shook hands with the woman.

"I'll be back shortly," the attorney said, closing the door and leaving Rachel and Mrs. Santiago together.

It was less a conference room than a private library, furnished with a provincial sofa in yellow silk, several club chairs, and a few tables. Mrs. Santiago was sitting on the sofa, and Rachel decided to sit next to her. They chatted for a few minutes, getting acquainted.

"I took care of her until the very end," Mrs. Santiago said. "I remember Ms. Winters talking about you."

"Oh, did she?" Rachel asked, surprised.

"She called you her protegeé."

"I . . . I'm really pleased to hear that," Rachel responded, moved by the comment.

"She was a very nice lady," Mrs. Santiago added, sighing.

Silence lapsed between them. Rachel wondered how to broach the question that had been on her mind since first learning of Julia's death. She stared at her summer high-heeled sandals, and made the totally irreverent observation that she needed a pedicure. Julia used to have her nails done religiously, Rachel recalled. She used to say it was like getting a brand new pair of hands or feet every two weeks.

"If you don't mind me asking, how long had Ms. Winters been ill?"

"Almost five months," the older woman said.

"Is that all?" Rachel breathed. It was such a short time.

"She was lucky," Mrs. Santiago said. "The pain only got really bad in the last three weeks."

Rachel didn't know what to say. She couldn't imagine Julia suffering and in pain. "But she did have painkillers, right?"

"Oh, yes. But she wouldn't take them. Not until the very end, just a few days before she died, when it was so bad she would sometimes pass out."

"But why?"

"I don't know. She didn't have to suffer, but she said the pain was her final punishment." Mrs. Santiago's eyes suddenly brightened with a thought and she grinned. "Ms. Winters said God pushed her into the world naked and screaming, and she guessed she'd leave the same way."

Because she could well envision Julia saying something irreverent like that, Rachel couldn't help chuckling.

At that moment the door opened and Kenneth Lehane entered. Lucas Scott was right behind him.

The smile on Rachel's face slowly faded under Lucas's cool gaze, making her feel that her display of humor was ill advised or, at least, out of place.

The attorney launched into a new round of introductions. Looking back and forth between Rachel and Lucas he said, "You two know one another."

Lucas said nothing as he took a seat directly opposite her. "We met on Saturday at the service," Rachel confirmed smoothly, determined not to let him ignore her.

Rachel realized too late that she would be sitting opposite Lucas. When he began a thorough examination of her long legs, she saw the mistake in choosing the sofa, which was too low. Lucas was dressed in a lightweight business suit, and the change it made in her physical image of him was dramatic. It was almost like seeing an entirely new man, but one who was still handsome and urbane. He presented a picture of such strong masculinity that she had to concentrate on keeping her breathing even. She missed most of the attorney's opening remarks. And when Lucas suddenly focused his attention from her legs to her face, Rachel felt herself react even more strongly. She knew it was ridiculous that she'd been thinking of him constantly when he gave no indication that he thought very much of her, especially now, when she was sure that he was probably thinking her skirt was too short for the occasion. And she should have worn pantyhose after all. Discreetly, she tugged on the hem and then crossed her legs into a comfortable position. She glanced up again only to find Lucas watching her with an unwavering stare from his beautiful eyes. His expression changed instantly, from thoughtful curiosity to being guarded. Trying to ignore him, Rachel gave her full attention to Kenneth Lehane.

But Rachel couldn't help herself from stealing covert glances in Lucas's direction, if for no other reason than to gauge his reaction to the occasion. He caught her looking at him twice. She continued to suspect that Lucas Scott was wound rather tightly with anger. But it was only after a while that Rachel realized it might not all be directed at her. After all, he didn't know anything about her, and had spent less than ten minutes talking with her.

Rachel also was inclined to give Lucas the benefit of the doubt when she remembered that he'd just lost his mother. Not that she totally forgave his obnoxious behavior, but she thought she understood where it was coming from. With that insight she, at least, was prepared to let bygones be bygones.

Nearly fifteen minutes were taken up with the protocol of recording the reading of Julia's will. Rachel listened with interest while previously unknown information about Julia's assets was laid out. Mrs. Santiago appeared to be daydreaming, and Lucas sat calmly with his emotions, for the most part, rigidly in control.

Kenneth Lehane read from one official document after another until, finally, he came to a multipage transcript of the will. He held it up and announced, "This is the final will and testament of Julia Winters, dated, signed and witnessed on . . ."

Without looking at him, Rachel knew when Lucas quietly changed positions in his chair. His body language spoke volumes. It occurred to her that this had to be very difficult for him.

"I, Julia Winters, being of sound mind and body . . . well, my body is a different matter. You, whom I've selected with love and deepest regard, to be present at this reading of my will, know by now that my body has been betrayed. It has been ravished by an insidious enemy invasion that has been the death of me. So be it. I accept God's hand knowing that, in His infinite mercy and wisdom, taking me is His way of forgiving me my sins, my shortcomings, my omissions of faith . . ."

Rachel was spellbound by the poignant and irreverent words. She could easily imagine Julia writing it with her trademark irony and amusement. To think that she may have suffered all alone, except for Mrs. Santiago, and with such humor and grace, struck Rachel as heartbreaking. As Lehane continued to read, she tried to avert her face, to use her hand as a shield against the threat of tears.

She was suddenly overcome by the reality of Julia's death and the realization that she'd never actually had a chance to tell Julia how much she meant to her. She especially didn't want Lucas to know when the slow fall of her tears began as Julia's own words were read and her knowledge of her own imminent death was revealed. Rachel was not ashamed of her feelings, and only wished desperately that she'd taken the time to call and speak with Julia again.

She listened as Lehane read the listing of Julia's assets. By her own admission Julia was not a wealthy woman in terms of money. But she'd written that she was very rich in the people she'd been fortunate enough to know in life.

"For Marguerite Santiago, my personal angel," Lehane read, "I thank you for holding my hand through many a torturous night of agonizing pain. I leave you the sum of $5,000 and my collection of theatrical tiaras." Mrs. Santiago finally broke down to sob into a handkerchief.

"For Rachel Givens, whom I call my Honey Child, for her bright inquisitiveness and fearless desire to experience all that life has to offer, I begin by offering my gratitude. Thank you for your sweet friendship and adoration, and for reminding me of myself at your age. Thank you for helping me believe I was as wonderful as you thought me to be."

The words were wrenching and bittersweet, and Rachel could no longer pretend that she wasn't deeply affected. There was a soft pat on her arm and she was stunned when Lucas bent forward to press a tissue into her hand. As she suspected, Julia had left her the painting of Highland Beach, along with an appraisal that authenticated the painting as the work of a nationally known African-American artist. Unexpectedly, Julia also indicated that a box of items had been left for her.

Not unsurprisingly, all of Julia's remaining assets, including stocks, cash, insurance policies, and all of her jewelry were left to her son, Lucas Monroe Scott.

"Lucas, these are not meant to make up for the years we spent apart. I pray that you will take the time to discover for yourself the reasons why."

Rachel stole a glance at Lucas to see if he had any reaction to this enigmatic confession. He was doing an excellent job of keeping his feelings to himself but even so Rachel could see the strain around his mouth and eyes. He was not completely immune.

The attorney paused to turn to the final page of the will.

"I have named my son, Lucas Monroe Scott, as sole bene-ficiary of my remaining personal effects, with the exception of my house on Highland Beach," Kenneth Lehane read, "which, along with its contents and all deeded land, is to be shared equally between my son Lucas and Rachel Givens."

Lucas repeated the final statement to himself several times to make sure he'd heard correctly. He looked quickly at Rachel and found her returning his gaze with the exact same expres-sion he'd seen when he'd first introduced himself as Julia's son. While he and Rachel sat dumbfounded, the attorney was giving closing remarks to end the reading.

"Wait a minute," Lucas interrupted. He leaned forward in his seat. "What was that about the house?"

Lehane reread the last page silently before speaking. "Ms. Winters left her Highland Beach property equally to both of you. That means half-and-half."

"Forgive me, but I don't think I understand," Rachel said. "It doesn't make sense. Why?"

Lucas flashed her a quick look when she agreed with him. "There's got to be a mistake. Is there another document, a letter that explains?"

"No mistake," Lehane said. He was standing and gathering his folder of documents. "You've heard everything Julia left with me that was to be read as part of her will, all of which was signed less than two weeks before her death. Believe me, Mr. Scott, your mother was very clear on what she wanted when this was drawn up."

"But it's impossible," Lucas said, standing to face the lawyer. He knew that Rachel was watching and listening to his argument, and he felt frustrated that he couldn't really speak his mind.

"Why is it impossible?" Lehane asked, genuinely curious.

"Because," Rachel stood as well. "Because Lucas and I don't know each other. We met just two days ago, and—"

Lucas cut her off. He knew she was about to say she didn't know that Julia even had a son until her death. "I don't think that matters. The point is—"

"Excuse me. It does matter," Rachel got in, annoyed.

"Is it okay if I leave now?"

Lucas turned his attention to Mrs. Santiago, embarrassed that he'd forgotten the older woman was still in the room.

"Yes, of course. I'll just ask you to sign right here," the attorney said, indicating the bottom of another document. "This says you were present at the reading and accept the terms of the will. I'll have my secretary arrange for the items left for you by Ms. Winters to be delivered."

Lucas helped her to her feet. "I'm sorry, Mrs. Santiago. I was rude to ignore you."

"That's okay," she smiled forgiveness. She reached for Lucas's hand, holding it as she gazed into his face. "Can I tell you something?"

Lucas couldn't begin to guess what she wanted to say, but he was acutely aware of both Lehane and Rachel waiting to hear as well. He realized he was a bit wary and he didn't exactly know why.

"Of course," he nodded.

"Your name was the last one Ms. Winters spoke at the end. She called for you over and over again," Mrs. Santiago said.

He didn't know what to say. Mrs. Santiago squeezed his hand as if to make sure he understood. Her sharing of that information left Lucas with a peculiar sense of responsibility. Like he had to do something. Like he had to feel a certain way now that he knew.

"She could have been delirious because of the pain," he offered.

"No, no. It wasn't pain that brought your name to her lips. It was love."

In the ensuing silence, Mrs. Santiago released his hand and signed the document Lehane indicated to her. Lucas stepped aside and found himself facing Rachel. He was expecting to see something cynical or righteous in her features, but he saw neither. He found, instead, that her expression was sober, her eyes gentle. Her chin, with its shallow cleft, quivered. Even though Lucas knew he was probably being unfair, it irritated him that Rachel might be patronizing him with sympathy.

"Thank you for coming in today, Mrs. Santiago," Lehane said, escorting her out of the room.

Rachel walked to the window and stood looking down on the traffic and antlike pedestrians. Lucas immediately turned his attention to her, studying her from a distance and trying to figure out if there was anything to figure out about her. She had a way of smiling with her mouth that came through in her eyes as well. And she talked with her hands.

"Lucas, I'm sure there's a simple explanation," she quietly offered.

"That's where I disagree with you. Julia never did anything simple," he said.

"Why do you keep referring to her as Julia? She was your mother."

"I don't need you to remind me," Lucas shot back. "But you and I didn't know the same person. Nothing was easy or simple with Julia. Her whole life was one big complex drama, and her will is just another example, as far as I'm concerned. She couldn't just make her decisions clear and be done with it—"

"I don't understand what you don't understand," Lehane said, walking back in.

Lucas took a deep breath and stood with his hands in his trouser pockets. "Like Rachel said, I think this is a mistake."

"What I meant by that was I'm not really family to Julia," Rachel corrected.

Lucas caught her disapproving glare.

Lehane pursed his lips as he considered their confusion. "Are you saying that you want to contest the will?" he asked both Lucas and Rachel. "Because if you do, it's going to take time, legal fees, and will pit the two of you against each other. It could get messy. There are any number of other things you can do instead."

"Like?" Lucas asked.

"First of all, I think you should let your mother's wishes stand. You and Ms. Givens share legal ownership. Make some sort of agreement between the two of you about who stays in the house when. Or you can agree to sell the house and split the proceeds. I have a current appraisal of its value. You both could do very well financially if you go in that direction."

"No," Lucas said instantly. Lehane regarded him with raised brows at his firm reply. But Lucas realized that he had surprised himself even more. "I don't think I want to sell."

"Alright, that's a start," Lehane said. "And what about you, Ms. Givens? How do you feel about that?"

Lucas turned to Rachel, who had stood by listening thoughtfully to the attorney's suggestions. She came forward, shaking her head and then shrugging.

"I don't know," she said.

"Well, it seems to me that you two need to talk this over. The only thing I can move on is if one of you absolutely wants to challenge the will. Otherwise, you have to work something out on your own. Let me know what you decide."

Lucas listened as the attorney gave instructions on what he needed to do to secure the money left to him as beneficiary of the various accounts his mother owned. He listened as Lehane repeated to Rachel that the painting and box of other items left to her by Julia were still at Highland Beach, and she could make whatever arrangements she wished to get them within the next thirty days. Lehane offered to be available whenever he and Rachel came to a mutual decision on what to do with the house. And he wished them good luck.

"You'll have to excuse me," Lehane said finally. "I have other clients waiting. Can you find your way out?"

"We'll manage," Lucas said. He shook hands with the attorney, thanking him for taking care of the final arrangements for Julia.

Lucas once again found himself alone with Rachel. She didn't seem anxious to leave and, as a matter of fact, appeared to be waiting for him to say something first. In other words, the ball was in his court.

"Well?" Lucas began.

Rachel raised her brows. "Well?" she threw right back at him.

Lucas was amused that she wasn't about to be challenged, and he silently gave her credit for holding her own. But her feisty demeanor wasn't helping to solve their dilemma. He shook his head with a slight smile, rubbing his hands together.

"Look, if I fight for ownership of the entire house I should warn you that I will win," Lucas said with confidence.

"I don't know any such thing, and I don't believe you can guarantee it," she said tartly.

"Really?" He tilted his head and regarded her with curiosity.

He watched as Rachel seemed to hesitate. She averted her gaze and moistened her lips before looking him in the eye again.

"I'm sorry but I have a feeling that I knew Julia better than you did," she said quietly, almost gently.

Lucas immediately stiffened at her sharp insight. Rachel had hit a nerve. The damnable thing was, he didn't believe that's what she was trying to do.

"That's a very good defensive move," Lucas said. "How did you come to that conclusion?"

He thought her whole persona softened, as if she really didn't want to hit below the belt or say something that would hurt unnecessarily. Lucas decided that it wasn't pity she grappled with, but an attempt to be fair-minded. It was a novelty, in his experience, from someone who was a stranger and with so much to gain.

"It was something you said after the memorial on Saturday. You said yourself you didn't know your own mother that well. That and the fact that Julia had never mentioned she had a son. That's an incredible omission, don't you think?"

"I couldn't agree more," Lucas said, his tone hard.

"Which brings us back to the house on Highland Beach," Rachel said. "You said you don't want to sell. What do you want to do?"

"Think about it. See the house. Maybe selling will turn out to be the best thing and the only way to settle the matter. But not yet."

"Have you ever been there?"

Lucas's eyes were distant and cold. "No."

"Then that's really the first thing you need to do. I have to go there to get my painting. And that box. The attorney said I could."

"Be my guest," Lucas said magnanimously. "You can ask him for the keys, but there's probably a set available somewhere at the house."

"So then, I guess that's it," she said.

"At least for the moment," Lucas countered. "This isn't over 'till it's over."

"Fine. But you know I'm not going to cave in so you can have it your way," Rachel said.

Lucas chuckled appreciatively. "Them's fightin' words."

"I meant them to be," she grinned wickedly. "May the best person win."

"You mean, the best man," Lucas said dryly, not giving an inch.

Five

"Hey, Manny."

The young man seated at the desk looked up from his computer screen.

"Yo, Lucas. It's good to see you, man. How you been?"

Lucas accepted the New Age handshake, which was nothing more than their curled knuckles touching. "Great, thanks. How about you?"

Manny grimaced, moving back and swiveling his chair from side to side. "Still here, man." He abruptly sat forward again, reaching to remove a stack of computer magazines and business folders from the extra chair. "Here. Sit down."

Lucas accepted, looking around the disorganized and cluttered cubicle. It was filled with a combination of adolescent sports paraphernalia, sophisticated technogeek accessories, and promotional items. Manny himself presented a picture of the young, urban, street-smart guy, a little out of place and uncomfortable in a downtown office setting. He had a tendency to wear shirts that were too big in the neck and too long in the sleeves, ties that were unbearably ugly and poorly knotted, and khaki slacks that were so long they bunched around his ankles. Lucas saw the look as hip-hop for the gangsta who held down a legit job. But Manny was a genius with computers and knew his way around cyberspace.

"What are you doing here?" Manny asked.

"I came to see you, man."

Manny laughed in disbelief. "Right. I'm serious, Lucas. You thinking of coming back, or what?"

"Why, you miss me?" Lucas grinned, settling into the chair and crossing an ankle over the opposite knee. He picked up a rubber exercise ball manufactured to look like the earth, and began squeezing it between his clasped hands.

"You better believe it. Like, it was good to have a brotha up at the top around here. Know what I'm sayin'?" Manny groused.

"Funny, I seem to remember when you pegged me for just another *white* suit. And you accused me of trying to act black on top of that. So, which is it?"

Manny squirmed, bouncing in his chair. "Come on, man. I couldn't tell right away. Look at you," he said, gesturing at Lucas as if it was still not a sure thing.

"Don't you know you shouldn't judge a book by its cover?"

"Yeah, I know, I know. I was stupid. So, what's the deal? How come you came back? The guys upstairs, they made you an offer you can't refuse?" he cackled.

Lucas uncrossed his legs and sat up straight. "Nothing like that. I'm not looking to practice law full-time anymore. Like I said, I came to see you. I have a favor to ask."

Manny perked up with interest. "Anything, man. You know all you gotta do is ask and I'm there for you."

"I need to get some information on someone. A woman. Background stuff, mostly. I don't want personal things like credit-card debt or outstanding bank loans. Whatever you can find out about her family, relationships. You know."

"Oh, man. You checkin' out a new girlfriend? What about that other one you was seeing? Jennifer."

Lucas knew from the young man's sly expression that he'd put the wrong spin on the request. He firmly brushed that suggestion aside. "We're just good friends. We go back a long way."

"Too bad. 'Cause she's okay, for a white girl."

"This is someone else."

"Who is it?" Manny asked.

"Her name is Rachel Givens. Probably about thirty, give or take a few years. I think she's from the DC area originally but I'm not sure if she lives here now." Lucas said, not unaware that Rachel Givens had grabbed his attention and exhibited a certain appeal, but he wasn't going to let that confuse the issue at hand.

Manny wrote down her name and other basic facts Lucas fed him. "No problem," he said. "When do you want this?"

"Soon as you can, but I may be out of town for a few days. Call me on my cell when you have something," Lucas said, standing up. He pulled his wallet out and opened it. "Here. Take this for your time."

"Naw, man. You know I can't take no money from you."

"Thanks. I don't recommend doing this during office hours."

"Okay. Maybe you can do me a favor, too."

"What? You have another cousin or brother in jail?" Lucas asked.

He knew it was an ongoing problem in Manny's large extended family, although Manny had never been in trouble, a fact of which he was enormously and rightfully proud.

"Nothing like that this time, man. Listen. I hear you're really playing your sax in front of people and that you're doing good, man. You're at some club down on Shaw and U Street?"

Lucas put his wallet away. "I get a gig now and then. I'm hooked up with a couple of small bands."

"I want to bring my girl down to hear you, okay? Like, we don't know anybody who's a famous musician or anything."

"I don't think I'm ever going to be famous, Manny."

"That's okay. I can say, 'see that guy? I know him. Me and him used to work together.' "

Lucas smiled at the compliment. "Sure. Any time. When you get back in touch about that information, I'll let you know where I'll be playing in the next month or so."

"That's cool. Thanks," Manny grinned. "So, how come you need me to check out this woman if you're not into her? What did she do to you?"

The question surprised Lucas because Manny had innocently touched on the heart of the matter. What, exactly, had Rachel Givens done to him? What was he hoping to find out that having met and spoken with her hadn't satisfied?

He playfully tossed the exercise ball to Manny, who deftly snatched it out of midair.

"Let's just say she has something that belongs to me. I want it back."

Rachel was getting used to waking up to the warm homey smell of breakfast food wafting from the first floor. She rolled onto her back, stretching and inhaling the comforting aroma of brewed coffee and crisp bacon. She glanced at the clock radio on the night table. It was after ten on Wednesday. She realized she was getting much too cozy in her mother's house. She was, maybe, much too excited about her drive later to Highland Beach.

Eyes closed, Rachel listened to the sounds of the morning. Mostly silence and summer stillness. She'd left the bedroom windows open the night before and she could hear some twittering birdcalls, but otherwise blessed silence. She felt lulled by it. In her New York apartment, the sounds of garbage pickup and traffic would have forced her from bed hours before. In contrast, her childhood home had a rhythm and peace of its own.

It used to be quiet like this on Highland Beach. Except the first thing she did each morning was to look out the window and stare at the water to make sure the Chesapeake Bay was still there. The memory brought a wave of sweet nostalgia. Ever since the meeting with Lucas and Julia's attorney two days ago, she'd been thinking about Julia's house. She was still in shock that she now owned half of it. The prospect of returning as a rightful owner filled her with an amazing joy, the likes of which she hadn't experienced in a long time.

Rachel finally got out of bed, washed, then dressed in a denim shift, combing her almost shoulder-length hair with her fingers and using a headband to hold it off her face. She'd learned over the years that a good shaping and cut, and letting her hair do its thing, were all she needed. She headed barefoot down to the kitchen. Her mother sat reading the papers and drinking coffee. Through the open basement door Rachel could hear the hum of the clothes dryer.

"Morning. Why did you let me sleep so late? I'm turning into a slug."

"You didn't tell me you wanted to get up early," Lydia replied.

"I should have. I feel guilty that you're up, made breakfast, doing laundry . . ."

"I cooked bacon. If you want eggs or anything else you'll have to make it yourself."

Rachel decided on toast and a few slices of bacon, not worrying about the nutritional value of what she was eating. For a while, conversation with her mother centered on family matters, in particular, Gordon, the baby of the family, and his latest adventures in dating. But mostly Rachel was aware that her mother seemed unusually nonconversational in the last day or so, since she'd told her about being left half of the house in Highland Beach.

"You know, I miss this. I forgot how much I used to love breakfast when I was little. Especially on the weekends. I remember when Sunday was Daddy's day to make waffles with sausages. And after church he'd take me and Ross to the latest Disney movie. There was something about Sundays that always made me feel warm and safe."

"Really?" Lydia asked absently, staring into space. "I seem

to remember you telling me often you couldn't wait to leave home and live your own life."

Rachel was thrown off guard that her mother would remember something like that. "I don't think I was saying I hated life at home. I think I just meant, you know—"

"What?" Lydia prompted, staring at her.

"There was so much I wanted to do with my life. I just wanted to . . . to get started. Like it would all disappear before I'd had a chance to experience anything," Rachel tried earnestly to explain.

"I thought maybe it had something to do with Julia Winters filling your head with nonsense about life being your oyster, or following your heart and wonderful things will happen to you. There was always something different you wanted, Rachel. Always somewhere else you wanted to be."

"You make me sound ungrateful and selfish," Rachel said, her voice laced with annoyance at her mother's scathing remarks. "What was so wrong with Julia encouraging me not to give up on my dreams? At least she cared that I had dreams."

Lydia slammed her cup down so sharply on the table that the coffee sloshed around and nearly spilled out. "Don't you talk to me that way, Rachel. How dare you suggest that I didn't care about you?"

"Mom, that's not what I meant. You know, sometimes it's just so hard to talk to you. You're the one that keeps bringing up Julia's name, and I think you're being unfair to her. You didn't know her the way I did."

Lydia sat wearily back in her chair and exhaled a deep breath of forbearance. "I knew her better than you realize."

"How is that possible?" Rachel asked, frustrated by her mother's innuendos.

" 'Cause you don't know everything that went on that summer, Rae," Lydia said in exasperation.

Rachel was about to go on the defensive when she caught

herself. She recalled the incredible revelation from her brother Ross that he'd known since that summer, for all these years, that Julia had a son. What other secrets were there?

"What do you mean?" she asked.

Lydia leaned forward to put her elbows on the table. She clasped her hands and used them as a prop that she rested her forehead against.

"Rae, I want to drop this. You're right. It's my fault for bring up Julia's name over and over. You don't need to know any more than you do, okay?"

Rachel knew there was no going back. Her mother's comments only fueled her curiosity because of the sarcastic undercurrent in everything she said. She couldn't imagine anything bad enough to have stayed with her mother all these years, something that was a well-kept and clearly painful secret. Rachel braced herself. She wanted to know, but was afraid of what the telling would mean, and what it might do to her.

"Mom, I really don't know what you're talking about," she said. "Tell me."

When Lydia raised her head, there were tears in her eyes. In her whole life, Rachel couldn't remember ever seeing her mother cry. She reached out and touched her arm. Anticipation was making her heart beat faster.

"Mom, what is it?"

"You know why Julia named you in her will leaving you half her house? It was out of guilt. She did it to make up for me and your father."

Rachel pulled away suddenly, as if she'd been burnt. "What did Julia have to do with you and Daddy?"

"Rae, haven't you ever wondered why your father and I got divorced?"

"Of course I wondered, but it didn't seem that it was the kind of thing I could ask you about," Rachel said. "It seemed like grown-up business. I was angry that it was happening. I didn't want Daddy to go, but I knew that what I wanted wasn't going to matter much. It was happening, and there was nothing I could do about it."

"No, you couldn't have stopped it. Your father and I were the only ones who could do that, and I just wanted it to end. Simon had a little fling with Julia that summer. I found out about it."

"No."

It was out before Rachel could even think. It was an immediate and instinctive reaction. She knew her father would never do something like that. Julia would never do anything to hurt *her.*

"No," she repeated, staring at her mother's haunted expression. Rachel didn't see anger so much as a deep wrenching wound.

"He didn't think I'd find out, but I finally figured out it was going on the whole month we were on the Beach."

"But . . . when? How did you find out?"

"I was suspicious the first time I saw Simon leaving Julia's house one Saturday afternoon when we'd planned on driving up to Ocean City. He said Julia had asked him to change a light fixture. Fine. The next time his excuse got kind of lame, but again I let it go. Then there was the time he said he was going to her house to bring you home. When you came in fifteen minutes later and said you had been on the beach with another family and not with Julia, I knew," Lydia finished bitterly.

In an instant Rachel saw the world she'd known, the memories she'd cherished and believed in, crash and burn. She felt a tightening in her stomach, then a churning queasiness. She got up abruptly, scraping the chair against the floor.

"No, *no.* Daddy wouldn't do that."

"So, now I'm a liar?" Lydia asked.

"That's not what I'm saying." She remembered the silence her mother had cloaked herself in after her father had moved out of the house. But the truth, once spoken, was too raw. "But how could Daddy do that to you? To our family?" Rachel asked.

"Rae, it's not that hard," Lydia sighed. She brushed her tears away impatiently. "In one little moment with the right place and circumstance, it happens. Your father said he didn't love Julia. He said he kind of felt sorry for her. If that was the case, he could have shown his pity some other way."

"Did he say he was sorry?"

"Oh, constantly," Lydia admitted. "But that didn't cut it with me. He had a choice, and he chose wrong as far as I'm concerned. An affair with Julia over loyalty to me and his family."

Julia and my father.

"I don't know what to say. I can't believe Daddy would do something like that."

"Stop saying you can't believe it, Rae, 'cause it wasn't just your father who did wrong," Lydia reminded her.

"I understand that." She used the back of her hand to wipe tears from her cheek. "Mom, it must have been so humiliating for you. Why didn't you ever tell any of us what went wrong between you and Daddy?"

"I was so angry at Simon for messing up like that, right under my nose. What he did hurt. But I didn't want his children to turn against him," Lydia said.

"I hated that he had to leave us."

"Believe it or not, so did I, Rae."

Rachel leaned forward, wrapping her arms around her mother's shoulders and letting their heads rest together.

"When I think about it now, your father was probably right. Julia was a sad person. She couldn't have been as happy and carefree as she let on to everybody."

"Why do you say that?"

"She lived by herself in that big, old house. She never let on she had a child. What was up with that? She always behaved like she was this internationally famous actress and singer, but what had she done in her life? You said she had a caretaker when she died. Well, how sad is that?

"Your father made a big trade-off when he got involved with her. He lost his family. I don't think Julia had anything to lose."

"Did you ever forgive him?" she asked.

"Long ago. You have to also, Rachel. He's your father, and he's not perfect."

"I know," Rachel said.

And neither was Julia, she was finding out.

It was a little after noon when Rachel heard the telephone ring as she descended the stairs. She was carrying a small tote and her shoulder bag. She reached the first floor as she heard her mother answer the call, so she continued out the front door to her mother's car, parked in the driveway. After putting her things in the trunk, Rachel returned to the house to say good-bye before starting on her drive to Highland Beach.

"Rachel, where are you?" her mother called to her.

"In the hallway," she responded.

Lydia approached from the kitchen. "It's for you," she said, holding out the cordless phone.

Rachel took the phone, placing it to her ear. For some reason Lucas was the first person that came to mind as the possible caller. "Hello?"

"Hey, big sis. How's it going?"

"Well, now I know I'm not on your A-list, Gordon. I've been at Mom's for almost a week and you're just getting around to calling me?" She sat down on the steps leading to the upper floor.

"You know how it is. There's a lot going on right now. Did Mom tell you I was taking summer classes?"

"She did. She also told me about your internship at the Justice Department. She's hoping it turns into a real job when you graduate from law school next year. *And* she told me about your newest sweetie. What happened to Alicia? I liked her."

"Man, she started talking about me working for her father and stuff like that. I know where that was leading," Gordon chuckled.

"Not ready for that walk, eh?"

"Not hardly. I'm too young. Got a lot of living to do before I take that bullet."

"I agree. So, it looks like I'm not going to see you this trip. I'm really disappointed, Gordon."

"Sorry about that. Mom just said you're getting ready to leave."

"Not back to New York. I have to drive down to Highland Beach. You were too young to remember, but we used to go there for vacations before . . . before Mom and Dad divorced," she said.

Unexpectedly, her voice caught on the word as she reacted to the recent conversation with her mother. The things that happened that last summer would mean nothing to him. Even though Gordon had a close relationship with their father, he seemed to get a perverse kick out of telling people he was from a broken home.

"Yeah, I've seen the pictures."

"Anyway, I have to take care of some business. I'll be back here in a day or two, but then I've got to get home."

"Now that you mention home, I was thinking of maybe driving up to New York—"

"And you need a place to crash. Sure, you can stay at my place. As a matter of fact, I have to fly over to Europe soon. If you come up while I'm away you'll have the place all to yourself."

"You don't mind if I bring Natalie, do you?"

"She the new girlfriend? I thought that was the whole idea?"

"Thanks, Rae. You're the best," Gordon said.

"I know," Rachel grinned. "I better get going."

"Okay. Again, I'm real sorry about not getting together."

"We'll work something out next time. Thanks for calling, at least. Bye."

"Talk to you soon—"

"Oh, Gordon! Wait, wait. Don't hang up," Rachel shouted. "I have to ask you something. Do you know how to use the Internet to find out things about people?"

Gordon laughed uproariously.

"What's so funny?" Rachel asked.

"Everybody I know Googles to check out new people they're interested in hooking up with. Standard operating procedure for dating. You've got to be careful. Who are you trying to track down? Good guy, bad guy?"

"How do you know it's a guy?" Rachel grinned.

"The only time it really matters is when you meet someone new."

"Well, it's not exactly like that, but I'd say he's a good guy," Rachel concluded. She didn't for a minute believe that Lucas Scott was going to turn out to be an ax murderer. "Anyway, this is business, not personal."

She gave her brother what little she knew about Lucas. Gordon promised to get back to her ASAP. Rachel finished the call and went looking for her mother. She found Lydia in the backyard, knitting.

"Getting ready to go?" Lydia asked, her fingers moving the knitting needles quickly and expertly.

"I think so. It's getting late. I should be back around nine tonight, depending on the traffic on 50 getting out of Annapolis."

"I may not be here where you get home," Lydia announced.

"Mom, sooner or later you're going to have to tell me about your secret other life," Rachel teased.

"No I don't." Lydia put down the sweater she was working on to stare at her daughter. "Are you okay with what we talked about? You know. Your father and Julia?"

"I don't know if okay is the right word, yet," Rachel said. "I think I'm angry and disappointed. I don't really understand how it could happen. Maybe I'm being naive."

"Maybe," Lydia nodded. "Maybe you're still seeing your father and Julia through the eyes of a thirteen-year-old."

"Then it's time I grew up," Rachel responded.

"Oh, my God. I'm back," Rachel murmured to herself.

When she turned onto Arundel On The Bay Road, she could literally feel her heartbeat quicken. She remembered the feel of making that turn when she was a child, and the excitement of knowing the family was almost there.

She wasn't as familiar with this lower end of the Bay community as she was with Highland Beach, but to her it was all the same. A magic place unlike any place she'd ever been to.

She drove slowly, her head swiveling from side to side as she took a brief glance at every single house along the next three streets. She could tell which houses were very old, as they had the look of deferred maintenance and long ownership. Others showed definite signs of work, like new siding or roofs, or landscaped front yards. One or two homes were not so much contemporary as just very new.

The trees and bushes growing naturally in profusion along the road and streets and between homes discreetly hid the fact that there was a beach and a shoreline behind each house. She drove up and down streets, knowing it was impossible to get lost. It was like a cocoon here, nestled on the very edge of the Chesapeake Bay. She remembered that somewhere at the end of one of the roads there lived a woman whose family had summered at Highland Beach for decades. With quick calculation Rachel guessed that the matriarch would have to be around one hundred years old.

"I bet she remembers everything that went on here," Rachel said to herself, wondering if the information would include her father's indiscretion.

But despite that concern, Rachel began to feel a lightness of spirit, a growing inner joy that she was actually back at the place that she'd loved so dearly. Every other response took second place to that.

She finally made her way back to Bay Highlands Drive and headed toward the shore. At the end of the street there was a gatehouse, a tiny enclosure with just enough room for one person. She didn't want to take the time to get out and read the plaque on the outside of the structure, which now appeared shuttered and deserted. Rachel seemed to recall her father telling all of them one year, after they'd finally arrived for their stay, that the gatehouse had been necessary back when the community was first founded for fear of attacks and harassment by surrounding white residents. For Rachel, the absence of anyone in the gatehouse was surely a sign that things had finally changed, and proof that that kind of defense was no longer necessary.

She turned left into Highland Beach. Going to the right would lead into Venice Beach, but she didn't want to take the time just then to drive through. She was anxious to reach her final destination.

Rachel turned left onto Wayman. The house her family used to rent was still there, but it didn't look the same. The cedar shingles were gone, and the siding had been redone. The house had been painted a lighter color and looked bigger. The porch had been enlarged. There was a new widow's walk at the top of the house, and huge new picture windows looking out across the Chesapeake Bay. It was now a house worthy of *Architectural Digest,* but Rachel knew she would always have a fondness for the way the house used to be. Comfortable, a little shabby, and lived in.

She continued her slow roll down the street and held her

breath. There it was, Julia's house. She slowed to a stop in front and just sat and stared at the three-story house. Everything looked the same. A smile formed on Rachel's mouth. It grew into a wide grin even as her eyes watered at the sheer unadulterated happiness she felt. Being back on Highland Beach felt like coming back home.

Rachel parked the car and removed her things from the trunk. Kenneth Lehane had told her exactly where to look for the set of keys that Julia had kept in a secret spot for all the years she'd owned the house. But the keys weren't there. She tried all the doors and windows, just in case one was open. No such luck. She searched other places that seemed a likely hiding place: under the welcome mat, in the planter next to the entrance. Nothing. Rachel couldn't believe that she'd made it all the way to Julia's house only to be locked out.

She sat on the porch steps with her tote. Digging out the envelope of official papers from Lehane, she carefully read every single page. Finally, there was a glimmer of hope. She found a list from the Homeowners' Association of local residents. Rachel recognized Harrietta Cousins, one of Julia's good friends whom she'd met at the memorial service almost a week ago.

Rachel left her things and walked to Harrietta's house, a narrow tri-level house which was actually on Douglass and a block away from the beach. She kept her fingers crossed that Harrietta was home and that she had the keys to Julia's house. She rang the bell but got no answer. She then walked around the side of the house to a fence that closed off the backyard. Rachel could hear voices on the other side.

"Hello," she called out loudly.

"Yes?" came back a voice indicating caution rather than curiosity.

"I'm hoping that Harrietta Cousins is home. I'd like to speak with her about Julia Winters's house."

"Well, who are you?"

Rachel sighed in relief. She recognized the voice. "It's Rachel Givens, Harrietta. Do you remember me from the service for Julia last week?"

After a moment, a door opened in the fence and Rachel found herself being ushered into the yard by a young woman. Although spacious, the yard was overcrowded with planters of every size and shape, giving the yard the look of a tiny botanical garden. Seated under a shady tree, Harrietta was ensconced like a queen on her throne.

"Course I remember you. So sad about Julia. But I already told you that." She pointed a gnarled finger at the woman who'd let Rachel in. "That's Mildred. She's supposed to be keeping an eye on me but I don't need any baby-sitter. She's younger than my oldest child. Come on and sit down. Over here, so I can see you."

Rachel smiled a silent thank-you to Mildred before taking the cushioned lawn chair next to Harrietta.

"Thank you for letting me in. I'm sorry to bother you like this."

"No trouble. I'm glad you changed your mind about coming to the Beach. Where you staying?"

"At Julia's house. As it turns out, I was named in her will as one of the owners," Rachel explained.

"No kidding! Oh, I'm so glad to hear that," Harrietta said. "Some of us around here were a little worried about what was going to happen to the house. We didn't know if it was put up for sale or not." She leaned closer, talking in a conspiratorial whisper. "We're concerned about who buys into the community, you understand. We like to know who our neighbors are going to be."

"Do you think I'll have any problems?"

"Of course not," Harrietta said. "I'll tell everybody around here you met with my approval. My word is good enough."

Rachel laughed. "I appreciate your support. I do have one

important favor to ask. Any chance you have keys to get into Julia's house?"

"Of course I do," Harrietta said. She turned toward her house and yelled in a bloodcurdling voice. "*Mildred*!"

Rachel hid her amusement. Harrietta was a character, and Rachel rather liked her. She was probably also a very good person to have as a friend.

In short order Mildred had been dispatched to find the keys, and she returned within minutes with them in hand. At the same time Mildred announced it was time for Miss Harrietta's lunch.

"Stay and join me," Harrietta invited Rachel, while Mildred stood by watchfully as she got up from her chair.

"Thank you so much, but I think I'll pass this time. I'm driving back to Baltimore later and I have a lot to do this afternoon."

"You can come by to see me anytime. I like being around you young people. The old folks around here just complain about being old. And watch out for Flo. She gossips, you know. By the way, did I hear you say you owned only half of the house?"

"That's right."

"Well then, who owns the other half?" Harrietta asked.

"Lucas Scott," Rachel said.

She saw the puzzlement on the older woman's face as she struggled to recognize the name she kept repeating softly to herself.

"Lucas is Julia's son," Rachel clarified.

Harrietta stood straight and gaped at Rachel. Her eyes were round as an owl's behind her thick glasses, and her small mouth formed a perfect O of surprise.

"Well, for goodness' sakes."

Rachel finally left wondering if Harrietta's surprise was at not knowing that Lucas would be deeded the house, or if it was not knowing that Lucas was Julia's son. Since Harrietta had already declared herself one of Julia's dearest friends, Rachel assumed her reaction was to the former. Despite Harrietta's belief that she was not a gossip, Rachel somehow knew that the news would spread like a brushfire before very long. But she couldn't worry herself about the fallout. Lucas would just have to deal with it.

She made her way back to Julia's house. When she unlocked the door and stepped inside, she held her breath. It was like a time warp to the past, and she was a little girl again. Of course, Julia was not there to greet her. The house was very silent and, because it had probably been closed up for weeks, extremely hot. Rachel slowly walked the old, familiar path through the open entrance hall into the large living room, and turned right to go through the enclosed solarium where the windows faced the bay. To her left was the kitchen. Rachel stood looking around in childish awe. Everywhere there was evidence of Julia. It was like she'd just stepped out for a while and was coming right back. There was a newspaper lying open on a lounge chair. It was dated three days before she'd passed away. A chenille throw was draped over the arm of a wicker club chair, and a pair of reading glasses was on the coffee table.

Rachel went from room to room on the first floor and started to open windows and prop open doors to let in the cool bay breeze. She inhaled deeply of the unique scent of the wood frame house, saturated with the smell of water, of trees and grass, of sand and sunshine. She refamiliarized herself with old things, and found the many additions that were new.

She walked out the back of the house into the brilliant daylight, squinting against the sun. Crossing Wayman, Rachel noticed that a park had been created on the other side of the road leading to the water's edge. There was a small playground jungle gym for little children, along with several picnic tables positioned for getting an optimum view of the Chesapeake. There was a narrow stretch of soft sand, and then the Chesapeake Bay itself. It rolled gently into the shore, but flowed faster south on its move to meet up with the Atlantic Ocean.

Rachel crossed the road, feeling the warm breeze off the water brush against her face and bare arms. She removed her shoes and sighed deeply with the visceral pleasure of sand squeezing between her toes. She lowered herself to sit with her knees drawn close to her chest. She'd left her sunglasses in the house, but even being forced to squint against the bright July sun was part of the experience. She was absorbing the summer day right into her pores.

It had been such a long time. Rachel closed her eyes, feeling languid and relaxed. She was being sucked into her own memories, her mind sinking into the past. She suddenly recalled every minute of the last day she'd visited Highland Beach . . .

Six

Rachel was sure that the steady downpour of steamy summer rain was a deliberate conspiracy to ruin the last day of her vacation, at least as much as her mother's determined efforts were to make the family leave Highland Beach earlier than originally planned. What was the big hurry, anyway? She sent up silent prayers for the rain to stop. Julia had told her that August rain on the Chesapeake never lasted for long. But as Rachel gazed anxiously from beneath the shelter of the porch at the gray mist that obscured the shoreline, she had the feeling that today was going to be the exception to Julia's rule.

She walked to the far end of the porch and leaned over the railing. From where she stood she could pretty much see Julia's house, the third one down, but there was no way to tell if Julia herself was home. For a moment Rachel calculated how wet she would get if she attempted to run the distance. And what excuse could she give her mother for defying her orders to stay away from Julia Winters' house.

"Rachel? Rachel! Do you hear me calling you?"

Rachel stood stone-still at the sound of her mother's voice. She felt the sudden chill of cool, damp air on her thin, brown face and bare legs, and hugged herself. She pressed back against the rough cedar shingle siding of the house, torn between obeying her mother's urgent summons and desperately trying to find a way to see Julia once more before her family *left Highland Beach and drove back home. She gnawed on the corner of her mouth, her stomach a roiling knot of ambivalence. She quickly made her decision, pulling the hood of her sweatshirt over her ponytail and heading for the steps. She was willing to risk the consequences. If she hurried, her mother wouldn't even know she'd been gone.*

But the door to the house opened behind her and her father stepped out onto the porch. Rachel stopped abruptly in her tracks, whirling around to face him. Simon Givens was tall and stocky and looked very much like the former college football player he bragged about being, and not at all like the pilot for a commercial airline he was. Rachel had always thought of her father as "the fun one." He was quick to tease her or to laugh, and a great buffer between herself and her strict, demanding mother. But as her father stood watching her, she could tell from the tension etched on his face that she'd better not take anything for granted. She held her breath as she looked for signs of disapproval from him.

"Didn't you hear your mother calling you?" her father asked.

He sounded stern but not angry. "Yes," she quietly admitted.

"Why didn't you answer?" She shrugged. "You're supposed to keeping an eye on the baby so your mother can finish getting our things together."

"I know," she murmured, stuffing her balled fists into the pockets of her sweatshirt.

"Then what are you doing out here?"

Rachel looked directly at him. "I just wanted to go and say good-bye to Julia."

"Julia," he murmured, his tone heavy with both resignation and understanding. "I thought you said good-bye to her yesterday?"

"No, I didn't," Rachel quickly defended herself. "I only told her we were leaving today."

"Then if you don't see her today, she'll understand, right?"

His logic confused Rachel, and was even annoying. How come he didn't tell her to go and be quick about it? How come he didn't offer to cover for her with her mother? Rachel gave her father what she hoped was a desperate and sad look of appeal. It would never have worked on her mother.

"Daddy, can I please go? Just for a minute."

He shook his head, at the same time beckoning for her to go back into the house. "There's no time. Now, come on."

"Please?" Rachel whined. "I promise I won't stay."

"Rae, I said no. She's probably not even home."

"Yes, she is."

"How do you know?" He walked toward the porch railing, peering through the sheet of gray rain in much the same way she had.

" 'Cause she told me not to forget to come by," Rachel said, joining her father.

They stood together gazing toward Julia's house as if some unnamed force held them captive there. Rachel waited for her father to change his mind and give her permission to go.

"You know how your mother feels about your going over there all the time."

"Yeah, but I don't understand why, Daddy. Julia's so nice. Don't you think so?"

He stared solemnly at her. "What I think is you forget that Julia is not one of your little girlfriends. She's a grown woman. You've been pestering her every summer we've been coming here. She's probably glad to see all of us leave."

Rachel frowned. "That's not true. She told me I could come to see her anytime I wanted to. She said I'm refreshing."

"Or just fresh," her father grunted. "Forget what Julia told you. It's more important for you to do what your mother tells you."

"But I have something to give her," she lied to her father.

"What?" he asked.

"A . . . a pair of earrings I made for her. From the bead kit she gave me last week."

Rachel could see her father's doubt, but maybe he was also weakening. Unlike her mother, he was not one to make imperial demands just because he was her father and in charge. She watched him as he thought it over, the movement of his mouth making his mustache twitch. He glanced toward Julia's house.

"Rae, I think you better forget all about—"

The door opened abruptly again and a woman came out. Rachel and her father turned to stare at her mother, Lydia, silenced by her dark, glaring eyes. Rachel looked quickly away from her, combating the guilt she always felt from comparing her mother to Julia. She wished her mother would lose some weight. She wished she would laugh the way Julia did. Julia was so glamorous and wore pretty clothes. She'd even been to Italy.

Her mother looked back and forth between her and her father.

"What's going on out here?" she asked.

Despite her body language, her mother's voice was calm and even. She had cultivated the kind of tone that Rachel had learned meant her mother always knew exactly what was going on, and always seem to know beforehand the answers to questions she asked. Therein lay the trap. If she lied, Rachel knew the consequences could be harsh.

She glanced at her father instead, still hoping that he would champion her cause. She didn't have the nerve to ask her mother if she could see Julia before they left. Most of her month on Highland Beach had already been spent trying to find ways to get around the limits her mother set on her movement and activities. On top of that, much to her aggravation, she'd found herself baby-sitting her younger brother Gordon during the whole vacation, and resenting it.

Rachel felt her mother's attention focus on her.

"I asked you a question."

"She came out to make sure she and the boys hadn't left any of their things lying around," her father responded. He put his hand on Rachel's shoulder and gave her a gentle push. "Go on in, Rae. There's a lot of work still to do."

Rachel obeyed. But she let the porch door slam shut behind her in protest. Helpless anger made her pout mulishly. She dropped onto a chair just inside the door.

"That's unfair," she muttered to herself, frustrated by her mother's lack of understanding.

There were half-filled bags, boxes, and suitcases all around the first floor, evidence that her family was leaving. Rachel felt tears sting her eyes. She didn't want to go yet.

There was a rumble of footsteps on the old wooden stairwell ending in the noisy landing of her older brother, Ross. He playfully hit her on the top of her head with his baseball cap.

"Cut it out," she ordered, annoyed with him.

"Mom was looking for you. We're almost ready to leave." He swept by, tall and lanky, headed for the kitchen.

Her parents were still out on the porch, and Rachel could hear them talking. First her father, then her mother. Her mother's voice was louder, but Rachel couldn't tell what they were saying. She had the feeling it was about her.

"Rae, here . . . half-pack."

Rachel focused on the toddler standing in front of her. He was holding an armful of his things and then he suddenly dropped them into her lap. Two stuffed animals, a plastic baseball bat, and the bottom half of a pair of pajamas with Spiderman printed all over. The bat fell and rolled along the floor. Rachel made a face at her baby brother, momentarily distracted by his small gestures and attempts to talk. She pushed everything he'd given her to the floor and lifted him onto her lap. She bounced him up and down, squeezing his warm, soft body against her.

"Gordon, Gordon, puddin' and pie, kissed the girls and made them cry."

Gordon giggled but quickly grew tired of the game and slid from her lap. "Where Mommy?" he asked.

"Talking to Daddy," Rachel answered. The voices on the porch had dropped to a muffled urgency. She wondered if they were arguing again. She stood up, retrieving her brother's things from the floor. "Come on, Gordon. Let's go find your suitcase."

The child picked up the bat and began beating it against the bare wood floor as he followed her down a short hallway into the parlor room. She patiently endured his little-boy need to make loud screeching sound effects to accompany his march. Rachel instructed Gordon to put his things into his bright yellow wheeled suitcase. But he was more interested in playing with a battery-operated robot.

Realizing the opportunity, Rachel reached for the nearby cordless telephone. She scrunched down on the floor next to an end table where she wouldn't be easily seen. She punched in Julia's number. There was no answer. Believing she may have entered the wrong number, she tried again. There was still no answer.

Rachel put the phone down and pushed aside the curtains to look out the window. Visibility was poor through the old glass, and the angle was even worse. She couldn't see Julia's house from here. Hearing her parents returning to the house spurred her into action, and she scrambled to her feet to finish packing Gordon's case.

"Did you get all of the baby's things from upstairs?" her mother asked her.

"I think so," Rachel said.

"Go on upstairs and look."

The impatience in her mother's voice propelled Rachel through the rest of the packing. Her father loaded their station wagon while Ross went through every room closing and locking all the windows, then drawing all the shades and blinds. Her mother dusted and vacuumed, making sure that their rented house was left in exactly the clean and neat condition in which they'd found it upon arrival almost a month earlier.

"I don't want anybody talking behind our back that we don't know how to act in someone else's home," her mother had said often during their stay.

Rachel had asked her parents the year before why they couldn't buy a house on the Beach. Her mother's response had been a flat and final "We can't afford it." So Rachel had decided that she was going to save all her allowance and buy a house of her own one day on Highland Beach.

When it came time to pack her own things, Rachel dawdled over all the things she'd acquired that summer, many of them from Julia. There was an old LP album from a Broadway musical called Timbuktu. Julia said she'd performed in it. She examined the old pocket mirror with the cover done in petit point. She'd found it at a local garage sale Julia had taken her to. She'd bought an old crocheted drawstring purse for her mother, even though there was a small hole in the bottom.

Then, way before she was ready, her father announced that it was time to go.

In a panic Rachel hung back, claiming a last-minute need to use the bathroom. She could see the suspicion in her mother's eyes as she returned to the house. Once inside, alone, Rachel headed for the telephone again.

There was still no answer at the house down the way. Finally, Rachel knew she was going to have to leave Highland Beach without saying good-bye to Julia. While using the bathroom she heard the car horn blast twice, reminding her that everyone was waiting for her.

In the car Rachel prayed that her father would take Chesapeake Road to get back to the main street heading out of Highland and Venice Beach. That way they'd have to pass the *house where Julia lived. But, as her father had suspected, Julia wasn't home because the house was dark. The family wagon drove down Wayman Avenue, past the children's playground with the Chesapeake Bay in the background.*

Unexpectedly, Rachel saw Julia on the side of the road, standing near a corner and waiting, waiting for her, Rachel was sure. She recognized Julia's Chinese paper umbrella. Rachel loved that umbrella because no one else had one like it. They drove closer and Julia waved at the car.

"Look! I think she's wearing the earrings I made her," Rachel said.

Nonetheless, her father drove past Julia without giving her a chance to say good-bye. Rachel turned in her seat to stare out the back window at the fading figure. She heard her name faintly, carried on the breeze, as Julia shouted good-bye.

"Daddy, could you stop for just a—"

"No," her mother interrupted. "Turn around and sit down."

But she didn't, watching through the rain-streaked window as Julia continued to wave languidly at the departing car. Like a greeting, not a farewell. Rachel waved back at her with both hands until the car turned a corner and Julia was gone.

No one in the car said a word. Ross was already engrossed in a magazine, pretending not to notice. For a while the only sounds were those of the windshield wipers, the rain, and Gordon's babbling from the front seat as he sat on their mother's lap.

"We should be home in a couple of hours," her father told them.

"Good. I'm sure glad to be leaving," her mother said.

"We could have stayed. We would be leaving in three days anyway," her father said.

"Of course, you would say so," her mother responded.

"I wish we could have stayed the whole summer," Rachel said, slouching in her seat and searching for a book to read.

"That's 'cause you like Julia Winters," Ross spoke up.

Her mother sucked her teeth impatiently. "I am sick of hearing about that woman."

"I think she's a little crazy," Ross voiced his opinion.

"She's nice," Rachel defended, angry at both comments. She leaned forward to talk across her father's shoulder while he concentrated on his driving. "You like her, don't you, Daddy?" Rachel asked.

"She's an interesting woman," he spoke carefully.

"But you like her, too, right?" she persisted.

"Rachel, enough," her mother said.

Rachel stopped. But not for long. "Julia says I'm talented. She says I should study art."

"You can't even draw," Ross chuckled, as if the idea was totally ludicrous.

"Shut up," she demanded.

Rachel stared forlornly out the window, watching as all the stores and businesses leading into Highland Beach gave way to Route 50 heading back toward DC. Miraculously, her mind was soon busy with the anticipation of all the things she wanted to try once she got home, things that Julia had showed her how to do. And she was going to start a journal. Julia has said that every girl should have a journal because it was a wonderful way to keep secrets and write down things you didn't want to ever forget.

"I can't wait until next summer," she said.

"What's happening next summer?" her father asked, glancing at her in his rearview mirror.

"We're coming back to Highland Beach."

"Oh, no. I don't think so," her mother declared.

Rachel sat straight. Her mother couldn't mean it.

"Did you hear what I said? We're not coming back next summer."

"Why?" Rachel asked.

"That's okay with me," Ross said. "There's nothing to do

here. I'd rather stay home with my friends next summer." It was a subtle reminder that in a year he'd be graduating high school.

"We don't know what we're doing next summer. Let's try to get through the rest of this one, first," her father said.

"We're not coming back," Lydia Givens repeated. "I mean it."

Rachel didn't know what she would do if her mother was serious. How was she going to change her mind? She'd already told Julia that she'd be back. They'd already made plans.

She resolved that she would help more with Gordon. She wouldn't complain or give her mother back talk or a hard time when she was told to do something. She'd do well in school. She'd go to Sunday School.

She spent the rest of the drive home coming up with countless ideas that would make it possible for her to return. She wanted to spend all her summers on Highland Beach, forever.

Rachel braced her arms behind her and leaned back, tilting her face up to the sun. Very little had changed. Although she remembered that there used to be more sand, coastal storms might have eroded the beach over the years. It didn't matter. She was finally back. She'd been hoping for this moment for twenty years.

She heard nothing but the sounds of nature. There was no one out walking, no roaming dogs, no one on the beach but herself. There was not even a visible sailboat on the water. For just that moment Rachel believed that she was the only human being in the universe. She finally stood, wanting to shout out to the world. Instead, she did something more outrageous.

Without a lot of thought, Rachel took a position with her legs spread wide and her arms straight out to the side at shoulder height. Taking one big breath she let her body fall to the right, reaching for the ground with her hands as she swung her legs into the air and rolled into a cartwheel. She giggled when she landed shakily, but on her feet. Giddy with success, she tried again. After the brief handstand her arms gave out and she collapsed. With a small squeal, she landed in an ungraceful heap in the sand.

"Very smart, Rachel," she chastised herself. She sat brushing sand out of her hair and from her clothing. Behind her she heard what sounded like clapping. Rachel glanced over her shoulder.

At the top of the steps leading back into Julia's house stood Lucas.

Seven

"Bravo," Lucas shouted, ending his applause.

He wasn't surprised that Rachel didn't react. He knew she wasn't aware she had an audience for her little maneuver. He leaned against the handrail of the back steps and waited for Rachel to join him.

She took her time, brushing the sand from her printed Capri slacks and sleeveless white summer blouse as she approached, barefoot with sandals in hand. He used the time to admire her lithe, agile body, giving Rachel kudos for being comfortable in her own skin. He'd noticed that in the attorney's office. Seeing her again reminded him that, as far as he could tell, Rachel Givens was pretty straightforward and uncomplicated. Watching her as she'd performed the cartwheel had raised his respect for her.

She was taking her time walking back to the house. He wondered if it was her way of showing how little she cared about what he thought of her, or her lack of surprise at seeing him. Or maybe something else was going on.

One thing was for sure, Rachel had succeeded in surprising him for the second time since meeting her. She seemed to have a strong sense of self-confidence. She was animated and playful. She was fearless. Lucas knew that the basis for her strength had to have come from a family where she felt safe and loved.

She reached the steps but stood at the bottom staring up at him. "What are you doing here?" she asked.

"I'm fine, thanks. It's nice to see you again, too," he said.

"You didn't say you were coming up this week," Rachel complained, starting to climb the stairs.

"I didn't know I had to check in with you. For that matter, you didn't tell me what your plans were, either," Lucas reasoned.

Now that she was closer Lucas could see that Rachel hadn't gotten rid of all the sand. There was still some in her hair, which the wind off the Bay had rearranged into something wild and rather becoming. He decided not to point it out to her.

"I was staying with my mother just outside of Baltimore. Since I was already nearby, I thought it was a good time to come and get those things Julia left for me. I have a lot to catch up on at home and I need to get back soon. At least for a while," she quickly corrected.

"Where's home?" Lucas asked, not moving from his perch on the railing and knowing that she was waiting for him to. Something perverse in him wanted to see if she would ask.

"New York," she answered.

"New York. I like New York. It's a great place to hang out."

"That's about what I think of it, too," Rachel said. She slowly rubbed her upper arm.

"Did you hurt yourself?" Lucas asked her suddenly.

"What?"

"When you came out of that cartwheel you landed pretty hard," he observed.

"I'm okay. It wasn't a very smart thing to do."

"I thought it was very brave. You didn't seem to care how you looked."

"Do me a favor. Don't tell me how I looked doing it, okay?"

"Fine. I was going to pay you a compliment," Lucas told her.

"Now why would you do that?"

"Because you deserve one. I would have been afraid of looking like a fool. You weren't, and you didn't."

Lucas had the small satisfaction of having caught her off-guard with his remark. Rachel didn't have a comeback.

"Do you mind?"

He gave in and moved out of her way, his gaze following her into the house. So he wasn't going to be there alone after all.

His decision to come to Highland Beach had been fairly spontaneous. He saw the advantage in doing it that way because planning would have led to anticipation. And anticipation would have gotten him all wound up inside again over the fact that he'd never been to Julia's house before. When he got there he was surprised to find a car on the property. The house was open, but no one was around. Lucas guessed that it had to be Rachel.

In a way he was glad. Being there alone, he realized, might have led him to the kind of deep reflection and rehashing of the past that would have made for a miserable stay. Rachel didn't have a clue that she was making it easy for him, and he wasn't going to let her know.

He could hear her movements inside. Clearly she knew her way around. He knew that on Highland Beach and in Julia's house, he was a total stranger, if not there under false pretenses. But he also wondered if Julia's leaving him part of her house wasn't going to turn out to be some sort of cruel purgatory.

Lucas wasn't sure where to begin the business of learning about Julia. He wasn't ready to go inside and be surrounded by her things. He wasn't ready to be sociable with Rachel as if they were both there for a friendly visit. Instead, he started down the steps and stopped to look up and down the street. He picked one direction and began walking.

Lucas took in the setting of the community, hugged against

the edge of the Chesapeake. His gaze swept over the size and details of the late Victorian-era houses that blended well with more contemporary designs. He began to enjoy the spectacular view.

He'd done his homework. He discovered that Highland Beach dated back to 1893, when the twenty-six acres that make up the community were purchased by the son of Frederick Douglass. Over the last century, Highland Beach had been the summer home or host to some of the most preeminent black talent of the Harlem Renaissance, and had been nurtured and maintained by outstanding black professionals. Julia had found a place for herself here. But could he?

Lucas began to breathe deeply, easier. He'd come to Highland Beach imagining the worst, and maybe that was still to come. But he allowed himself an ironic smile. What, exactly, had he been afraid of?

Perhaps there were no ghosts here, after all.

Okay, so I wasn't expecting Lucas to turn up. Rachel tried to calm herself. That was no reason for her to behave like he was trespassing, or that he was in the way. Or that he was the devil incarnate. As a matter of fact, she knew that Lucas could make a pretty compelling case for having more right to be there than she did. That only made her ask herself for about the hundredth time, what had Julia been thinking?

Lucas's sudden presence had rattled her. His witnessing that embarrassing display on the beach added to her annoyance. The dark shades may have blocked his eerie gray-green eyes, but she knew that he was trying to dig past her defenses and search out her weak spots. She wasn't going to make it easy.

The joy of having the house to herself was gone, but she decided she wasn't going to let Lucas undermine her right to be there after so many years away, or deny her what Julia wanted her to have.

Rachel found the painting still hanging on the wall in the living room. When she saw it, she again experienced all the reasons why she liked it. It was small and simple and sweet. It depicted two very young black children on the beach, standing in water up to their ankles. They held hands and were bent forward staring at their reflection in the wet sand made as the water washed away from the shore. She carefully removed it from the wall, carrying it to the window where she could examine it under direct light. The picture was one more tangible evidence of the great appeal of Highland Beach, and she was suddenly infused with a deep gratitude that she'd been fortunate enough to have had many summers here. And maybe her mother was right. Maybe Julia was trying to make up for her part in what ultimately happened that last summer that changed all of their lives forever.

Finding the box proved more of a challenge. Julia had more than a dozen stored all over the house, most filled with memorabilia Julia had saved from her early career as a singer and actress. Some boxes were filled with old clothing and household items, clearly earmarked for donation to charity. Rachel found the box with her name written on it in blue marker at the bottom of a hall closet.

She removed it to the living room along with the painting. There, she found that Lucas had left a weekend duffel, and that he'd brought his saxophone as well. She wondered where he'd gone off to, but appreciated that she had some time by herself in the house.

In the meantime, she looked through the box. Inside she found some of the projects and crafts she had constructed during many summers. There were books, boxes of card games, crayons, and plastic molding clay. There was a long flowered box that Rachel didn't remember, and when she opened it she found the beautiful lace fan that she'd always admired. She took it out and spread it open, fanning herself. With a smile she remembered pretending to be a Spanish dancer while Julia played flamenco guitar music on her cassette player.

When Rachel heard voices and laughter outside, she went to the window to investigate. She peered out just as Lucas was coming back into view. He had stripped off his polo shirt and tucked it by the hem into the back of the waistband of his jeans. His torso was thin but muscular, and there was a patch of dark curly hair across his chest which funneled in a thin line down to his navel. She was surprised to suddenly see Lucas casually half-dressed. Rachel stared in fascination, baldly enjoying the view.

Lucas carried his athletic shoes while strolling in his bare feet, as she had done earlier. The legs of his jeans were wet up to his knees, and it was obvious that he'd walked through the water on the beach. And he'd picked up company along the way. He was accompanied by two attractive black women about her own age. Rachel was incredulous that in about an hour or so these two woman had managed to find and attach themselves to Lucas. Or vice versa. But she also noticed that he seemed to be enjoying himself, demonstrating a gregariousness she had not seen before. If he was not flirting, he was at least being incredibly charming.

The picture the trio made annoyed the hell out of her.

In a move that was wicked and calculating, Rachel went outside and sat on the top step and made her presence known. She was ignored. She pretended to be indifferent to their tête-a-tête, but waited for Lucas to introduce her. He didn't. She couldn't hear what was being said, and it was another ten minutes before Lucas and the beauties parted company. He put his shirt on and made his way back to the house. Instead of going inside, as Rachel thought he might, he sat down next to her, one step lower. Lucas leaned forward, resting his arms on his knees, and silently stared out at the Chesapeake.

He was close enough for Rachel to see the way the sunlight gleamed over his dark, finely layered hair. She could see the developing tan line around his neck and upper arms, marking the outline of his shirt. His mouth was relaxed, and the scowl lines were gone from between his brows. It had only taken a few hours. She found that the silence was not uncomfortable.

"I remember you telling me that you loved it here," Lucas suddenly spoke.

"That's right. To me it's the best place in the world."

"Tell me what it was like when you were a kid."

His interest surprised her. Rachel settled more into a comfortable position and warmed to the subject.

"Well, my whole family would come down. My father was a pilot for an airline, so he came back and forth when he had days off. We used to rent a house down there," Rachel said, pointing to the right. "We'd go to the beach almost every day, or play around on Blackwalnut Creek. Some of the other houses had backyard pools, and the families would invite anyone's kids to use them. We went boating and fishing. Sometimes at night there would be a community barbeque on the beach. That was fun because the kids got to stay up late. I didn't even mind if it rained, and I never wanted to go to bed at night. I was afraid I'd miss something."

Lucas just listened, but Rachel knew he was waiting to hear all about her summers.

"I was eight when I first met Julia. I was heading home one day with my brother Ross after we'd gone fishing on Walnut Creek. On the way I stepped on something and cut the bottom of my foot. I was sort of limping and hopping, trying not to put pressure on my foot. My brother told me I was walking too slow, so he left me to make my way home alone. Brothers can be mean and stupid like that." She was pleased when Lucas smiled a little. "Anyway, as I was passing Julia's house she came out and stood where we're sitting, and I remember she was laughing. She yelled to me, 'What kind of dance is that you're doing?' Well, I was crying because my foot hurt and I didn't think that was very funny, which only made me cry harder. She told me to come in so she could see what I'd done to my foot. I did, and Julia took care of it. She washed it and put iodine on it and a Band-Aid so I wouldn't have to dance all the way back to my house. I remember that all the time she was taking care of me she was saying things that made me laugh. In fact, she always told me that when something hurts or goes wrong, don't cry about it. Instead, the thing to do was figure out what was funny about it and laugh. I never did get very good at doing that. But when I was with Julia, we seemed to laugh all the time."

Rachel forgot that she was supposed to be explaining to Lucas what was special about Highland Beach. He hadn't asked her to tell him about Julia, but in her mind there was no way to separate Highland Beach from Julia. Her experience on Highland Beach *was* her relationship to his mother. He didn't say anything and didn't interrupt to ask questions. His attention seemed focused on the water, the way the sun sparkled on the surface, the way the water was dotted in the distance with sailing boats, and the way the Eastern Shore sat on the horizon.

"I'm sorry for going on and on," she said simply. "I hope that answers your question. I loved it here as a child."

"I'm beginning to see why," Lucas murmured. "It's isolated and it's beautiful. It feels peaceful."

"Yes, that's what I was trying to express. I didn't realize how much I missed it here until I came back today."

Lucas glanced over his shoulder at her. His glasses still hid his eyes, but Rachel had the sense that if she could see directly into them they would reveal more than he wanted her to see. She could appreciate that, not only was this place all so new to him, but that being here might allow him a glimpse into the Julia who was his mother but whom he'd apparently never really known.

"I thought I'd stay a few days," Lucas said. "I need to let some of this"—he lifted his arm to indicate everything around him—"sink in."

"I think that's a good idea. I'm driving back to my mother's tonight, so I won't be in your way."

"It wouldn't bother me if you stayed," Lucas said, returning his gaze to the water.

Rachel was a bit surprised by his magnanimous comment, and decided to take advantage of it.

"I don't know if this is a good time or not, but I'd like to ask you something."

Lucas laughed quietly. "What do you want to know?"

"About you and Julia." She got that far and stopped, trying to gauge his reaction to the subject. His expression and position never changed. "Why do you say you don't know her? How come you're so . . . angry with her?"

"Julia," he said, sighing. "What about Julia? She walked out of my life when I was about three or four. I don't know why. For a long time I had no memory of her, no sense that I even had a mother. I was raised by my father and my grandparents. I understood that he was divorced, but when I was very young I couldn't make the connection to having a mother somewhere. They never talked to me about Julia. I never asked questions. I don't think I had any curiosity. But then as I got older and began to make sense of my family arrangements, I decided that she just didn't want me. By the time I was able to ask questions for myself I no longer cared. She didn't hang around to be a mother to me, and I never was given a chance to know anything about her. That's all I needed to know."

Rachel held her breath as she listened. It was a horrible story, and it so contradicted her own experience with Julia that she didn't know how to react. Julia had always treated her like a daughter. How could she have been less a mother to her own son?

"No comment?" Lucas asked dryly when she took so long to say anything.

"What you describe doesn't sound anything like Julia at all."

"One and the same person."

"Then something's wrong. We're talking about two different people."

"Both are gone now, so it doesn't matter, does it?" Lucas said.

"Of course it does. Almost from the minute I first met you, you've been cutting and cold at the very mention of your mother's—"

"Okay, time out—"

"name. I remember at the reading of Julia's will how she wrote that you were important to her, and how much she hoped—"

"Rachel, stop. Enough."

She obeyed. There was no mistaking the tension in his voice, and she didn't want to witness an abrupt mood swing. She believed that Lucas was really starting to enjoy himself here, and she didn't want to spoil his first visit.

"Sorry."

"Thank you."

"You know there's more to the story, right? There has to be."

She was glad he still wore his sunglasses. They were a very effective shield against the warning glance she knew Lucas shot at her.

"Let me deal with it."

"Will you?" she persisted.

"I'm here, aren't I? Why does this bother you so much?"

"Because I don't believe your mother abandoned you. And because I know that . . . that sometimes things happen and people do things without thinking of the consequences," Rachel said, ever-mindful of what went on between her father and Lucas's mother.

"Are you saying I should give Julia the benefit of the doubt?"

"I think that's better than believing the worst of her, or hating her," Rachel said.

Lucas shook his head. "I don't hate her. You had it right the first time. I'm angry."

"Fine. So do something about it."

She waited for Lucas to lash out at her, but that didn't come. Despite the flexing jaw muscle and the tightness of his mouth, he seemed to be honestly considering his options. It was a start.

A phone began to ring and they both started.

"I think that's my cell phone," Rachel said, getting up and reaching for the door.

"It could be mine," Lucas said, following her inside.

Rachel hurried to her tote bag and dug out her unit. She thought it was probably her mother.

"Hi, it's Rachel."

"Prego, it's Claudio."

Rachel's first reaction was to hope that Lucas was not in earshot. She watched as Lucas wandered into the kitchen looking for something cold to drink. She turned her back to him.

"Oh, hi," she said, talking softly into the phone.

"*Raquel!* Mia bella, how are you? Why you don't come to Claudio, eh?"

In the background, Rachel could hear the chatter of conversation in Italian. She could imagine the entire scene. A wide promenade with lots of pedestrian traffic. A dozen open-air cafes, side-by-side along the street, each with its own distinctively colored umbrella.

"It's good to hear from you," Rachel said, acutely aware of Lucas's presence right behind her. She was experiencing a momentary disorientation, trying to switch gears after the conversation they'd begun.

"I make big plans for you and you not here. I miss you, cara."

Claudio lapsed into a soft rumble of Italian endearments. Rachel closed her eyes. She didn't understand much of what he was saying, but she understood what he meant. She loved his exuberance.

"Yes, I know," Rachel said carefully. "I'm so sorry I had to postpone the trip. There's something I have to take care of here before I can come."

"Not your mama, eh? Your family?"

"No, no. Well . . . yes, in a way."

"Como?"

Rachel dropped her voice. "A very dear friend of mine from when I was a little girl, has died."

Claudio groaned. "Cara mia, I am so sorry for you. I should be there for you."

"Thank you, Claudio. That's so sweet. There was a service, and then the reading of her will."

"But when do I see you? I think we go to Taormina for a few days, me and you."

"That sounds great," Rachel said. She was distracted, and couldn't recall where Taormina was.

"And I find place for your work. There are many shops where you leave your jewelry and it will sell. *Italian Vogue* would like to show you in the magazine. You see what I do for you, bella?"

"You've taken care of everything."

"Racquel. Cara mia," Claudio crooned, his voice slipping into a cadence that was caressing and provocative. "No more talk of work. Only of love, si? Come, we go to Sicily, have a good time. Stay at my uncle's hotel on Isola Bella, eh? Remember Rome last year?"

Rome. Claudio again turned to his native language to express himself. She remembered the first time she'd gone to Rome with three of her best college friends, Desiree, Carly, and Allison, for a post-graduation reunion. Julia once told her that to experience romance, every woman should have an Italian lover. Rachel had taken that advice to heart, as she had everything Julia told her. She and Claudio had collided near the Trevi Fountain. Within ten minutes he'd asked her to marry him, which she found very romantic, if foolish. Carly and Allison thought he was crazy. But Desiree, also an art major with the soul of a romantic, had encouraged the courtship.

Yet Rachel found it hard to pay attention to Claudio's long-distance lovemaking because she was wondering if Lucas was eavesdropping, and what he might be thinking. She wasn't in Italy, but in Highland Beach with another man whom she couldn't ignore or shut out, and she didn't want to.

"Claudio, it all sounds fantastic, but I can't talk about it right now," Rachel said.

"Si, si. But there is more."

"You can tell me the rest when I get there."

"Mia bella, listen. You come quickly, eh?"

"As soon as I can. I'll call you in a few days."

"Ciao, cara mia. Arrivederci."

"Bye."

Rachel closed the cell phone. Lucas was nowhere around. She wondered if he had left the house again. She retraced her steps from the living room and found him standing at the window staring out. His duffel bag lay open and he'd removed a pair of rubber flip-flops, a digital camera, and a box covered in a fancy pink fabric that he'd placed on the dining table.

He turned to regard her when she came back into the room. She knew from the look in his eyes that he had listened to most of her conversation with Claudio.

"Long-distance business call."

"I hope business is good."

She wasn't sure if he was being sarcastic, but Rachel ignored his remark. "I found the box Julia left for me, and the painting. Would you like to see them, so you know I didn't remove anything else?"

"I don't think that's necessary. I know you wouldn't take anything you're not supposed to, Rachel."

It seemed an odd statement. She decided not to make an issue of any underlying meaning. Rachel retrieved the painting, holding it up in front of her chest she stood so that Lucas could see the details. Rachel was impressed that he actually took his time.

"You like this picture?" he asked.

Rachel smiled. "I *love* this picture."

He nodded. "It does a nice job of showing the innocence of being a kid, when the biggest challenge is building the perfect sand castle."

She raised her eyebrows. "I didn't figure that out until I'd seen the picture dozens and dozens of times."

"That's because you were actually living that kind of a childhood every summer. Art imitating life."

"Yes, that's it."

"What are you going to do with it?"

Rachel put the painting back in a safe place. "Not sell it, if that's what you want to know. I have the perfect place to hang it in my apartment. In my bedroom."

"Which is where?"

"Manhattan. Morningside Heights. It's near Columbia University on the Upper West Side."

"I know the area. I've performed at St. John the Divine."

"Really?"

"Really. I thought of moving back to New York to live."

"But?"

"I think the crowds and traffic and tight spaces would make me crazy after a while. And . . . there are other issues," he confided but didn't explain.

"I feel the same way. I love the city. I just don't want to stay there forever. It serves my purpose for now."

"Which is?"

"It was easier to start up my business from there. I met a lot of helpful contacts, and it has great outlets for my work."

"What's your business?"

"Artist and designer extraordinaire."

Lucas chuckled at her lack of modesty.

"My company is called Honey Child Accessories."

"Interesting name," he observed.

"That's what Julia used to call me," she admitted.

He studied her features thoughtfully. "I can see that. What did she have to say about that cleft in your chin?"

"Nothing. But my mother used to tease me that I was Michael Douglas's love child." Rachel hesitated. "If you promise not to read anything into what I tell you, the truth is I've always had a fantasy about living on Highland Beach and creating my work from here."

"I'll accept that at face value," Lucas responded. "And I don't blame you."

Rachel found that she was suddenly studying him. This close, she could now see how he resembled Julia. She realized that she'd been so stunned for the past week to learn that Julia and Lucas were mother and son that she hadn't really tried to make the physical connection. Their faces were shaped the same, long and a bit square around the jaw. Lucas had his mother's high cheekbones and slightly hollowed cheeks. The eyebrows were hers and, of course, as she'd discovered, the laugh. That was easily the most startling characteristic because Rachel remembered Julia laughing all the time.

"You have something you have to do right now?" Lucas asked her.

"Not particularly. Why?"

"Would you show me around the house?"

Eight

The request took Rachel by surprise. There was something a little poignant and vulnerable about Lucas asking, since it would have been so easy for him to wander the house freely without having someone watching for his reaction.

"Sure, if you want," she replied.

They started on the first floor. There were only three large rooms, plus the solarium and a bathroom. Rachel managed to keep up a comfortable stream of conversation reverting, when she had to, to anecdotes from her childhood. That kept the mood light. She was aware that Lucas didn't ask any questions, but he was paying very close attention to everything she told him. His expression was a study in concentration and hidden emotions.

By the time they reached the second floor, climbing stairs that squeaked with each footstep, Rachel felt more natural about moving from room to room. There were four bedrooms: two at the top of the stairs on other side, each facing the Bay, a smaller room, which they both guessed had been originally meant for a nanny or live-in help, and Julia's room, with its own bath converted from a closet years before. There was another full bathroom and several walk-in closets. She hesitated before going into Julia's room, especially with Lucas, but again he showed no emotion when they entered.

It was an old-fashioned and traditional lady's room, with floral prints, handmade quilts, and gilded mirrors, as well as a shrine to Julia's career. The room was decorated with props, programs, posters, and pieces of costumes from her very short reign on stage. Rachel stood by the door but Lucas walked around the room, which was dominated by a queen-size four-poster bed, examining every detail. But he didn't touch anything.

Her heart went out to him when she realized that he looked at each framed photograph as if hoping to see one of himself.

"She talked a lot about her career, but now that I think about it, it wasn't very long. Five years at most. She used to say she was almost famous," Rachel confided quietly.

"Very talented, but not good enough," Lucas suddenly observed.

"Exactly," Rachel responded.

He joined her at the door to the room. "This it?"

"There's one more floor. I've never been up there."

"Let's have a look," he said, letting Rachel once again lead the way.

The staircase leading to the last floor was narrow and dark, and when they reached the top floor, it was basically empty except for a small cluster of things in one of the corners covered over by a very dusty sheet. There were windows on all of the four walls, and each allowed an overview of the neighborhood. The most dramatic scene was the one of the Chesapeake Bay. Lucas walked from window to window to spend a minute looking through each one.

"Now you've seen everything," she told him as they descended back to the first floor.

"Thanks. I appreciate you taking me through the place."

"I enjoyed it, too," she answered. Lucas was looking at her thoughtfully.

"Having you show me everything made the house more alive to me. I started to see it the way you do."

"Well, I haven't been exactly shy about my feelings."

"You're definitely not shy," Lucas commented. "You can

take that as a compliment. Any suggestions about which room I should use while I'm here?"

"Julia's room is the largest in the house, but I don't guess you're ready for that."

"No, I'm not," he agreed emphatically.

"Then use one at the top of the stairs. It's a corner room so you'll have a window view from two sides of the house."

"Sounds good."

"We better find the linens or make sure there are clean sheets on the bed up there."

"I can do that later."

Rachel realized it was getting dim inside the house now that the sun was behind the tree line.

"I didn't even check to see if the electricity is still on," she said, moving to test a lamp.

"It has to be. I can hear the refrigerator." He walked into the kitchen and tried the faucet. "We have running water."

"And lights," Rachel said, relieved when the lamp went on.

She turned on several others, and the house took on a soft and cozy aura in the fading daylight. She'd never been in Julia's house after it got dark.

Looking around, she spotted the box Julia had left her, and the painting. She decided to load them into her car.

"I'll be right back," Rachel called out, lifting the box and heading for the door.

When she returned Lucas was coming down the stairs again.

"I took my things up and checked out that bedroom."

"You forgot the pink box," Rachel said.

He shook his head. "I didn't forget it. What else do you have to do?"

"Wrap the painting. I'll see if I can find some old newspaper."

She found about a week's worth in the kitchen, along with a spool of lightweight string. She came back to the living room and, on her knees, spread several sections of the paper open on the floor.

"Let me give you a hand," he offered.

"Thanks, I could use one."

He began to applaud.

Taken aback by his sudden show of humor, Rachel started laughing. He joined her on the floor watching what she was doing. "That's not going to work. You're wrapping that like it's a birthday present."

She sat back on her heels. "Okay, you do it."

Rachel watched as he efficiently padded the glass of the painting with extra paper before wrapping and tying it with the string. He handed it to her with a self-satisfied grin on his face.

"You missed your calling," she said dryly. He was studying her. "What? Why are you staring at me?"

"Lean forward."

"Lean forward? Why?"

He took her firmly by the shoulders but gently forced her to lower her head.

"Lucas, what are you doing?"

Before she could resist or protest, he began brushing his hands back and forth over her hair. Sand sprinkled out onto the remaining newspaper on the floor.

"You still had sand in your hair from your gymnastics this afternoon."

When he was done, he sat back. Rachel used her own fingers to haphazardly restore order to her hairdo. But she felt a little odd by the liberty Lucas had taken. It was a simple intimacy that stripped away a fundamental barrier between them. In an instant she was now aware of him in a different way. She was suddenly more sensitive to the strength and gentleness of his hands, to the fact that he was tuned into her every move and gesture, that he was capable of uncharacteristic sweetness. "Why didn't you say something before?"

"Maybe I was looking for an excuse to touch you," he said lightly. "Now say 'Thank you, Lucas.'"

"Thank you, Lucas." She meant it.

He got to his feet and reached out a hand to help her up as well. Rachel accepted, but she started to feel as though she were being seduced. Emotionally, if not sexually. Even that thought made her acutely alert and on guard. She used the moment as an excuse to put the now-wrapped painting in her car as well. It gave her a chance to catch her breath.

Quickly re-entering the house, she caught a glimpse of Lucas holding the pink box. He stared at it, as if trying to decide whether or not to look inside. She watched his thoughtful consideration for a moment longer, but guessing what his hesitation was all about gave Rachel an idea. Quietly, she went back upstairs to Julia's bedroom.

She knew that Julia had been big on keeping albums and scrapbooks. She was sentimental in a way that wasn't surprising to Rachel, given her short career. But Rachel was looking for something else in the room. She spotted two more albums on the lower shelf of Julia's nightstand. She removed them and, without opening either, returned to the first floor. Lucas was now sitting on the sofa with the box resting on his thighs. Sitting adjacent to him, she put the albums on the coffee table. His gaze rested on them briefly, but he said nothing.

"I should be leaving soon. Are you going to be okay here by yourself?" she asked him.

"Why wouldn't I be?"

She could hear some strain in his voice, more than had been apparent the entire afternoon.

"This is all strange and new to you. Highland Beach, the house, even what you might learn about your mother. She's gone, and you'll never have a chance to ask her face-to-face what happened. This isn't Psych 101, but I'm trying to say I sympathize with what you must be going through," she responded. "But feel free to jump in at any time and tell me to mind my own business."

"A lot of good that will do," he murmured caustically.

"This house is like a giant Pandora's box for you. The issue of ownership aside, I know it must be hard to tackle your mother's memory and years of questions in a few days."

"That's not exactly right. I've been dealing with this my whole life, in one way or another."

"I thought you said you didn't care?"

"When I was a kid I had no choice. But Julia has managed to put me back into her life only now that's she gone, like you said. I'm not convinced that going to all the trouble to dig through the past will make a difference." He looked at her with a slight frown. "You think I should give her the benefit of the doubt?"

"I think you shouldn't try to make up the story until you have more information," Rachel said. "Isn't that the whole point of your trip to Highland Beach? To dig up clues and ferret out secrets, and put together the thousand-piece puzzle? Yeah, I do think your mother deserves the benefit of the doubt until you find out otherwise. It seems to me you probably have a pretty interesting history."

"Does it? So what do you think is my interesting history?"

Too late, Rachel wished she'd stopped while her opinion made sense. "I don't want to do what I just told you not to."

"I'm asking you to. Go ahead."

She carefully studied him and then took a deep breath. "Well . . . for starters, I would guess that you're biracial. A lot has changed in the last twenty or thirty years, but maybe that was an issue when you were born. I don't know if you ever bothered to look, but you resemble Julia in the face. You seem well educated, and you're a talented musician. When you take time to think about it, you probably also got your musical talent from her." She had the satisfaction of seeing Lucas's surprise. He hadn't considered that. "You're a good observer.

And a good listener. I don't think you have any sisters or brothers. If you did, you'd have someone else as a sounding board for your feelings about your mother, and not feel so . . . so isolated." She shrugged. "That's it. That's all I have to say."

"I appreciate your honesty."

"Am I right about anything I just said?"

"Do what I'm doing. Find out where all the skeletons are buried on your own." Lucas pointed to the albums. "What are those for?"

She picked up the albums. "I got these from Julia's room. I figured if she was so into keeping photographs and saving things, maybe you'll find something in these about yourself." Rachel held them out to him. "Here. They're yours in any case." Lucas took the albums but, as with the box, did not open them. "What's in there?" Rachel finally asked, pointing to box.

"Don't worry. I don't have a weapon, and I don't plan to off myself."

"That's not even funny." She glared at him.

"I wasn't trying to be. Just wanted to be clear about that. I don't know what's in the box," Lucas confessed. "My grandmother gave it to me."

"Which one?"

"On my father's side. My white side, to be blunt. I was at my grandparent's house when I learned about Julia."

"Maybe it has things that belonged to your mother," Rachel offered.

"I can't imagine what they could have had all these years that belonged to her."

They had you, she wanted to remind him.

"When my grandmother gave this to me, she said it was time I got it."

"Are you afraid of what you'll find?" Rachel asked him.

"I guess I am," Lucas confessed without embarrassment.

"Whatever it is, obviously your grandparents believe it's

important." She stood up. "It's time for me to get going. And I don't think you'll want an audience when you get around to looking in the box."

Lucas put the box on the floor and stood as well. "Yeah, it is getting late. Did you find everything you came for?"

"Pretty much," Rachel said, heading for the entrance and grabbing her purse on the way. "Don't worry. If I've forgotten anything, I'll get it on my next trip. The next time I'll try to spend more time with Harrietta Cousins. I have a standing invitation."

"What's a Harrietta Cousins?"

"One of the Highland Beach elders. And one of your mother's best friends. As a matter of fact, don't be surprised if Harrietta comes looking for you. I think it might be worth your time to get to know her. She probably has all kinds of stories to tell."

"I'll keep that in mind."

He walked her to the car and then stood back while she got into the driver's seat. The air had gotten cold. Belatedly Rachel wished she'd brought a sweater or jacket.

"Thanks for showing me around," Lucas said.

"No problem. I hope you enjoy your stay. Feel free to call if you have questions . . . or if you're afraid of the dark."

Lucas shook his head ruefully at her quip.

Rachel inserted her key in the ignition and tried to start the engine. There was only a sluggish churning noise. She turned the ignition off and tried again, with the same results.

Lucas opened the driver-side door. "Step out and let me try," he ordered her.

Rachel reluctantly complied. "Maybe I just need to pump the gas pedal."

Lucas did just that and tried the ignition again.

"How old is this car?" he asked when the engine refused to turn over.

"About nine years. It belongs to my mother."

"It may be time to put it out of its misery."

"I'd like to get it back to my mother first. Can you get it started?"

"It's not sounding good," Lucas said, listening carefully to the sounds the car made. Finally he gave up and popped the hood. "Do you belong to AAA?"

"I don't own a car. I live in Manhattan, remember?"

"Okay. Do you have a flashlight?"

"I don't know. I'll look."

There was no flashlight in the trunk, glove compartment, or anywhere in the house. Rachel felt vindicated when Lucas discovered that the batteries in his flashlight were dead.

By now it was dark. There was not a street light near the house, and they could barely see each other.

"I don't think I can do much to help you in the dark," Lucas concluded. "Looks like you may have to stay until morning when I can see what I'm doing under the hood."

"What do you think the problem is?"

"My guess is the alternator may be failing. Either it's not charging the battery, or the battery is so old it's not holding a charge. You need to get the car to a service center as soon as you can. If I don't see anything else that could be wrong when I check in the morning, I might be able to give you a jump start."

Lucas closed the hood of the car and suggested they return to the house. Hugging herself against the sudden drop in temperature, Rachel reluctantly followed.

"I didn't come prepared to sleep over. I don't have a change of clothing, no toothbrush, nothing," she complained.

"I don't see what the big deal is," Lucas said indifferently. "So what if you have to wear the same outfit again tomorrow? I won't tell anyone. As far as needing a toothbrush, haven't you ever gone camping? Do what the Indians did. Chew on a piece of tree branch."

"Oh, that's nasty," she grimaced.

"It works. Anything else? A bedtime story? Warm milk?"

"You're making fun of me."

"I'm merely suggesting that you relax. I'm the one who has a legitimate reason for feeling uncomfortable about staying here. You're the one who told me to get over it."

While Rachel tried not to pout about the unexpected turn of events, Lucas wandered off to the kitchen. Finally resigned to staying the night, she called her mother but ended up leaving a message on her answering machine. She couldn't believe that her mother might be out on yet another date.

When she finished, Rachel went in search of Lucas. He was rummaging through the kitchen, opening and closing cabinets.

"What are you looking for?"

"Something to eat. Aren't you hungry?"

At that precise moment her stomach chose to demonstrate the lack of a recent meal by emitting a rumbling sound of hunger.

Lucas glanced at her in amusement. "I heard that."

"Sorry."

"Instead of apologizing, help me find something to eat."

Rachel discovered that there was actually plenty of canned or boxed sundry items, but nothing that alone or in combination would make for a satisfying dinner. Lucas declared victory when he found a bag of store-bought Swedish meatballs in the freezer, and she located a glass storage jar in the pantry with spaghetti. Further investigation turned up a dusty but good bottle of red wine.

The kitchen, oddly enough, created an environment of compatibility between them. And she was impressed to find that he knew his way around a saute pan and Cuisinart. He knew how to use spices. All she could do was stand around looking inept.

"What kind of black woman are you who doesn't know how to cook?" he challenged.

"The kind who's discovered the joys of restaurants and takeout. What kind of man are you that you're not embarrassed to be seen mincing garlic?"

"I have a father who's an accomplished chef and restaurant owner—"

"Really?"

He seemed to take his time rinsing his hands, sprinkling a squirt of lemon juice on his fingers to rid them of any lingering odor of garlic and onions. Then he wiped his hands with a towel, leaning back against the counter while the spaghetti cooked.

"I also learned early on to take care of myself."

"That's admirable, Lucas, but I can tell you I suffer no guilt from not being a fabulous cook."

She redeemed herself, however, by setting the table and finding a box of tapered candles for their impromptu feast.

Unfortunately, because she had done little to contribute to the preparations for dinner, Rachel also got stuck with the chore of cleaning up.

"I'll toss you for it?" she suggested.

"Forget it," he said firmly, and retreated to the living room.

Doing the dishes was not as distasteful as it might have been. Rachel quickly recognized the benefit of time to reflect on the day. All of her expectations had been turned upside down, but the afternoon held many nice surprises. Lucas had been easy to be with, and he'd shown a sense of humor under what had to be difficult circumstances for him. Rachel had to admit that Lucas was capable of incredible charisma and magnetism. But the prospect of spending the night with him, so to speak, raised her interest to new heights and activated her imagination.

From the living room, the silence was broken by the sudden riff of musical notes, scaling rapidly in a playful tune. Lucas was on his saxophone, and the sound of the horn produced a warm and sensual feeling in the house. Hearing

Lucas's performance in the background made the rest of the cleanup easy and painless. It made her feel, oddly, domestic and content.

By the time Rachel made her way back to the living room, Lucas had segued into a piece that had that same mournful cadence she'd first heard at the memorial. Maybe that's what he was thinking of as he played.

Lucas was not in the living room, however. The back door was open, and he sat on the top steps with his back angled against the side of the house. He was facing the pitch-black night. The gentle sounds of the Chesapeake rolling onto the beach accompanied him. She didn't want to disturb him, so Rachel quietly sat on the floor by the open door, closed her eyes, and listened.

She wished that Julia could have been there to hear her son.

Rachel wondered what Lucas was feeling, what was going through his head. She could only guess at how wrenchingly lonely and confused he must have been growing up, suffering for all intents and purposes, the loss of his mother. She wanted to know, herself, what could possibly have separated mother and child. Why was Julia's death the only way for her and her son to bridge the past? When had he started referring to her as Julia rather than as his mother?

Lucas finally stopped playing, but it was another fifteen minutes before he came inside, closing and locking the door behind him.

"That was a great recital," Rachel told him. "I enjoyed hearing you play again."

"Thanks," he said.

He sounded a bit embarrassed, as if he'd forgotten there was someone listening to him play. She suspected that Lucas had fallen back into reflection. Maybe the day had been filled with revelations too deep for Lucas to easily climb his way out of it.

"I think I'm going upstairs and get myself settled in the other bedroom," she said.

"I'm going to hang out down here a while longer," he said, placing his horn back into its case. "Goodnight."

Rachel felt a little let down. After finally getting comfortable with each other, his goodnight felt abrupt and indifferent to her, until she once again remembered that he was a stranger in a strange place. She headed toward the staircase, but stopped to speak to him.

"Lucas? Are you okay?"

"I'm going to be," he said cryptically.

After stripping the bed the next morning and stuffing her few personal belongings into her tote, Rachel made her way down to the first floor of the house. It was another beautiful day on the bay, but she felt too tired to appreciate it. She hadn't slept well the night before.

The room had turned out to be drafty and cold, and she couldn't find extra blankets. She'd gone to bed with most of her clothes on, but had been unable to sleep. Rachel had also lain awake well into the night waiting to hear when Lucas came up to his room. She'd fallen asleep before that actually happened but had awoken off and on, restless with concern for him.

Rachel walked the length of the hallway and passed the corner room at the top of the stairs. She found the room already empty. There was no question that Lucas had eventually slept there. The bed was unmade, and the clothes he'd worn the day before were in a pile on the floor.

The first-floor rooms were literally flooded with sunlight that was almost painful to her eyes. A quick walk through the rooms proved that Lucas was not in the house. Rachel checked the time. It was a little after ten, and she was anxious to get on the road. She was already twelve hours behind the schedule she'd planned, and she was concerned about whether she'd even make it back to her mother's with the car acting up.

In the kitchen Rachel found that Lucas has made coffee and English muffins that they'd discovered the night before in the freezer. His empty cup sat in the sink. Returning to the living room, Rachel noticed that the box and the three albums she'd taken from Julia's room had all been removed. She wondered why, and she wondered where to. She stood at the window anxiously looking out. There were children in the playground across the street. Rachel opened the door and took in some of the fresh, warm morning air, sorry that she had to leave. She glanced at her watch. She *really* did have to leave.

Then she saw Lucas. He was making his way up from the beach, bare-chested again, in a bright pair of orange and white jammers and his flip-flops. There was a towel around his neck, evidence that he'd actually been in the water. Rachel found it exciting that he was physically fit enough for an early-morning swim, but the idea made her shiver. He crossed the road and saw her standing at the back door. Without a second thought Rachel waved at him, and then tucked her hands under her armpits, a little embarrassed by her own actions.

As he got closer, she could see the shadow of his beard. He reminded her of the pro basketball player Rick Fox, but with gray-green eyes.

"Good morning," he spoke first.

"Hi. How was your swim? The water must be freezing."

"I call it bracing. It was more fun than a cold shower." He took the steps two at a time until he stood next to her.

Rachel detected shadows under his eyes. She doubted his night was any more restful than hers, but Lucas at least appeared calm. Despite his appearance, wet and disheveled and sandy, she also felt a powerful awareness of him that made her suddenly edgy. She tried to keep her focus on his face, rather than on his provocative state of undress.

"How did you sleep?" he asked.

Rachel shrugged. "Okay."

He stepped past her into the house. "I'll take that to mean not well."

Rachel followed him. "What about yourself?"

"Okay."

"I'll take that to mean, not much. I was a little cold."

He turned to arch a brow at her comment. "You could have done something about that."

For some reason Rachel's mind quickly formed a short list of options that didn't include finding extra blankets. She wasn't even going to go there.

"I really should be going. Could I trouble you to take a look at my mother's car?"

"Sure." Lucas pulled on a T-shirt he'd left on the sofa and headed right out to the car.

"What are you going to do today?" she asked. She found that he had already pulled his car next to hers so he could use jumper cables between the two automobiles.

"Check out the neighborhood. Take some pictures. Try to figure out what to do with Julia's things."

"What was in the pink box?" she boldly asked.

"I still haven't opened it. There's no rush. It's waited this long."

By his tone she knew the subject was now closed. He didn't want to talk about it. Or wasn't ready to.

She waited anxiously while Lucas set things up to get power to her car. Finally, he tried her ignition. The engine turned over instantly. She breathed a sigh of relief and stopped short of throwing her arms around him in gratitude.

"Oh, what a lovely sound," she said. "I owe you big time."

"I'll add it to your tab," Lucas said flippantly, removing the cables and putting them back in the trunk of his own car. Then he moved his car once more to give her room to back out.

Soon she was all set to leave. Lucas came to her driver-side window and leaned forward to talk to her.

"I recommend that you don't stop anywhere until you're either back at your mother's or close to a service station. You might not get the car started again."

"I got it."

"Another thing . . . I was thinking, with you living in New York, it's going to be hard to manage the upkeep of this house. You're five hours away, and you travel a lot for your business. And owning a house could get to be expensive. You get the idea."

"And your point?" Rachel asked.

"I've decided that I want the house. I'd like to have full ownership. I know Highland Beach and this house means a lot to you—"

"And?"

"I'm prepared to make you a generous offer."

Rachel slowly smiled at him. "Lucas, that's such a cliche. As my younger brother would say, 'I ain't down with dat.' My answer is no way. But nice try."

Nine

"This piece was inspired by the traditional cameo," Rachel explained. She lifted the silver pin from the felt-lined cubbyhole in her sample case so the shop buyer could examine the details. "You can insert a photograph in this space, but it doesn't have to be a portrait. It could be a flower, or a pet, or a miniature work of art."

"Oh, this is lovely," the woman crooned, turning the piece several times.

Rachel knew that she was checking the craftsmanship as well as the kind of materials used. "You'll notice that there's a safety catch so there's no chance that the pin might come undone and fall off."

"Yeah, I see what you mean. I like the way you've done it here. You do quality work."

Rachel smiled, taking the pin back. "I've applied the same technique to the backs of my necklaces."

"Excellent," the woman said. She smiled broadly at Rachel. "Well, as usual I think you've made a sale, my dear."

"Wonderful," Rachel said politely. She'd learned over the last several years not to be too eager or too grateful. "How many would you like?"

"I'll take a dozen of the pins. These will sell very nicely to our artistic customers. The folks in the West End will snap these up. How soon can you make delivery?"

"If it will help you out, I can sell you some of my samples. I have duplicates, so it won't leave me short."

"That would be great, luv. Do you mind?" the woman asked, her hands already sifting through the sample case for the pieces she wanted.

In the meantime, Rachel began writing up the order. She also did a quick calculation of how much profit she'd cleared so far to put toward bankrolling her purchase of the house on Highland Beach. She'd been in London for three days, and not an hour went by that she didn't wish she could have postponed her business trip even longer. She still hadn't recovered from Lucas's astonishing attempt to buy her half of the house, but it put her on alert that he was serious. On the one hand, it infuriated her that he would be so selfish as to try and squeeze her out. On the other, Rachel wished she'd thought to make an offer to him first.

She wasn't surprised that he wanted the house. How could he not? She could tell from that first day they'd both arrived on Highland Beach that he'd quickly fallen under its spell. He had good reasons for wanting to be there. Far better than her own. While she patiently waited for her client, Rachel lamented that she would love to damn Lucas to hell for what he was trying to do, if it weren't for the fact that she'd recently discovered she liked him.

"Now then, luv. I'll take these fifteen pairs of earrings, and five necklaces. Is that too much?"

Rachel kept her demeanor calm and accommodating. "Not at all. Choose as many as you want."

Ka-ching, ka-ching.

"Good! I've also taken a fancy to these bracelets. I think I'll get this one for myself," the store manager giggled.

With the sale completed, as well as the promise of future orders secured, Rachel left the trendy shop on St. James Street and headed toward Covent Garden, just a block away. Checking her watch, she realized she was nearly twenty minutes late for lunch with her friend Amanda. She tried to hurry, but found her way thwarted by the pressing crowds of strolling tourists who wandered aimlessly all over the street. Trying to maneuver around a tour group of young girls, she collided with a large man and bounced right off his arm. Rachel dropped her sample case and it popped open, spilling some of her work.

"I'm sorry," Rachel apologized to the man as she squatted down to pick up the scattered pieces.

"Here, let me help," the man offered.

Soon, three or four other passers-by were also lending a hand. One teenager, the man's daughter, in fact, paused to admire a pin similar to the ones she'd just sold to the last boutique.

"This is so pretty. Did you make this?"

"Yes," Rachel smiled, reaching to take the piece and return it to its place in the case. She checked her watch again.

"Wait a minute. Daddy, I like this," the teen said, showing it to her father.

"Very nice," he agreed. "What is it?"

"It's a pin. But it's also like a tiny picture frame. Can I have it?" the girl asked.

Rachel sat back on her heels, taken by surprise. Before she had time to think, she'd made a sale on the spot. But the man and his daughter bending over her sample case drew even more people curious to know what she was selling. Another twenty minutes later, and she found herself rushing up the enclosed staircase bordering what used to be London's central flower market. Looking around, she spotted a young woman with brown hair in a short shag cut calmly smoking and people watching over the balcony of Chez Gerard.

"Amanda, I'm so sorry I kept you waiting. I know you're ready to kill me," Rachel said, breathless as she dropped into a chair and propped her case against the wall.

"Not at all," Amanda said.

"You'll never believe what just happened to me."

"You're American. I'll believe anything," Amanda said dryly.

"I just made a great sale with a store buyer, and I was rushing to meet you. I had an accident in the middle of the street, and I sold two pins, a necklace, and a pair of earrings!"

"Congratulations. Things like that never happen to me. But I did get a callback for that part I read for, and that wouldn't have happened if you hadn't pushed me to do the audition. I should make you my agent. You're far more effective than the one I have."

"You'll get the part, you'll see. You're a great actress. I think this calls for a drink."

Rachel signaled for the waitress and ordered two glasses of wine.

"Do you really have to leave tomorrow? We've barely had time to really visit, you know," Amanda said after they'd toasted each other's success.

"Yeah, I do."

"You've been here four days, and you planned on staying a week. Why the rush?"

"Overcommitted, I guess you could say. I conducted a lot of business and got three new accounts. And I got to see you. Thanks for letting me crash at your place. I hope I didn't mess up your plans by coming a week late."

"Look, you do the same for me when I'm in New York, and it's not like I have a hot lover at the moment. One of the best things that happened when I was in the States studying at Juilliard and working at Bloomingdale's was meeting you."

"Aren't you sweet for saying that," Rachel cooed.

"Just carefully protecting my interest," Amanda chuckled, blowing smoke into the air. "You remember what we always say."

"Cultivate your friends all over the world," they responded simultaneously, and then laughed.

"I was sorry to hear about this friend of yours who died. At least you didn't cancel coming altogether," Amanda said. "So, business is good? You're making a lot of money?"

"I'm doing okay. I took your advice and contacted the buyer at the Tate Modern. He wasn't interested in my things but he did send me over to a number of great shops in the XO building. That's one of the new accounts I picked up this trip."

"Sounds like you're going to become independently wealthy in no time. Can I persuade you to support me?"

Rachel laughed. "I'll keep you in mind. I'm working on a new project right now, and I need the extra money."

Amanda sat forward. "Really? Don't tell me you're finally going to open up a shop in New York. How cool is that?"

"I'm afraid not."

"What then?"

"I don't want to jinx it by talking about it too much, but there's this house I want to buy," Rachel said, excited.

"A house?" Amanda was incredulous. "Huge responsibility. Why would you want to saddle yourself with that?"

Rachel smiled. "This is a very special house, Amanda. This is a house I've wanted since I was a little girl. It belonged to the woman I told you about who died. And . . . there are a couple of complications, so it's not exactly a slam dunk."

"Oh, God. Is that another one of your American catchphrases? What does it mean?"

"That the deal is not guaranteed. I have to move quickly. I don't trust Lucas not to—"

"Lucas? Who's that? You've been holding out on me, Rachel."

"It's not what you think. It's . . . well, Lucas has a personal interest in the house as well and—"

"Is he cute? Straight? What does he do?"

Rachel shook her head. She didn't want to get onto the subject of Lucas. For the last hour she'd managed to keep him out of her head. It was enough that he'd thrown her a curveball by calling her on her business line just before she'd left the States. Why?

"I'm going to begin getting rid of some of Julia's personal effects. I just wondered if there was anything else that belonged to her that you'd like to have?" he'd asked.

Rachel had been touched. And suspicious. "What's the catch?"

He'd laughed. "This is not a trick. Remember, I didn't have to call you at all. But I'm sure there were probably other things that belonged to her you would like to have."

"Since you asked, Julia had a pair of earrings she used to let me wear when I visited her. They were long and dangling and glittered. I'm sure they were real diamonds," she added, testing him.

"They're yours."

Rachel had gasped. "Lucas, I was only kidding."

"I'm not."

"They're probably worth a fortune."

"Probably."

"You could sell them for a lot of money."

"So could you."

"I *really* want them."

"I said, they're yours."

"Why are you doing this?"

"Because I don't look good in diamonds, and they don't match a single suit I own."

She'd gotten a huge laugh out of that.

"This doesn't cancel the 50-50 split, I hope you know," she told him.

"I didn't think so. So it's still a Mexican standoff, I take it?"

"To the bitter end."

"You're on."

"Never mind about Lucas," Rachel said to Amanda, returning her attention to their conversation. "He's not important. But

I need to wrap up business here, get to Italy, and go back home as fast as I can."

"Oh, yes. Claudio," Amanda drawled wickedly.

"Yes, Claudio," Rachel sighed.

Amanda began to laugh. "You are truly amazing. I'd love to know what you do to find these men who get all tangled up in your life and then fall in love with you."

"I don't know what men you're talking about. Claudio is not in love with me. He's fun to be with, and the sex is great. He's been really good about helping me get established in Italy, but he's getting something out of it, too."

"Hardly sounds romantic."

"It is . . . and it isn't," Rachel said. "It just is what it is."

"Would you ladies like to order lunch?" the waitress asked, reappearing again.

"I can't," Amanda said, reaching for her purse. "I've got to be at the theater in about fifteen minutes for this afternoon's matinee."

"We'll just have the check, please," Rachel said to the waitress. "I'm sorry about lunch. If I hadn't been delayed and had that accident—"

"Don't worry about it."

"Since this is my last night, let me take you to dinner after the show," Rachel suggested.

"That would be lovely. I accept."

They left the restaurant and headed toward Leicester Square and the theater where Amanda was performing in a short-run production.

"Have you been seeing someone else at home? Or met anyone new?" Amanda asked.

Rachel was about to shake her head but recalled that Lucas was certainly new. Her brain, with a willpower of its own, had constantly conjured up the image of him coming out of the Chesapeake, dripping wet and provocatively undressed. When he'd leaned in through the car window to speak to her she'd thought, unbelievably, that he was actually going to kiss her. She'd been prepared to let him, responding almost instinctively. That would have to count as a salient moment. So was watching him play his sax, blowing out his unspoken feelings. And she couldn't forget when he'd unexpectedly brushed the sand from her hair.

Rachel had to admit that she wasn't exactly indifferent to him.

"I have recently met two men. Both interesting and handsome in their own way."

"Well, do you like one better than the other? In other words, which one do you spend the most time thinking about?"

"Well, Lucas. But only because the truth is, he's the man trying to buy this house out from under me. I think he's capable of being underhanded and succeeding by any means," Rachel explained.

"Oh. You mean you've just been thinking about what you could do if it would help you get the house."

Rachel shrugged. "That's true. By any means possible. This is war. As in, all is fair."

"Well, I wish you luck. Getting the house, I mean. But you should remember there's very little difference between love and war."

Long after Amanda had disappeared through the staff door of the theater and she had started out to her next appointment near the British Museum, Rachel was wondering if it was possible to get Lucas to agree to a truce.

"Lucas, it's only been two weeks. I suggest you give it a little more time. What's the big rush? Ms. Givens is away on business, and nothing can be done until she returns anyway," Lehane said.

Lucas, sitting opposite the attorney in his office, shook his head. "I disagree. I've been reading up on past cases and doing a little research into this kind of arrangement between Ms. Givens and myself. There are ways out of the terms in Julia's will."

"I know there are. I told you and Ms. Givens that when we went over the will. But I think I also said a decision doesn't have to be either, or."

"Frankly, I don't understand why you object to me wanting to gain complete ownership of the house. Julia was my mother. I have a right."

"Well, to be honest," Lehane frowned, looking uncomfortable. "This is the first time I've ever heard you make that claim."

"You want to explain what you mean?" Lucas asked, his voice low and hard.

"I'm not trying to be impertinent, but I know quite a bit about your personal history, Lucas. I know, for instance, that she didn't raise you, nor did you ever previously seek her out. I know that she felt an incredible amount of guilt over the way things worked out, but it's wasn't my business to try and piece together the how or why. I only know that Julia was very specific about the house on Highland Beach going to both you and Ms. Givens. I don't know why, you don't know why, but maybe it would make more sense for you, at least, to try and find out why."

"So she left nothing that explains things?"

"Nothing legal. I handled Julia's legal matters, not her personal ones," Lehane said kindly. "You know, it's possible she left a file of papers or other documents in the house. Take a look and see what you can find. I'll be happy to advise you on anything you find."

Lucas agreed to do that, but he did not tell Lehane that he already had a mysterious box, contents as yet unknown. But he also knew he had one other avenue to explore. Perhaps two, both of which he'd so far been avoiding.

"Let me ask you something," Lehane said, leaning over his

desk, with his hands clasped together. "Do you suspect Ms. Givens may have influenced your mother somehow? Maybe connived to have the house left to her?"

"I don't think so," Lucas said without hesitation.

"I don't think so either. I think she was as surprised as I've ever seen a person who gets that kind of news. There was nothing false about her reaction."

"I agree."

"If you don't mind my saying so, I like her. I've had a chance to speak with her several times, the first when I called to tell her about Julia's death. Ms. Givens was deeply affected. I also know she postponed an important business trip so she could travel down here for the service. Your mother meant a lot to her. After meeting her myself, I see why she meant so much to Julia."

"And you believe she can walk on water," Lucas drawled. Lehane grinned. "This is still an unusual arrangement."

"People about to die sometimes do odd things. Look, you could do worse. Ms. Givens could have been less than agreeable, less than cooperative, less easy on the eyes. Give yourself a chance to get to know her. What would be the worst thing that could happen?"

Lucas held back from responding, even though he pretty much knew the answer. It had begun to hit him when he'd gone down to Highland Beach on the spur of the moment and found Rachel already at the house. It was the cartwheel, and the sand in her hair, and her trying to bargain with him over doing the dishes. The worst thing that could happen was that he'd find out she wasn't anything like what he thought she'd be like. She wasn't even like any other woman he'd ever met. Frankly, Lucas liked that he couldn't intimidate her, especially after his attempt to make an offer on her half of the house.

So much for plan A.

Which is how he came to be in Kenneth Lehane's office

discussing plan B. The fact that he liked her raised the potential for complications and temptation.

"Tell you what," Lucas said, rising slowly from his seat and preparing to end the meeting. "I'll give it a shot. I'll try to get to know her. But I still want you to find a precedent for having the deed revoked and a new one drawn up. I just want to be ready."

"Ready for what?"

"For when Ms. Givens and I find out that whatever Julia had in mind isn't going to work."

Lucas left Lehane's office, disturbed and irritated that the attorney had done a number on his head. Rachel didn't need an endorsement from Lehane.

She was a class act. She was smart and feisty and compassionate. And she was sexy, not by design or calculation, but by movement and body language. Just being herself was working better than either could imagine.

As he was heading to a parking garage to get his car, his cell phone rang. It was Jennifer on the line.

"Just calling to see if you're free tonight."

"Why? What's happening tonight?"

"I have to attend a reception at the National Gallery, and I can bring a guest. Care to be my date?"

"I don't think so, Jen. I have a lot to do today, and I'm running late. And I have a rehearsal tonight with one of my groups."

"Oh, pooh. You know, I've hardly seen you in the last two weeks. What's up?"

"Just busy, that's all."

"Okay, if you say so. I was beginning to think maybe you met someone and you're were too busy for friends anymore."

"Maybe," Lucas said cautiously. Rachel came to mind. But that was different.

"Well, have you or haven't you?"

"Have I or haven't I, what?" he asked, a shade impatiently.

"Met someone?"

"Hey, come on. What is this?" Lucas questioned. "Why all this sudden interest? My personal life is not public domain."

"I'm not the public, Lucas. I'm your best friend, and I care about you. You seem very touchy lately."

"Like I said, I have a lot on my mind. Sorry about tonight. Have fun. I'll make it up to you some other time."

"I'm going to hold you to that."

Lucas put Jennifer out of his mind and quickly brought his focus back to Rachel. It occurred to him, as he drove to the law offices where he would have been named a partner had he stayed, that he'd spent the entire day with Rachel Givens, without actually having the pleasure of her company.

The pleasure of her company.

The notion was spontaneous, but he did question when it had come to that. At what point had he determined that Rachel was not manipulative, but someone who loved his mother? How could he blame or dislike her for being the fortunate recipient of his mother's love in return?

When Lucas pushed through the revolving door, he saw Manny waving to get his attention. After greeting one another, Manny held out a manila envelope to him.

"Here it is. All the goods I could find on that woman."

"That's great," Lucas said.

"There was no file on her, man. She's clean."

"You mean, like a criminal dossier or an FBI record?"

"Yeah, that's right. I found a whole bunch of stuff from magazines. Articles and pictures, stuff like that. I didn't read all of it. I just printed out what I thought would help you."

"Anything particular stand out while you were searching?" Lucas asked him, fingering the envelope and anxious to see what was inside.

"Yeah. She's a babe, man. You sure she has something that belongs to you? She don't look like no player to me."

"I just want to make sure. I really appreciate this, Manny.

By the way, I haven't forgotten about getting you and your girlfriend down to see me play."

After offering some dates, Lucas left the building. Any guilt he'd felt about covertly digging around in Rachel's life was overcome by a new desire to know more about her.

Lucas settled down at an outdoor café. It was past the lunch hour so it wasn't very crowded, and he knew he could sit and read through Manny's research without rushing. He ordered something to drink and opened the envelope.

The information had been garnered from articles in magazines like *ESSENCE, Ladies' Home Journal* and *Marie Claire*. Newspapers like the *Washington Post*. He was instantly intrigued.

Lucas learned that Rachel was talented and creative. She'd been singled out as an African-American designer with innovative use of materials in her work, and her appeal was to a crossover consumer base. She had a degree in fine arts from Howard University, making her first money from her classmates on campus.

There was an interview in which she talked more about her background and family. She was the middle child and only girl in her family. Her father was a retired airline pilot, and her mother worked as a college administrator in Baltimore. Her parents had been divorced for many years. Rachel admitted that she was the only one in her family with a leaning toward the arts, but said that she was greatly influenced by a woman who was like a second mother to her, Julia Winters.

Lucas felt a peculiar twist in his gut at that admission. He could read in the remark Rachel's pride in that relationship. For the first time he was beginning to accept that there was a real basis for the general consensus that Julia was distinctive. He was beginning to see her as a free spirit herself, talented and very ambitious. This became clear as he read about Rachel's life. It was Julia who encouraged Rachel to pursue art, travel, be independent, and stay curious. The interview went on to reveal that it was Julia who told Rachel that she had to live in New York because that's where things happen, although Julia herself had given up her career to settle in Highland Beach, Maryland.

"That's where I first met her," Rachel said in the article. "I did ask her why she left New York, and she said she went wherever there was work and opportunities. But she also told me that she didn't have what it took to succeed. She told me I did."

Lucas put the article down and became pensive. His head was spinning with the revelations not only about Rachel, but also about Julia. He remembered Rachel's analysis that he'd probably inherited his musical talent from her. He saw, more than he'd ever considered before, that he *was* his mother's son.

It was quite a while before Lucas finished the material. He'd found what he was looking for, and there was no need to go further.

Lucas stretched out his legs, crossing them at the angle, and settled into a contemplative slouch. He was oblivious to the traffic, pedestrians, and the once-bright day quickly turning overcast and threatening. When the waiter approached to ask if he wanted anything else, he switched from drinking cola to Long Island iced tea. And he sat and read every one of the articles over again.

It began to drizzle before Lucas could rouse himself and leave the café, which was already lowering an awning over the outdoor setup to protect die-hard customers. He drove to the club just outside of Georgetown where he was to rehearse with his quartet. He was the first to arrive. He played his sax alone, using the music to meditate about what options were open to him.

Much later, during the two sets scheduled for that night, his fellow musicians could hear that there was something a little different about his solo performances. They were heartfelt and soulful. His playing and interpretation was pure musical magic. It was an exorcism. That night Lucas got a standing ovation. That night he became the full-fledged artist and musician he was meant to be.

The next morning he felt differently about a lot of things. And he made another decision.

"Good morning, Kenneth. Sorry I'm calling so early," Lucas said.

"It must be important. I've barely gotten to my desk. What can I do for you?"

"It's about what we discussed yesterday."

"You mean ownership of your mother's house?"

"That's right. Forget about mucking around to change what's in her will. I've decided not to contest."

"Well, I have to tell you, Lucas, I'm glad to hear that. What made you change your mind?"

"I want to find out why Julia set it up the way she did between me and Rachel Givens."

Rachel strolled the narrow, medieval streets of Taormina. The buzz of conversation was incessant, the sound making her feel like she was surrounded by a swarm of bees. Most of the talk was in Italian, but she also heard a lot of German, French, and Spanish. And there were virtually no African-Americans. The sun was so intense that she'd found it necessary to limit her window shopping to the shady side of the Corso Umberto, the main street, which was packed with summer tourists.

She stopped when she realized that Claudio lagged behind. Adjusting her sunglasses, she turned to see if she could glimpse him through the hoards of visitors. She was no longer annoyed that he had a tendency to stop when he encountered friends to spend time talking, and it seemed that Claudio knew every single person under forty in Sicily. But it was also her time that was being used.

He was tall, although not as tall as Lucas. His smiling face below a cascade of slightly-too-long curly hair was easy to spot. He was deeply tanned and his tan showed beautifully against the dazzling white of his short-sleeved shirt. Rachel saw his arm waving in the air when he spotted her first. He beckoned for her to return so he could introduce her. She merely smiled and indicated she wanted to go into the nearest shop. She didn't want to stand by while Claudio and his friends rattled away in a language that left her on the sidelines. Not his fault, of course.

Unfortunately for Rachel, the store she entered was one of the many shops that sold the colorful traditional painted ceramics for which Italy was famous, and which dominated the hundreds of shops throughout the historic town. After less than fifteen seconds of looking around, she turned to leave.

"Signorina, I help you, yes?" the cheerful shop owner offered.

Rachel smiled as she left. "No, thank you. Nothing today."

That was when she made her decision.

She didn't blame it on the crush of hot, sweaty bodies with their bulging knapsacks, or the aromatic profusion of smells wafting from cafes that lined the street, or even on Claudio who was a high-spirited but exhausting companion. She blamed it on a not-so-sudden revelation that she was lonely here. And it was more than being isolated by the language, which she truly enjoyed hearing even though she knew very little Italian. And it wasn't about being in a foreign country, because she loved Italy and had found Taormina and the lower shore community near the Isola Bella to be stunningly beautiful. It all came down to Highland Beach. And Lucas Scott.

Rachel grew impatient. She retraced her steps to find

Claudio was chatting with a different person now. A young woman. Slender and stylish and flirtatious. This was probably someone Claudio *didn't* know, but no matter. He would introduce himself and dazzle the new acquaintance and they would become fast friends or instant lovers. Rachel understood this. He was so Italian. But he made the fatal error of ignoring her while he tried to impress another woman.

That's when her decision was cemented.

Without warning, Rachel walked away. Immediately she began to feel relief. She walked briskly and with familiarity through the town, back to the ancient arch that marked the entrance into the city. She squeezed her way along the too-small sidewalk and purchased a ticket for the five-minute cable car ride back down to Strata Olympia. From there she walked, easy and carefree now, along the side of the road, passing shops, restaurants, and even people she'd become familiar with during the week. She walked down the steep driveway entrance to the hotel where she and Claudio were staying, owned by one of his many uncles.

Rachel smiled and waved at the staff on her way to the room, a separate little cottage-in-the-round and only fifty feet or so from the beach of the Ionia Sea. Once inside the dim room, she began to pack her bags.

She was arranging for a cab to the airport in Catania when Claudio came racing down the grotto-like entrance, breathless and talking very fast.

"What happened? What are you doing? You leave me like that and—"

"Claudio, I thought I might miss you," she said calmly.

Then he saw her bags and that she was dressed for traveling, not in a skimpy sundress and cute thong sandals, but in black Gap stretch pants, and a Banana Republic peasant blouse.

"Raquel, mia cara . . . what is this you do?"

"I'm going home."

"Como? Raquel, tu—"

Rachel placed her fingers over his mouth and laughed at his astonishment. "English, please."

But he was so confused that he began talking rapidly in Italian. Rachel waited until he ran out of breath.

"Why you go? It's beautiful here, we have a good time, si?"

"I know. Con te partirò, Claudio."

"Cara . . . You break my heart."

He said it with such theatrical flair that Rachel had to struggle not to giggle.

"Claudio, I don't doubt for a moment that you will survive. Five minutes after I leave, you will be planning what to do for the evening. You certainly won't lack for company." She kissed his cheek. "I did have a good time. You were right about Taormina. It's wonderful. But I know a place just like this back in the States."

"But Raquel . . . you, me . . ."

"That's right. There's you and there's me. There's no *us,*" Rachel said kindly.

"What can I do to make you happy? What do you want?"

Rachel spoke slowly so there'd be no mistake. "I want to go home."

Ten

"Welcome back. It's good to see you again."

"Thanks," Rachel said to Reid Dixon, accepting the glass of wine he offered. Then he stood, poised with his own glass.

"Here's to the conclusion of a successful export agreement, and to a great future."

She said nothing as he carefully tapped his glass against hers. She knew that he expected some kind of encouraging reaction, but instead she took a long, slow sip of the wine, knowing she could hardly be expected to drink and talk at the same time. She certainly didn't want to say anything she didn't mean.

"Hmmmmm. I like the wine."

"Good. I guessed that you probably wouldn't want anything too dry," Reid said.

"That's right. What else do you know about me?" she asked, curious.

"That you're a very busy lady. I'd been trying to call you for a while until Malika told me you'd been doing a lot of traveling lately for business. Europe and Maryland. Quite a contrast," he said.

"Different kinds of business," Rachel said. She took another sip of wine. "I have to say I'm surprised."

"Why?"

"Well, when we finally talked and you arranged for me to pick up the painting I wanted from your show in July I wasn't expecting to be wined and dined. It's not necessary. We hardly know each other."

"I'm hoping that will soon change."

Rachel smiled graciously, but her stomach registered apprehension. Not because the idea of being pursued by Reid was so unpleasant, but because it was inconvenient. She also immediately found herself drawing comparisons to Lucas. Actually, there was much that was the same about both men except for one important difference. She thought about Lucas a lot.

". . . be a total surprise."

Rachel realized her gaze was blank as she stared at Reid. She tried to focus. "I'm sorry. Could you say that again?"

He pursed his lips. "It wasn't anything important. Just making conversation."

"And I wasn't paying attention. How embarrassing."

"I'll let it slide this time. Maybe you're dazzled by my savior faire and great looks. Or you could still be jetlagged."

Rachel smiled, appreciating that he was not taking her lapse in good manners seriously. "This won't sound very flattering, but I do have a lot of things on my mind right now."

"I can deal with that, as long as you're not daydreaming about someone else."

She hid her reaction by glancing around. "I do think your apartment is fabulous. How did you find a place this big?"

He lightly touched her elbow and indicated they should sit down. She took one of the modern leather and chrome chairs rather than sit on the sofa, which seemed a little too intimate for Rachel. If he noticed her maneuver he didn't let on.

"First of all, I was willing to leave Manhattan. Second, I looked in neighborhoods with pre–World War II buildings. They were built better, and the rooms were twice the size of your average new apartments. Do you like it?"

With that one simple question Rachel felt he'd managed to make the conversation personal again. *Or maybe I am just being overly sensitive,* she considered. There was this troubling idea that had planted itself in her head that she was cheating on Lucas. Where did that come from?

Rachel shook her head slightly to clear it, and tried to catch up to Reid's commentary on the fine points of renovating. His apartment consisted of a very large, open, loft-type space, created by removing several nonload-bearing walls. The space was then divided to provide separate dining and living-room areas and a kitchen by the clever placement of furniture, artwork, collectibles, and large potted plants.

"What a luxury to have this much room all to yourself."

Reid leaned forward to place his wine on the low coffee table, which was composed of four towers of stacked books with a large sheet of plate glass for the surface. Then he sat back and crossed his legs.

"I didn't always live here alone. I was married."

"So, you're divorced?"

"Almost. We've been separated almost two years."

This new information, while unexpected, quickly served the purpose of making Rachel feel much more comfortable with Reid. He wasn't really available. At least in her mind. She knew that being married or separated would not necessarily stop a man or woman from having other relationships or affairs. But she was a monogamist down to her toes. Claudio was no longer an issue. Then there was Lucas. *That's crazy*, she told herself. She only knew him a little better than she knew Reid. But she'd already spent a night with Lucas. So to speak.

" . . . if that's okay with you."

Rachel blinked rapidly. "Excuse me?"

Reid chuckled ruefully and dramatically clutched his chest. "Oh, man. A stab to the heart. I must be losing my touch."

"I'm so sorry. It's not you, I swear. I don't know what my problem is. Maybe I should—"

He leaned forward and took her glass from her hand. "I

know what it is. I should have fed you first. The wine is going to your head."

"That's really sweet of you to make excuses for me. I'm glad you don't have a fragile ego."

"I didn't say that." Reid stood. "I am determined to remove any and all obstacles so you and I can get to know one another. The first thing is to take care of business. Come over here."

Rachel followed him to another room. It was a small space with photographs, paintings, and prints on the walls, good lighting, and several comfortable chairs. There was a table with books and magazines. She smiled as she looked around.

"It's like a private little gallery."

"That was the idea," he nodded.

"I really like it."

"You'll have to come and enjoy it again," he said. "I believe this belongs to you."

He picked up a painting that was leaning against one of the chairs. Reid held it so that she could see the entire frame of reference. "Still like it?"

"Oh, yes. Even more now that I know I own it. And I can still see how much it reminds me of Highland Beach."

"I'll have to get down there and check it out sometime," Reid said. "I'll wrap this for you."

Rachel immediately recalled Lucas doing the same thing with the small painting his mother had left her.

". . . you won't have to struggle home with it on the train. I'll drive you home later."

"You don't have to do that," Rachel quickly demurred. "I'll grab a cab or call a car service."

"No way. I don't want to risk anything happening to you or the painting."

She laughed. He really was very likable. "I have something for you also."

She found her tote bag that she'd left near the apartment

entrance. By the time Reid joined her, she had removed an artist's black presentation box. Rachel sat on a chair and opened the box. Reid sat next to her, bending forward to see the contents.

"I hope it's what you wanted."

"Yes. This is just what I had in mind for my mother."

"I tried to create something unique and simple. She doesn't need a lot going on around her neck. And I wanted to design something that would enhance whatever she wore with it, while letting it stand out on its own."

"This is beautiful." He lifted it from the case to examine it more closely. "I know my mother is going to love it."

"I hope so, but I'll be more than happy to exchange it if she doesn't."

"That's not going to happen."

"There's one more thing that goes with the necklace," she said, removing a folded wad of tissue paper. Inside was a pair of earrings. "Now she has a set."

"That wasn't the deal."

"Tell her these are from the artist as a special gift for her birthday."

"Why don't you come to her birthday celebration? I know she'd love to meet you."

Her warning bells went off again. "Thank you, but I can't. I'm leaving in another day or so on a trip."

"More business?"

"Well, in a way."

"You'll meet my mother some other time," Reid said confidently. "Now that the business is out of the way, let's go have dinner."

"You really don't have to. The painting is enough, and—"

"Maybe it is for you," he interrupted. "But I've been looking forward to this since the night of my opening. I was disappointed when you couldn't join the group afterward. You'd just received a call with some bad news."

Rachel smiled, genuinely moved by his thoughtfulness. She knew now that if she hadn't already met Lucas, if she hadn't already begun to see and appreciate and like the man, Reid would have stood an excellent chance of getting to first base.

"Girl, what have you been up to? I haven't seen you since you got back," Malika said, entering Rachel's apartment and closing the door. "What's going on?"

Rachel sighed, retracing her steps to the living room, where she was writing checks to pay bills, making lists, and checking them twice. "Too much. Things are a little complicated right now. I haven't unpacked from Europe, Claudio's been calling me almost hourly . . . I broke up with him."

"It's about time. I told you long-distance romances are doomed."

"That's only part of why it ended. Then I have all these new orders to fill for accounts in London and Italy, and I have to go down to Maryland as soon as possible."

"What's in Maryland?"

"Maybe my future," she murmured.

"Reid is going to be upset, you know. He likes you."

"I like him, too. He's talented and I really love his work. He's a gentleman, he has good taste, and he's more than just cute. But I don't think I can give him what he wants. Me."

Malika laughed. "Yeah, he's definitely going to be upset."

"What's up with you and what's-his-name?"

"Ken. We got it goin' on. He's even giving me a show at his gallery in November."

Rachel cut her a look. "Is that what getting next to him was all about?"

"No, I really like him. The fact that he owns a gallery was a plus, that's all."

"Maybe that's what I need to do," Rachel reflected mostly to herself.

"Do what?"

"Play nice. Bat my eyelashes. Show a little thigh. Isn't that what women do to get what they want from a man?"

Malika laughed again. "Girl, I don't even want to know what you're talking about."

"That's okay. Maybe I don't, either. I'm just . . . thinking out loud."

How far would Lucas go to get the house? she asked herself, nonetheless.

"Listen, you can tell me all about it at dinner. Since you can't cook and I don't want to, let's go out."

"Fine."

"And don't think I'm going to let you off the hook from telling me what went down between you and Claudio," Malika commented, waiting for Rachel to get her purse and slip on a pair of sandals.

"Nothing much to tell. What we had ran its course, and I didn't want to be the seasonal love interest anymore. There was never any expectation where he was concerned, and I never loved him. But he was sweet and great for my ego. My Italian stallion. My friend Julia said when you walk away from something or someone, keep walking. No regrets, no second-guessing, no strings. Oh my God . . ."

Her voice trailed off as the significance of Julia's philosophy sunk in. No strings. Julia had none beyond her Highland Beach house. But what had her life been like? Singular. No family. A self-imposed exile in a house big enough for a dozen people, located on land's end. The constant reliving of a career that, by any measure, had been brief and undistinguished. Joie de vivre by day, tears and memories by night, all alone.

Rachel was glad that Malika had enough news and conversation to carry them through dinner. They went to a local café to catch up on the few weeks since they'd last seen one another. Mostly, all Rachel had to do was listen. But she didn't even do that very well, faking her way through the evening, laughing when it was called for, but all the while trying to figure out why Julia had chosen to live such an unbearably lonely life.

Rachel's cell rang as she and Malika were finishing dinner and waiting to pay the bill. Malika excused herself to go to the ladies' room. It was Gordon and, judging from the noise in the background, he wasn't at home quietly studying to get a head start on the coming semester.

"What's going on?" she asked. "Are you calling to borrow money again?"

"I'm calling 'cause I have that information you asked me for."

"What information?"

"Didn't you want to know about a guy named Lucas Scott?"

Rachel felt a little odd at her brother's announcement. When she'd first asked Gordon to help her, it seemed like a smart idea. What was wrong with wanting to find out about Lucas Monroe Scott? Now it somehow seemed like an invasion of privacy. Now it made her feel like she didn't trust him.

"That's great, Gordon. But I have a problem."

"Oh-oh. I don't like the sound of that."

"It's not you, or anything you did. It's just that . . . I think I changed my mind. I don't want to know what you found."

"*What?* Rae, come on. Why'd you make me go through all that work?"

"I know, I know. I'm sorry."

"It's not like he's done anything terrible. And there wasn't a whole lot anyway. Are you sure you don't need this? What am I supposed to do with all the printouts?"

"I'll pay you whatever it cost."

"No, it's not that. I did it at work during lunchtime."

"There's one thing I'm curious about. Was there anything bad?"

Gordon laughed. "Define bad."

"What I mean is, is there anything embarrassing?"

"Not exactly. I mean, I found out the guy's been arrested a few times."

That was a total surprise.

"He's not a crook or anything dangerous, but he kept getting busted at these rallies and political demonstrations."

"That's interesting," Rachel said.

"Not really. He's a civil-rights attorney, so it kind of—"

"Attorney? Lucas Scott is a lawyer?"

"You got it."

"Are you sure?"

"Give me a break, Rae. I'm good at what I do."

"A lawyer. I don't know what to say."

"Then don't. Just listen. Here's something else. He chucked it all to become a musician. I didn't get that on-line. I found that out from a friend of mine who's heard him play. I can't remember what instrument—"

"Saxophone," she said automatically.

"I thought you didn't know anything about him?"

"I never said that. I wanted to find out more."

"It's a good thing you're my sister."

"Is that it?"

"Here's one last thing. He was once married. His ex was white. Did you know that?"

"No, I didn't," Rachel said. "How long?"

"How long was he married or how long since the divorce?"

"Whichever."

"Married about three years, divorced a little over six."

Rachel had to admit she would have been more surprised if it turned out that Lucas had never been married. She imagined that women were after him all the time. The two women she'd seen walking with him on Highland Beach weeks ago came to mind. It also didn't especially surprise her that his wife was Caucasian. What she knew about his background would have made that more plausible than not. And it was over, in any case.

"I also found out that—"

"Gordon thanks, but that's enough."

"If you say so. How come you need to know about this guy? Is he bothering you or something? I don't care if he's a hot-shot lawyer. If he messes with you, I'll have to take him out."

Rachel grinned affectionately at her brother's staunch protectiveness, even though he was some ten years younger. Malika returned to the table then, and Rachel wrapped up her call.

"It's not what you think. I've had some . . . er . . . business dealings with him recently and I wanted to know what kind of man he is."

"On paper, he looks like a straight shooter. I mean, he's willing to go to jail for what he believes, so he's probably cool. That takes some guts and integrity, right?"

"I agree," Rachel said.

Rachel hated the mad scramble for seats on the early-morning Acela train from New York to Washington, DC, but she joined in the race.

She got a seat at the end of the car next to the luggage rack, where she could easily keep an eye on her bag. Despite what seemed like an endless round of travel in the last month, she was already feeling excited about returning to Highland Beach. It was different this time because now she had a real claim.

Rachel settled back in her seat with an inward sigh of satisfaction. She carefully took a paper bag from the top of her tote that contained her breakfast. The train began its slow move out of the station, and there were still people moving through the car getting settled. She took a bite out of an over-buttered bagel, and glanced up in time to see Lucas walking the aisle searching for a seat. Finding something available halfway through, he was about to take the seat when he saw her.

For just an instant, Rachel didn't know what to do. She could look away and pretend she hadn't seen him. She could acknowledge him with a polite smile. The sudden liftoff of butterflies in her stomach signaled her that she wasn't ready to face him yet. She didn't know if it was due to a sudden shyness or anticipation. It had nothing to do with what Gordon had told her about Lucas. It was all about what she already knew because she'd spent time with him.

Rachel could see that Lucas also hesitated before making a decision. He continued down the aisle toward her. But the connecting door behind her leading to the next car opened, and two businessmen came through. They were going to claim the two empty seats facing her.

"I'm sorry, but these are taken," Rachel said as Lucas reached her. The two men moved on.

It wasn't until they'd gone that she realized Lucas was not alone. Right behind him was a woman, attractive and blonde. Rachel studied her briefly, recognizing her from Julia's memorial service.

"What a coincidence," Lucas said. "Mind if we join you?"

"Of course not. Sit down," she said, including the woman in the invitation.

Lucas stepped in first to take the seat by the window that was opposite her. The woman sat on the aisle. Rachel saw immediately that this arrangement presented a problem. For the next two hours and twenty minutes she was going to be knee to knee with Lucas. Had he sat there on purpose?

Rachel tried not to stare, but she wanted to see if she could find any changes since the last time they'd been together. Was he angry at her for drop-kicking his plan to buy her out? Was he going to try to persuade her? Or did his smug look mean he was actually pleased to see her? Her opinion of him, at least, had shifted.

His gaze locked onto hers, and Rachel guessed that Lucas was also assessing her. She imagined that something was communicated between them, fundamental and private. She relaxed. Whatever it was made her glad that she'd gone with her instincts to let him sit with her for the trip south despite the fact that he had a traveling companion.

"Rachel Givens, Jennifer Cameron," Lucas introduced them.

"Hi," the blonde smiled.

"I guess you made it back to your mother's okay," Lucas said.

Rachel was surprised by the question. There was an intimacy and concern implied.

"Yes, I did. Barely. I took care of the repairs since she was nice about letting me use her car."

"Is that where you're headed? Back to your mother's place?"

Rachel smiled broadly. "Not this trip. I'm going straight to the beach."

"Oh, I'm so jealous," Jennifer said dramatically. "I haven't taken a vacation this entire summer. Right, Lucas?"

He nodded, but both he and Rachel knew she had been speaking of a very specific beach. His look, however, indicated instant interest in her plans.

"For how long?" he asked.

"I don't know. Maybe three or four days. I need a break from all my recent business trips, but there are also things that I need to do down there."

"Like?"

She heard a little edge in the question. Not hostile, just very curious. "Oh . . . little things. This and that."

Jennifer glanced back and forth between Rachel and Lucas. "What are you two talking about?"

"Sorry, Jen. I don't think I told you that Rachel and Julia were good friends."

"Oh, really?" She frowned. "How long have you known each other? I know that Lucas and his mother—"

"We only met recently," Rachel explained.

"How interesting," Jennifer murmured.

"What were you doing in New York?" Rachel addressed Lucas. "Club date? Concert? Court appearance?" She bit her tongue.

His eyes became instantly alert and suspicious, but he never got a chance to answer.

"It was work," Jennifer spoke up. "Lucas was invited to speak at John Jay College, and I talked my way into coming along so I could play in Manhattan."

"John Jay? That's where they teach criminal law, isn't it?" Rachel asked with great interest.

"Right. Lucas is a great teacher and he's had a lot of experience as an attorney," Jennifer again spoke for him, with obvious pride.

"I was going to say that you wouldn't find it interesting, but maybe I'd be wrong," Lucas murmured, watching her closely.

Rachel's expression was inquisitive and innocent. "I didn't know you were a lawyer."

"So am I. Lucas and I went to law school together," Jennifer volunteered.

"How interesting," Rachel said, repeating Jennifer's comment.

"It's funny you should mention going to the beach," Jennifer said. "Lucas found out recently that his mother left him this fabulous house somewhere near Annapolis. He's already been there twice to do work, but I'm still waiting for an invitation to spend a weekend," she said, hinting broadly and nudging him with her elbow.

"You will. Maybe next year," Lucas said.

Rachel raised her eyebrows at him. Immediately she began to wonder what he'd done while she was away. And with whom. She focused her attention on Jennifer, who was friendly and very pretty, wondering what the relationship was between her and Lucas. *Of course he comes with accessories*, she thought sarcastically, not inferring high maintenance but that he was a magnet for the opposite sex, black or white. Until recently she'd had no interest in his personal life. But she wasn't going to be unfair and jump to conclusions.

Rachel spent the train ride carefully watching the small interplay and dynamic between Lucas and Jennifer. Harmless and affectionate for the most part, with an underlying tension. There was no question that they were comfortable in each other's company, proof of a longstanding relationship. Jennifer had a tendency to touch Lucas's arm or hand or thigh during conversation. To hold his attention? Or to stake a claim?

After more than two hours of this, Rachel was glad when the announcement came that they were entering Union Station.

"Can I give you a lift anywhere?" Lucas asked as the three of them departed the train.

"No thanks. I've rented a car, and I have a few boxes I have to collect from shipping before I get on the road." She saw his interest sharpen.

"You planning on doing more than just R & R while you're on the Bay?"

"Maybe one or two things. Not much."

"Lucas, wait for me, will you?" Jennifer headed for the ladies' room.

The minute she was out of earshot, Lucas turned to her.

"Just what do you have in mind?"

"Why do you want to know?"

"I have a vested interest, remember?"

"There's no need to get worked up, Lucas. Simple house

chores like cleaning out the refrigerator. Dusting the floors and furniture. Sorting through the closets," Rachel explained. "It has to be done, and I'm sure you haven't given much thought to them."

"Don't you think you should have discussed any changes with me first?"

"Just like you did with me? I appreciate that you thought of me when you went through Julia's personal things, but what else have you been doing at the house since I was away? Did you deliberately wait until I was in Europe to sneak down there?" she asked tartly.

"I didn't need your permission, Rachel," Lucas said tightly. "I own—"

"Only *half* the house. The other half is still mine, and you better get used to the idea," she got right back in his face.

"This is not going to work."

"Possession is nine-tenths of the law," she quoted righteously.

"That's an old wives' tale," he shot back. "The law is not that simplistic. I know."

"Fine. Then we might end up in court after all." She pivoted and walked away.

"Don't do anything that's going to make this more difficult," Lucas called after her.

"Last one there is a rotten egg," Rachel said with deep satisfaction, leaving him standing there.

It had taken him two days, but Lucas felt relief and an easing of the tension in his arms and back when he made the final approach to Highland Beach. The drive had taken nearly an hour longer than usual, due largely to a steamy late-summer downpour and several accidents that tied up traffic getting out of DC. He'd also gotten started later than he'd hoped. His dashboard clock read that it was now a little after three o'clock. The good news was the weather had begun to clear up.

He drove the now-familiar street leading to the house, glimpsing the Chesapeake less than five hundred feet to his right. Off in the distance, even beyond the western bank of the Delmarva Peninsula, a line of threatening clouds hovered above the horizon. Directly overhead, however, the sun seemed to welcome him back with a warmth and brightness he needed.

He saw the silver-gray SUV parked in the driveway and pulled in behind it. He'd promised himself that no matter what, he wasn't going to let the situation with Rachel undermine his right to downtime at the house, even though he was having trouble defining the situation. He only knew for certain that she had an incredible knack for getting under his skin and detonating his nerves.

He glanced around as he unpacked his satchel and saxophone. He could hear the voices and laughter of children carried on the light breeze from the direction of the playground. Katydids provided a welcome noise, as were various musical birdcalls, none of which he could identify. Lucas carried his things up the back steps. He found the door open but the inside screen door closed. He entered and found the house still and very quiet.

"Rachel?" he called out.

There was no answer.

He put the sax down in the living room and carried his suitcase to the room he'd taken over on the second floor. The windows had been opened and a fresh breeze blew in. Lucas set the bag aside, then stood considering the room with a frown. Something seemed changed. He looked around slowly before the first thing hit him. There was a handmade quilt folded at the foot of the bed, and an area rug had been placed along the side. He wasn't absolutely sure, but the shade of the lamp on the bureau didn't look familiar either.

Lucas felt annoyance begin to build, at war with his inward acknowledgment that he'd been meaning to do something about the lamp and about the cold floor when he got out of bed in the morning. He backed out of the room.

He passed Julia's old room. The door was closed. Right now it was mostly empty except for the bed frame, bureau, and armoire, and a rocking chair. Weeks ago, he'd tackled the stressful job of dismantling the room, boxing most of her personal things like clothing and accessories. He'd put everything on the third floor until he could make some decision about what he might want to keep.

Lucas walked to the end of the hall to the room Rachel used. He didn't feel like he was violating her private space since it was clear that she'd trespassed on his. Lucas stood in the open doorway and looked around.

The added touches in his room were nothing compared to what Rachel had done here. Her room was smaller than his, but it was much cozier. She'd accomplished this not by feminizing the decor, but by putting in things that were eye-catching, placed there for comfort as well as aesthetics. Unconsciously, Lucas took several steps into the room.

The room had not been painted, but some of the things they'd found in July had been removed. The original curtains, too frilly and fussy, were gone, replaced by a simple contemporary shade that allowed in lots of light while providing privacy and protection from the intense daytime sun. Her bed had new linens in a solid color, and there was also a handmade quilt at the foot of the bed. And an area rug. And a basket under the window filled with magazines and books. Pictures were tastefully arranged on all the walls.

Lucas was thrown totally off guard by what she had done. And while he was a little bent out of shape by the liberty she'd taken in his room, he couldn't help feeling a little cheated that it was nothing compared to the thorough overhaul she'd done here.

He returned to the first floor and stood at the screen door wondering where Rachel had gone. A hunch propelled him to leave the house and walk across to the park. He turned left, heading toward the beach. It was not as crowded as he thought it might be, but there were still plenty of people under umbrellas reading paperback novels, or gathered in small groups talking and laughing. Children ran about with a clear sense of safety and freedom that he'd already discovered was one of the luxuries of the isolation of Highland Beach.

With his hands deep in the pockets of his shorts, Lucas stood taking in the scenery. The sun heated his skin, and sand filled his dock shoes. The air quickly evaporated the sweat moistening his skin under the white open-neck polo shirt he wore.

"Hi."

He looked around.

"I'm over here."

He spotted Rachel to the right, seated in a legless beach chair resting on the sand. She was in a one-piece turquoise tank suit, and a broad-brimmed straw hat. With her brown legs bent at the knees, she was using her thighs as a prop for the sketch pad she was drawing in. Lucas casually approached, aware that there was a coiling of tension starting in his gut.

Rachel tilted her head back to gaze at him. "You just get here?"

"Yeah, just." He glanced around, rather than staring at her and the picture she made sitting on the beach. "It was raining when I left DC."

"It's more overcast now than it was this morning. If you brought the bad weather with you, you'll have to leave."

Lucas held back the instinct to laugh. "Mind if I join you?" he asked instead.

"Be my guest. Sorry I don't have another chair."

"I don't need one," Lucas said, dropping to sit next to her in the sand.

He took off his shoes, pouring the sand out of them. He was aware that Rachel had gone back to her sketching. It didn't bother him. He didn't feel like she was ignoring him so much as it seemed she was giving him his space. He could do with it what he would, enjoy it or not. The tension that had started to build relaxed and faded. He was very content not to do or say anything. As the silence continued, Lucas found himself focusing less on her sleek body, so close to him, and more on his surroundings. He came to a sudden and startling admission. He loved it here.

It was a place of refuge. Each time he drove past the old gatehouse guarding the entrance to outsiders he had the eerie feeling of entering a lost colony. Some place not on the map. Some place like the end of the world. Like *Brigadoon.*

And Rachel was here, an inadvertent part of the package. They were tied together by odd circumstances, and he wondered if things might have been different for him if he'd had to experience Highland Beach and learn about his mother without her.

Now he understood why Julia had loved the house so much. He reluctantly recognized that at least they had that much in common.

"So I guess I'm the rotten egg," he said.

"What? Oh. I don't know what made me say that. It was so childish."

"It served its purpose, actually. You made me see that the tit for tat we seem to get into all the time is also childish. I apologize if I came across a little heavy-handed."

Rachel closed her pad and looked directly at him. "Apology accepted. But if you start up with me again I'm bringing out the silver cross and garlic." He burst out laughing. "I'm probably guilty of being a little imperial myself."

"Yeah, but on you it looks good. With me, it seems mean tempered."

"Not really," she said carefully. "Maybe you've been a little suspicious. Maybe you felt you had reason to be."

His admission took him by surprise and succeeded in

producing silence between them. But that was okay. He was relaxing and found that he enjoyed being able to sit quietly, to let his mind roam with a mix of feelings, thoughts, and ideas. And dreams. He was starting to have new dreams about his future.

"What have you been up to since you got here?" he asked finally.

"Well, I took it upon myself to work on the kitchen like I said I would. I reorganized the cabinets. You know. Dishes over here, pots under there, glasses to the side. I hope that was okay," she ended.

"Did you do only your half of the kitchen?" Lucas asked. She got it after a moment and made a face at him. He continued, "Sounds good to me. There are a lot of things that need to get done in the house."

"I noticed that you painted the foyer. It looks nice and fresh," she said.

"Thank you. You approve?"

"Well . . . I might have picked a different color, but what you did is fine." She leaned forward in her chair, holding her straw hat down with one hand as a gust of wind threatened to rip it from her head. "I'm been thinking. Why don't we build some sort of deck out from the back of the house? We could put in a rolldown awning so it could be used even if it rains. What do you think?"

"Sounds like a good idea, but I wouldn't put it at the top of the list. The house needs a good painting on the inside. That first-floor bathroom needs to be redone. I want to see if the fireplace in the living room can be made to work."

Lucas tried not to react to the fact that she'd asked his opinion, or to her clear intentions to be around for a long time. He didn't feel like arguing the point. Instead, he was aware of the warm, humid air producing a certain lethargy in him. He stripped off his shirt and used it to wipe the sweat from his chest. Then he leaned back on his elbows, tilting his face to the sun and closing his eyes. He felt liberated and content. He didn't know how long it was going to last, but for right now, being on Highland was the whole world.

"Here. Use some of this," Rachel said.

"What?" He opened his eyes to find her holding out a bottle of sunblock. "You're right, I should." He recognized the irony of being a black man in need of sun protection. Accepting the bottle, he sat up, unscrewed the top, and began applying the lotion to his arms, face, and chest.

"What are you working on?" he asked.

"I was playing around with some new designs. The flowing of the Chesapeake gave me an idea for some hair combs that might work for a line of summer accessories. It's been slow going since I'm really just hanging out and working on my tan."

His back presented a dilemma. Lucas knew he couldn't reach it himself. Rachel took the bottle out of his hands.

"Let me do it. Turn around," she ordered.

Lucas shifted, presenting his back to her. He anticipated the first touch of her hands, but was unprepared for the electric charge that coursed through his body. He started involuntarily.

"Is it cold?" she asked.

"It's fine." He hunched forward. On the contrary, the lotion seemed hot as she slowly rubbed it into his skin with small circular movements. The lack of pressure from her hand made the contact feel like a caress. Lucas closed his eyes, breathing slowly as he found the smooth strokes seductive and stimulating.

She methodically covered every inch of skin, curving over his shoulders and traveling lightly across the back of his neck. Her touch sent a shock wave through him. Sliding down his spine, her long, uninterrupted movement caused a spasm of tension in his stomach and he could track the exact moment that the tension shifted from sensual to erotic. Lucas pulled away.

"I'm not finished," Rachel complained.

"That's good enough. Thanks. Will this wash off as soon as I hit the water?" Lucas asked, springing to his feet.

"No, it's indestructible. You'll have to melt it off," she smiled up at him.

Lucas silently emptied his pockets of his wallet, keys, and cell phone, unceremoniously handing them to Rachel. "Hold these, will you? I'm going in for a swim."

Before Rachel could respond, he was jogging to the water's edge, his well-developed leg muscles showing a man who was fit and vigorous and physical. Rachel watched as he ran right into the gentle surf, pushing off into a dive headfirst as his outstretched hands and arms neatly cleaved the surface. When his head finally popped up above the water, he was already some distance from the beach. She watched as Lucas treaded water and oriented himself before he began swimming in a smooth, leisurely crawl parallel to the shore. She watched for a long time expecting him to quickly tire and return. But he showed no signs of stopping, performing lap after lap parallel to the shore. The sun slipped behind the clouds that, once far away, seemed to be rolling in toward land, turning the sky dark in its wake.

The first splash of rain was heavy and quick, dotting the sand and pelting her skin. There was an instant scramble among other holdouts as blankets and towels were tossed into beach bags, chairs collapsed and folded up, calls went out for children to hurry and get their things, and everyone made a mad dash for cover. Rachel quickly followed suit, expecting Lucas to appear as the rain began coming down in a relentless torrent. The beach was almost deserted and she didn't see him, nor could she tell if he was still in the water. She hoped not. She grabbed his shoes and shirt, adding them to her things, and ran for the shelter of the house. She managed to get everything up the steps, except for the beach chair that she left at the foot. Rachel was thoroughly wet by the time she got inside the house. Standing in the open doorway, she searched again for Lucas. She felt a twinge of apprehension. Did he get a cramp? Was he sucked beneath the water by a phantom undertow? Had he taken refuge somewhere else?

Rachel deposited her wet towels in the bathroom and went to get more dry ones. She came right back to the door when it suddenly opened and Lucas hurried in, water running from every part of his body.

"What happened to you?" she questioned frantically.

Lucas used his hands to wipe the water from his face. His shorts were plastered to his body.

"I'm glad you were smart enough not to hang around out there waiting for me," he said.

"Lucas, you scared me. When you didn't come back after the rain started, I didn't know what to think."

He stood with his hands on his hips looking at her while water dripped to the floor. "Were you worried about me?"

"Yes," she answered, annoyed. She left him there to return to the kitchen, to a closet that had been converted into a laundry space and outfitted with stacked washer and dryer. She pulled another clean towel from the pile on top of the dryer.

"I got invited to share a large umbrella with some people who decided to wait out the worst of the rain."

"I hope you had a good time," she said, returning with the towel and tossing it to him.

"Yeah, I did. People are friendly around here. As a matter of fact, I ran into some ladies I met my first time here. They remembered me."

"I'm not surprised."

He was scrubbing the towel back and forth over his head and then bending to dry his hairy legs and chest. She watched the play of muscles in his arms and across his shoulders. When he stood up straight again, his gaze seemed to roam her body as she stood in front of him in only the turquoise swimsuit and flip-flops. Her hair was twisted to the back of her head and held there by a claw clasp. His eyes were particularly drawn to her chest, and she realized that the cold rain had forced her nipples into turgid little peaks that were probably visible through the Lycra of her suit. She did nothing to conceal herself, feeling a peculiar power and desire that Lucas stay focused on her. Slowly he dragged his attention up to her face, and Rachel met his stare with open frankness.

"Did you have a good swim?"

"I did. It was just what I needed." He began to haphazardly fold the towel, still studying her with his bright gray-green eyes. "Were you really worried about me?"

She heard the genuine curiosity in the question. She heard a kind of surprise bordering on disbelief. She listened closely and imagined that she even heard something hopeful. It was a loaded question, and a minefield.

Suddenly feeling awkward, Rachel lowered her gaze. Turning, she headed for the stairs. "I'm going up to change into something dry," she said, leaving the question unanswered.

It was forty-five minutes later when she left her room and returned to the first floor. There was a CD of mellow jazz playing from the living room. Hearing it reminded her of something she realized she should have done earlier. Too late, she entered the room and found Lucas, who'd also changed in the interim, standing in front of a long landscape hung on the wall. He appeared to be viewing it solemnly and with his undivided attention.

"Lucas, I'm sorry. I meant to tell you about the painting, but—"

"Where did you get this?" he asked.

"From the artist. I saw it at an opening last month in New York. It was the night I learned about Julia," she added softly. When he didn't respond she rushed on. "If you don't like it I'll take it down. I just wanted to see how it would look on—"

"Was it expensive?"

"Expensive? I guess so. But I didn't pay for it."

Finally he turned to regard her closely. "Since I don't believe you would steal it, you'll have to explain that."

"I bartered for it. Actually, the artist wanted something from me in exchange, so I agreed. I made a necklace for his mother's birthday. I accepted the painting as payment."

"Nice deal," he said.

"I know how you feel about me taking over and not telling you when I'm doing something. I can put the painting upstairs on the second floor. Or even in my room—"

"I like it." Lucas turned to look at the painting again.

"Are you sure?"

"You know what it reminds me of? When you're driving in toward the gatehouse and the road splits between Venice and Highland Beach, there's a little break where you can see beyond the trees to a patch of sky, and you know that just below it is the Chesapeake."

"That's pretty much what I thought, too," she agreed, standing next to him.

"So, we'll leave it here on this wall?"

Rachel glanced at him. "If it's okay with you."

"It's okay with me. See, that wasn't so hard. Maybe we're getting the hang of this after all."

"Maybe," she smiled, enjoying the light in his eyes shining down on her. "Why did you ask if the painting was expensive?"

"Well, if you'd paid a lot of money for it, I'd feel I should pay for half since we're both going to enjoy it."

She laughed. "I hadn't thought of it that way."

"Any more surprises for me?"

"Well, up in your room—"

"I saw the quilt and the rug. It would have been nice if you'd asked first, but I'm getting used to you. And I like the new touches. So thank you. I appreciate that you were thinking of me."

She shrugged almost shyly. "I thought those few things would make the room more comfortable."

"I'll reimburse you for whatever you laid out," Lucas said.

"The shade is from a lamp I found in a closet. The rug was from a discount store in New York. The quilt is mine. I have several that were made by my grandmother."

"Are you sure it's okay?"

"I'm sure. She would be very happy to know they're being used. So, what are your plans? How long are you staying?"

He sighed, strolling away as he considered her question. "A couple of days, I guess. Not as long as a week. And you?"

"Same thing. I needed a break, but I have so much work to catch up on."

"Then let's not waste our time talking about work or leaving," Lucas grinned.

"Good idea."

"How do you feel about driving into Annapolis this evening? I thought we could find some place that serves up decent crab cakes."

Her smile faded and she knew her face looked stricken.

"Don't like the idea?"

"Lucas, I'd love to go, but I have plans for the evening."

"Do you?" he asked, managing to look surprised and accepting all at the same time.

"Harrietta Cousins invited me to have dinner with her. I think I mentioned her to you. I know she's been hoping to meet you. Come with me."

He shook his head. "I don't think so. I don't much want to be put under a microscopic lens and have my life dissected. Your Harrietta is going to want to know what the deal was between Julia and me. Not yet."

"If I'd known you were driving down this afternoon—"

"It wouldn't have made any difference. I would still say no."

"What will you do?"

"I'll be fine, Rachel."

"Maybe you'll have the time to look through that box your grandmother gave you. I noticed it's still on the table over there in the corner."

He turned away restlessly. "Not tonight."

"But how do you know there's not something really important in there for you?"

"Because if there was, Julia could have given it to me a long time ago. What's the big rush for me to find out now?" he said, almost shouting.

Rachel was stunned by his sudden vitriolic reply. She stared wide-eyed at Lucas and decided she wasn't going to let him get away with that.

"You're avoiding it."

"So what?" he asked, trying to gain control of his sudden outburst.

"That box has been sitting there for weeks."

"Let it go, Rachel. Don't push." His voice was now dangerously low.

"What are you afraid of?" she persisted, despite knowing there might be consequences.

"I don't know if I'm ready to forgive her." His tone was loud, hard, angry. "I honestly don't know if I can. And if I can't, then I'll have to live with that for the rest of my life. Right now not knowing is manageable. Do you understand?"

Slowly her fear subsided, and her sympathy for Lucas increased. He sat heavily on the old sofa and she followed to sit next to him, but not too close. He still needed space.

"I think I do understand. You know, it wasn't until Julia was gone that I finally saw how little I knew my own mother and how little credit I gave her for being just who she is. That was my fault because I was always comparing her to Julia and thinking my mother didn't measure up. I made Julia into a superwoman in my mind and gave her all kinds of mythical powers. I made Julia bigger than life, and it wasn't fair to her, me, or my mother."

Lucas regarded her closely. "What are you trying to say?"

"Julia was a beautiful, lively, kind person. But she was also very sad and very lonely. I didn't know that until I met you, but now I see how her choices made her who she was. Her choices even made you who you are because someone else raised you.

"Look, what I'm *really* trying to say is, life is about choices. I think your mother lived long enough to deeply regret hers. That's kind of where you are now. To forgive, or not to forgive. To move on, or stay lost in the past."

Lucas didn't respond at all. She wasn't even sure he'd been listening to what she said. She wasn't sure she'd made any sense. Rachel gazed at him a moment longer and got up, heading toward the door. She didn't want to keep Harrietta waiting. But she regretted having to leave Lucas alone. She turned one more time to speak to him.

"You're a musician. Music speaks to you in a special way, doesn't it? There's a line in a song that goes, 'If you're given a choice to sit it out or dance, I hope you dance.' Lucas, I hope you dance."

When Rachel returned just before ten, the house was almost completely dark, except for the outside porch light and a counter lamp in the kitchen. It was so quiet she thought that maybe Lucas had gone out after all and not come back. She went from that to the possibility that he had left and wasn't going to return. But she didn't believe that was really the case.

She could hear faint music coming from somewhere outside the back of the house. When she passed through the living room and solarium, she saw that the back door was open. Approaching, she stood in the opening and looked out.

The moon was high, and it cast light that rippled over the surface of the Chesapeake and created shadows on the beach and in the park across the street. The music she heard was coming from another house, slow background melodies playing behind low conversation and laughing. It took a few minutes for her eyes to adjust, but even then she couldn't see much of anything in the dark.

She cautiously descended the steps, walking a little bit away from the steps to stand in the warm summer air. It was quiet and peaceful. The thought came to Rachel that sooner or later she would have to return to New York. She had a business to operate, obligations to meet, and projects to develop, but in that moment she was as happy as she'd ever been, and it was getting harder and harder to imagine herself anywhere else. There was only one thing that would make it perfect, but she was convinced that the chances were slim to none that it was possible to have everything. Julia had tried and ended up alone and unfulfilled. Rachel had decided not that long ago that although she loved and admired Julia dearly, she didn't want to be like her. Perhaps that was the most important thing she'd learned from her.

"How was dinner?"

The disembodied voice startled Rachel. She detected Lucas coming toward her out of the darkness. She was glad to see him, glad that he'd not been scared off by ghosts.

"Entertaining."

"You're home early."

"It's not like it was a date. She's an elderly woman set in her ways. Dinner at seven, in bed by nine-thirty. She was probably asleep before I got back here."

Lucas stopped in front of her and Rachel noticed at once that he seemed more relaxed than when she'd left him.

"I thought about maybe going over there to walk you back, but I figured that chances were slim to none that you'd have to worry about being mugged or kidnapped on the street."

"Thanks for the thought. Harrietta's granddaughter offered to drive me, but I told her I was going to be okay. Besides, Harrietta guaranteed that Highland Beach does *not* have crime."

"She sounds opinionated."

"Oh, very. She loves to talk, knows everything and everyone, and will gladly get into your business. She says she's glad that you've come to take your place in the community. I'm also to tell you that you have a standing invitation to come to see her and have dinner, and she expects you to be prompt. She doesn't like to be kept waiting, and no is not an option."

"Wow. I'm scared of her," Lucas commented, making her laugh.

"She did have one other question, but I feel embarrassed to even repeat it."

"What?"

"She asked if you and I are having an affair. She's heard rumors about the two of us being alone together in Julia's house."

"And you said . . ."

"I told her not to listen to rumors."

"I bet that's not what she was hoping to hear."

Rachel searched his face to see what kind of mood he might be in, and how he might be feeling after the earlier dustup.

"What did you do all evening? Did you drive into town? I wish I'd gone with you—"

"I'll ask you again sometime." He reached for her hand. "Come on. I want to show you something."

"Where are you taking me?" Rachel asked, curious but not concerned. His hand felt warm and strong.

"Not too far." They crossed the road to the park, and walked toward a picnic table placed under the branches of a tree. "Right . . . here," he said.

Rachel looked around. "What are we doing?"

"Listen," he said, falling silent and following his own instructions.

"You mean the music? Yes, I hear it."

He gently pulled her around to face him and held out his other hand. "Will you dance with me?"

Click.

She felt the shift instantly. Rachel tried to see Lucas's eyes but couldn't see his face clearly. She felt a little breathless, a little giddy, and hugely satisfied. "Yes, I'd love to."

Lucas slipped his arms around her and led her into the beat of the distant music. The music was slow and Rachel could feel his hand hold hers, his other hand resting on the curve of her waist. He held her close enough that their bodies barely touched, but she could feel the heat emanating from him. As the music played, the dance seemed more intimate and less formal. Their thighs touched and her breasts pressed lightly against his chest. She gave up trying to see his face and concentrated instead on the message his body was giving off. His hand, splayed against her back, gently drew her in little by little until their bodies swayed together.

The music faded but Lucas did nothing to release her, and Rachel made no move to step away. Instead, they seemed to be trying to get closer together in a subtle, more tantalizing manner. Finally they were just rocking in place, groin to groin. Then they stopped altogether. She raised her face as his bent toward her, and Rachel let her eyes close. She parted her lips and then waited for the inevitable contact of his mouth. It was more than that. Lucas, with an erotic slow deliberateness, covered Rachel's mouth with his and he wasted no time in letting his tongue divide and conquer. She felt a searing response in the coiling tension in her stomach and in a delicious spiraling of desire between her legs. She wanted to press even closer but didn't want to be the aggressor. Yet the intimacy of their kiss and the suggestive darting of Lucas's warm, rough tongue left her lightheaded and soft and yielding.

Lucas slowly ended the kiss, but in such a way that signaled it was really just the beginning.

"What brought that on?" she asked.

"I looked in the box," he said simply.

Eleven

"I think I remember where this one was taken," Lucas said, holding the photograph so that both he and Rachel could see it.

"Are you sure? You couldn't have been more than three at the time," Rachel said.

"Pretty sure. Tompkins Square Park in New York. I know my parents lived nearby when they first got married, and I remember that park. Actually, I might have forgotten all about that forever if I hadn't seen this picture to remind me."

Rachel took the picture out of his hand to examine it more closely. It showed Lucas as a laughing toddler. Squatting down beside him was Julia. Even as a baby he had her smile. She knew that this was the earliest picture she had ever seen of Julia. She was beautiful. Her son had inherited his share of her genes. As he'd come to adulthood, it was also clear that his skin tone had become more tan, somewhere between the caramel and olive tones of his parents.

"You were a pretty baby," she said softly.

"I'm not so bad now," Lucas answered.

Rachel made a face at his conceit and gave him back the photo. Lucas placed it on top of a pile of others they'd already seen. He continued sifting through the box and pulled out several more, holding up yet another.

"Look at this one. That's all three of us."

"What a great picture. Your father is a handsome man. I see

you got the Scott hair," she laughed, referring to the riot of dark, curly hair that covered his head.

Lucas smoothed down his hair with its slight wave, shorter and coarser than his father's. "I went through a period in high school when I locked my hair and wore dreads. My grandparents didn't understand. That's pretty much when I realized that I needed to learn more about the other half of my life."

"Julia's side."

"Well, it was more than that. At that point I started feeling I didn't belong anywhere. I didn't fit."

"Identity crisis?"

"Maybe. Or just wanting a full history. My grandparents are great people, but they're only half of the story. I recently learned from my father how much he still loved my mother years after they divorced, and I thought, what happened? Why didn't it hold together? Whose fault was it that they split up? Why didn't she want me?"

"I don't believe Julia didn't want you. The answer has got to be more complicated than that."

"My father gave me some clues when I talked with him. He said you can't stop someone from following a dream. He never come right out and said Julia walked away because she didn't love him anymore, or that she didn't want the responsibility of a kid. I don't know. I'm trying to read between the lines. I'm trying to respect his feelings while still trying to come to grips with my own." He picked up his wineglass, but it was empty.

"I'll get more," Rachel offered.

She uncurled herself from the sofa and padded barefoot into the kitchen to open a second bottle of wine. She was still experiencing an odd disorientation. Back at the house after their moonlit dance, he showed her what had brought on the sudden change in his attitude. He'd offered to show her some of the pictures he'd discovered in the box his grandmother had given him. She had been astonished by his willingness to share his personal secrets, and it was not lost on her that Lucas was also showing considerable trust in her. What was in the box was all the pictures that had been removed from the album she'd found in Julia's room more than a month earlier.

It seemed clear to Rachel that if Julia had walked away from her son, she certainly had not forgotten all about him. She may not have been able or willing to seek him out once he was older and risk his scorn, but she had found a way to let her son know there was a lot more to the story.

Just as powerful as Lucas's discoveries was the fact that a new thing was happening between the two of them. Somehow time had compressed, and they had taken a quantum leap right out of the past and skipped a whole bunch of primary steps in their relationship. They had gone, in a heartbeat, from friendly adversaries to intimate friends. She wondered what was coming next.

Rachel thought that the dance and kiss under the moon was romantic enough, but did it pave the way for them to take their relationship in a whole new direction? The kiss had been wonderful. Delicious, to be exact. She'd enjoyed kissing him, experiencing his ability to jolt her sensibilities into full alert, to make her feel languid and willing. As they made their way, hand in hand, back to the house, she already knew that whatever happened, there would be no turning back.

Rachel returned to the living room to find that Lucas had set the box aside on the floor. He was reclining on the sofa, his butt on the edge of the cushion. He was frowning at two envelopes in his hand.

"Thanks," he murmured, accepting his refilled wineglass from her.

She sat next to him but kept her distance, at least for the moment. There were too many things happening at once, and she didn't want to confuse the issue.

"Are those letters?" she asked.

He nodded. "I found them in the same box. There's about

fifty, maybe more. They're addressed to me from Julia," he said. "This is the first time I've ever seen them or knew anything about them."

"Like the photographs."

"Right. Like the photographs."

Rachel could see that the letters had never been opened. He regarded her with a thoughtful expression.

"The big question is, why would my grandparents not want me to have letters and photographs from my mother? Isn't this proof that she didn't forget about me?"

"Maybe they thought they were protecting you."

"From my mother?"

"From being confused. Maybe it wasn't about you. Maybe your grandparents had issues."

"They're terrific people. I've never felt anything but love from them. But it must have been difficult raising a biracial grandchild and dealing with other people's questions and negative comments. It wasn't always a walk in the park for me, either."

"What do you mean?"

He turned his head to look at her, his gaze distant and reflective. "Being raised by a white father and grandparents didn't make me white. School was sometimes difficult. Some of my classmates and teachers, didn't quite know what to make of me. Which side of the fence was I on? My first two years of college were . . . enlightening, shall we say? That's when I learned that calling myself black came with some pretty rigid parameters. At least according to the other black students and some of the friends I tried to hang with at the time."

"What about dating?" she asked carefully.

"Never a problem. But it had a peculiar spin on it where I was concerned, if you know what I mean." He chortled with a touch of irony and disbelief. "I once dated a woman who told me flat out she'd love to have a baby with me so it would have my eyes." He sat forward, tapping the envelopes against the palm of his hand. "I was married, you know."

"Really?" Rachel more surprised that Lucas had mentioned it on his own than by the guilt she experienced at already having that information.

"She was white."

She thought she heard a bit of defiance in his voice. "So? Was that relevant?"

"Looking back on it after we divorced, I think it was."

"Did you love her?" Rachel questioned.

"I did at the time. Probably for the wrong reasons. I certainly wasn't exempt from making bad decisions."

"I was almost married, once," Rachel suddenly confided. She wasn't sure why, except it felt right, and seemed fair. Why should he take all the risks of baring his soul?

"What happened?" Lucas asked, interested.

"I think I scared him off," she said. He grinned at her, as if he could well believe it. "I had all these plans, and he was pretty laid back. I forgot that marriage is supposed to be a partnership. I never kept him in the loop, so I guess he felt, what does she need me for?"

"Are you sorry about how it worked out?"

"Actually, after I got over wanting to rip his heart out, and feeling totally humiliated when he called the wedding off, I realized he did me a favor. He didn't intend it that way, but he set me free to do what I really wanted to do. Be a designer and have a career and travel, and be free."

He was looking steadily at her and Rachel suddenly realized exactly what she was saying. She wanted the life she believed Julia had. A life, which it now appeared, had been mostly smoke and mirrors.

"Is that what's most important to you?"

Rachel smiled and shook her head. "No. What's important is finding a balance. My career is not the be-all and end-all of my life." She averted her gaze. "Of course I'd like to have a relationship, maybe next time with someone who has a life so that mine doesn't overwhelm him."

He didn't say anything until she looked at him again. His light eyes were focused and serious. Then he turned his attention to the envelopes in his hand. "What do you think happened to Julia's plans?"

"I don't know. But I think it's fair to say things didn't work out as planned. And maybe other things happened she hadn't expected." She watched as Lucas ran his fingers over his name, written in a looping script on the envelope. It was almost as if by doing so he'd actually touched Julia.

"Are you going to open them?" she asked.

"Not right now," he murmured. "I'm coming across one too many Pandora's boxes, and it's got me a little freaked. I'm wondering, what else am I going to find?" He dropped the two envelopes into the open box on the floor. He took her hand and threaded their fingers together. "Julia's life is a lot to process in a few weekends, but I feel like I can't afford to lose any more time."

She liked that he kept touching her. "Time for what?"

"Living."

Rachel smiled at him. "Since you've been coming to Highland Beach, you seem to have gotten the knack." He didn't return her smile but she felt as if he was. It came through in his eyes, and from the warm enclosure of his hand.

"I think it's maybe more than Highland Beach."

"You like it here?"

"Yeah . . . I like it here."

"What?" she asked, when he continued to study her.

"We have a problem, you know."

"We?" she asked.

"You, me, and the house. You've made it clear you don't want to sell your share."

Rachel wanted to pull her hand free, but he held it fast. She thought he was going to say something different. "Why should I?"

"I'm not going to sell, either. I think Julia meant for me to have this house. Maybe she was trying to make up for all those years of not being around in my life. I don't know."

"I feel the same way, Lucas," Rachel said. "No one was more surprised than I was when I got the call from her attorney saying that I'd been named in her will. But like you, I also believe Julia meant for me to have the house. Or at least, half of it."

"But you see how that can't work indefinitely, don't you?"

Rachel wondered if he was thinking the same thing she was. It wasn't about the house at all. With the imprint of his kiss still fresh on her mouth, with her body awakened to his touch and the possibilities, she was already wondering what a full frontal attack would be like between them.

"I'm still hoping we can work something out. I don't mean to be difficult, but I've never hidden that I've *always* loved it here. It didn't take you very long to see why I feel the way I do."

He conceded that point when he sighed deeply. "Highland Beach is my strongest connection to my mother, besides a handful of photographs, and the letters."

Rachel got up impatiently. "Then is that what that kiss was all about? Are you trying to play me? Are you going to use your knowledge as a lawyer to try to win?"

He slowly sat forward. "The kiss stands on its own. Unless you were acting, I'd say by your response that you enjoyed it as much as I did. I kissed you because that's how I was feeling at the time and it was right."

"So we fast-forward to a few hours later. How are you feeling now?"

"I'm still glad I kissed you. I like to think I'm mature enough and experienced enough to know when something is right. I also like that you didn't make it easy for me. I worked for that kiss." Rachel grinned. "I'm really attracted to you. If you can't tell that the way I feel has nothing to do with the house, then you haven't learned anything about me. As for me being a lawyer, if I wanted to use that against you I could have. I'm trying to find a way to honor my mother's wishes. I can promise it's not going to happen through a lawsuit."

Rachel wondered if Julia really knew what she was doing when she tied them both to her house, with neither of them having total control. She felt a little foolish for getting so defensive. Maybe he was struggling with the same things she was.

"Alright, I believe you. I'm sorry for suggesting—"

"The only thing I care about right now is if you think I didn't mean it when we kissed."

"It felt pretty real to me," she admitted softly.

"It was. Which is why I said we have a problem. I wasn't talking about the house, Rae. I was talking about you and me together in the house."

"You just called me Rae."

"Did I? I was thinking out loud. It suits you," he told her.

"That's what my family calls me," she said.

"Can I call you Rae?"

"If you like," she said, accepting that Lucas had touched on the growing attraction between them.

"Do you agree with me?"

Their attraction had been slow but sure, and somehow in-evitable. It was their kiss that brought their feelings to the forefront.

"It doesn't have to be hard if we respect boundaries." She saw the skepticism darken his gray-green eyes.

"You mean the half-and-half rule?"

"I mean not letting the . . . our attraction get out of hand," she said honestly.

"Rachel," he said in a tone that was quiet and understanding, but amused.

She knew what was meant by his reaction. He closed the distance between them. In one smooth motion he'd slipped his arms around her, drawing her against his chest. He was kissing her before she could even think of protesting, which, of course, never entered her mind. She must have been hoping for this, or at least expecting it, she reasoned, because her lips parted just as his mouth fitted to hers.

The first kiss had been spontaneous and exploratory, thrilling because it was not expected. This second kiss had upped the ante, and her response was disconcertingly instant. Within seconds Rachel felt herself drifting into a euphoria stimulated by pure desire. She wanted to get closer. Closer . . .

The telephone rang and shattered the mood. It rang a second and third time before Lucas even deigned to move or release her.

"Hold that thought," he whispered to her, touching his lips briefly to hers once more. He withdrew his arms and went to the kitchen to answer the wall unit.

Rachel stood rather dazed, annoyed by her eagerness, missing him. Lucas was back quickly.

"It's for you." He still detained her, holding her by the arm. "What was that you were saying about boundaries?"

Rachel didn't answer because she couldn't. She did know that she was going to have to do more than lecture Lucas if she didn't want to go up in flames. It was clear to her that the two of them were potentially combustible together.

"Hello?"

"Rae? Who was that man? I thought you were at the beach by yourself."

Rachel tried to gather her wits, because the one person she definitely couldn't fool was her mother. "Hi. Is everything okay?"

"Yes, everything is fine. Answer my question. Who answered the phone?"

Rachel lowered her voice. "That was Lucas Scott, Julia Winters's son. I'm sure I told you about him."

"What's he doing there with you?"

"Well for starters, the house belonged to his mother. He has a right to be here. Second of all, he's the executor of her estate, and there are still things to settle according to Julia's will."

"You mean you two are staying there together?"

"It's a big house. We hardly even see each other," Rachel lied easily. God would forgive her. "Why are you calling?"

"I want to know what you're doing down there on Highland Beach for more than a week. What's going on?"

While her mother probed and prodded, she watched as Lucas gathered his box of photographs and letters from Julia, turned off the CD player in the living room, and grabbed his glass of wine.

"Has it really been more than a week?"

"Seemed to me that you were never going back to New York and your work."

"I will. It's pretty and relaxing here and—"

As he passed her, Lucas suddenly bent to nuzzle her jaw and the side of her neck with his mouth. Rachel felt the way her stomach muscles contracted with the teasing of his lips. He jerked his thumb to the ceiling to indicate he was headed upstairs before walking away.

"I want you to explain how owning half a house works. Not tonight, of course. I just wanted to call and make sure you're alright and to find out when you plan on going home."

Rachel found that an odd question. She'd been thinking for the past ten days or so that she *was* home. Maybe that's why she hadn't thought much about New York. But she couldn't go on ignoring her career, and her other life, forever.

"Thanks for calling, but I'm okay here. I'll be heading back to New York soon."

"I've been thinking of going up to New York myself, maybe for a long weekend."

"Really?"

"Why do you sound so surprised? I love New York."

"Mom, as long as I've lived there I don't remember you coming to visit a single time."

"Well, I wouldn't really be coming to visit you. I'd stay at a hotel."

"By yourself? That's crazy. You can stay with me."

"Rae, I didn't say I'd be by myself," Lydia corrected politely.

"Oh."

"We'll talk about it when I see you."

When Rachel got off the phone, she wasn't sure what to think about the possibility that her own mother was keeping company with someone. It made her feel naive and backward that she hadn't realized before that Lydia had no qualms about being romantically involved and sexually active, maybe even being in love.

So what's your problem? she asked herself.

Rachel was afraid to go upstairs. Somehow, her bedroom being at the end of the hallway felt like a dead end. Like, she could get backed into a corner with no way out. Suddenly, the prospect of being alone with Lucas began to take on larger implications. Not that she was opposed to any, but he was right. They did have to be careful. She deliberately stayed on the first level, hoping he would retire to his own room before she went up herself. There were boundaries to be maintained. She had told him so. And there was still that thing about attraction.

She was already in serious trouble.

It grew quiet. After turning out all the downstairs lights and locking the doors, she started up to her room. She'd just made it past the bathroom when the door opened. A waft of steam curled out, followed by Lucas. He'd just stepped out of the shower, and there was one towel wrapped around his waist, while he used another to dry his arms and chest.

"It's all yours," he said.

"Thanks. I think I'll shower in the morning," she said.

She couldn't pretend that she wasn't aware Lucas was standing there practically naked. But it was particularly provocative because of the sexual innuendos that had passed between them all evening. She kept her focus on his eyes. And his mouth, the part of him she knew best. She smiled.

"What's that for?" Lucas asked her.

"You're so different from when I first met you."

"Which me do you like better?

The one who kissed me. "The one who's learning to let go of the past," Rachel said, heading toward her room.

"I don't know if I'm there, yet."

"Want to know how I know?" she asked over her shoulder once she reached the door.

"Okay. How?"

"You started calling Julia your mother tonight." She could see he hadn't been aware of that happening.

"Okay. Now let me give you something to think about that I just figured out," he said.

Her expression showed mild curiosity.

"My mother knew exactly what she was doing when she left the house to both of us."

Lucas finished reading another letter and closed his eyes against a wellspring of emotion that had already formed a knot in the middle of his chest. He sat up from the half reclining position he'd taken in bed and glanced at the night-stand clock. It was almost one-thirty in the morning. Adding the handwritten pages to the other letters he'd already opened and read, he swung himself to the edge of the bed. He needed to move. He needed to get away from an overload of sadness and disappointment from the past. Not his, but Julia's.

Lucas left his room wearing only the boxer shorts that he

slept in. Without second thoughts he started down the hall toward Rachel's room. He needed to talk. He wanted to tell her about what he'd read. The contents of those letters had begun to set him free, but broken his heart in a different way. He stopped before he reached Rachel's bedroom door and changed his mind. He decided that this was not a good time, after all, to try to get his mind around his mother's history and failed dreams. Maybe what he really needed was a drink. Maybe it would help him to shut out the words going round in his head so he could get some sleep. Lucas turned around and headed, instead, for the kitchen.

He unlocked and opened the back door and sucked in the chilly bay air to clear his head. Everything had a preternatural quietness. The house was so still. He tried to imagine his mother here, alone with memories, self-recriminations, and terrible losses. No wonder she had been drawn to the little girl named Rachel, whom she could impress and influence and mold . . . and love. She had given up everything else. The tragedy, as far as Lucas could determine, was that it didn't have to be this way.

Lucas found the half-finished bottle of wine in the refrigerator and poured himself a glass. He stood in the open doorway nursing it, feeling tense and helpless. He wanted to understand and forgive his mothert, but something was still wrong. Something still did not make sense, and it wasn't clarified in the letters. He knew he had to continue to pursue the whole story. He was tired of feeling like part of his life was missing.

He was about to pour himself a second glass when he heard a peculiar groaning sound from above. Lucas finally identified it. His grandparents' house made shifting noises all the time because it was old. The second time the sound was louder, and it made him stop and put the wine bottle down because he felt something different was happening. Suddenly, the noise started spreading into a loud, crunching roar. In the middle of it he heard Rachel scream.

Lucas put the glass down so hard the stem broke. He raced back for the stairs.

"Rachel!" he yelled, taking the steps two at a time.

He stubbed the toes of his right foot on the top step and stumbled. He cursed soundly at the pain that shot through his foot but kept running.

"Rachel!"

He made the sharp turn onto the hall and was met with whirls of dust bellowing out of Rachel's room. The noise quickly quieted down and he could hear her coughing and gasping for air.

"Lucas, help me."

Lucas rushed into the room and promptly stumbled again on a pile of rubble.

Reaching out blindly, he searched for a light. He was able to turn on the dresser lamp. Looking around, Lucas saw that he was standing in broken plaster, sheetrock, and wood chips. "Are you hurt?" he asked her.

"I don't know." She began coughing again. "There's dust in my eyes."

"Take it easy. Don't rub them."

Lucas made his way to the bed, climbing over and staggering through debris. Rachel was partially covered by rubble from the ceiling, which had given way. He was grateful most of it had ended up at the foot of the bed or on the floor. He gripped her around her back as she locked her arms around his neck. Slowly Lucas dislodged her, pulling her from the bed.

"Oh, my God, what happened?" she croaked, trying to clear her throat.

"The ceiling collapsed. Are you okay?"

Now clear of the mess in her bed, Rachel stood up, testing the strength of her legs. "I think so."

"Let's get out of here. If I'd finished what I started, I might have prevented this."

"Started to do what?"

"Never mind that now. Hopefully you suffered only a few scratches."

Lucas helped her to the bathroom where they could better see any damage. Besides being covered in chalky powder from the plaster, Rachel had only suffered a minor bruise on her shoulder and neck.

"Go ahead and take a shower," Lucas suggested. "I'm going to see if I can find out how bad the damage is."

But after putting on shoes and a pair of jeans, Lucas quickly found out there was nothing he could really tell without a tall-enough ladder, proper light, and knowing what he was looking for. By the time he had finished his investigation, Rachel had finished her shower and left the bathroom dressed in a long summer robe.

She'd combed the plaster out of her hair and managed to look none the worse for wear.

"How are you feeling?" he asked her as they met in the hallway.

"I'm okay. Did you see anything?"

"It'll have to wait until morning. We'll have to call someone to come in and make repairs. There's no way you can sleep in there tonight. Unfortunately, I've already cleared everything out of my mother's room."

"I can sleep on the sofa downstairs; that's not a problem."

"No, you take my room. I'll sleep on the sofa."

"Lucas, I don't mind—"

"You won't find any cookie crumbs in my bed or girlie magazines under it . . ." Rachel giggled. "I'm feeling a little restless anyway."

"Are you sure? I feel so badly about taking your bed."

"If it bothers you that much, you can make up for it some other time. Like, not suing me for what almost happened."

Rachel stood in front of him with her arms crossed over her stomach and her hands tucked under her elbows. He peered into her face, and although she tried to smile, Lucas realized that she was more shaken than she was willing to let on. He gently folded her into his arms, stroking her back while she rested her cheek against his chest.

"Thank you," she said softly.

"I'm glad you didn't get hurt. The ceiling can be fixed. Okay now?"

"Yes, I'm fine."

But he continued to hold Rachel just a little longer before stepping back. As much as he knew she needed some comforting, he needed that moment for himself as well to make up for not following his inclinations earlier. Lucas went to the linen closet to find another pillow and a lightweight blanket. At the top of the stairs, he turned to her.

"I'll see you in the morning."

"Thanks for giving up your room. Goodnight."

He waited until she'd closed the door before descending the stairs, where he tried to fashion himself a place to sleep on the sofa.

Rachel entered Lucas's room feeling strange about having taken it over. She looked around slowly, finding parts of him everywhere. The shirt and slacks he'd worn earlier that evening were now on a chair. She saw several books he'd brought to read while on Highland Beach that she was sure he hadn't opened yet. Sunglasses, a pair of fifteen-pound hand weights, and swim trunks.

She also noticed that he hadn't actually gone to bed at all, but had apparently been lying on top reading. She found a handful of papers which had been folded, now spread open and stacked in a pile. Upon closer inspection, she realized that they were probably some of Julia's letters. She lifted one to look at the date on the top page. She figured that Lucas would have been about seven when that one was written. She leafed through and pulled out one from the middle of the stack. This had a much later date. He would have been eleven.

It didn't appear that Lucas had made any attempt to put the letters in chronological order, but had opened them randomly. She also found greeting cards. Age-appropriate birthday cards for turning five, eight, nine. Several Christmas cards, one for Halloween . . . another when Lucas graduated high school. In it Julia had scrawled, "Please send me a picture of you in cap and gown."

It was wrenching to know that Julia had never gotten that photograph because Lucas had never received the request. Yet, despite years of never getting a response from her son, she continued to reach out to him. Rachel was curious to know when the last letter or card had been sent. When had Julia decided to give up? Had she?

Rachel could see that all of the letters and cards were Julia's attempts to interject herself into her son's life. To live the role of his mother vicariously, to love him long distance. She knew that Julia could only have succeeded if Lucas allowed her to. What had he felt, reading these letters so many years after they had been mailed? And did reading them now change the message, or the intent, in any way?

She risked the violation of his privacy to look through a few of the letters. Just enough to read between the lines and suspect that Julia had regretted being absent from Lucas's life until the day she died. Rachel gathered the letters and cards and placed them carefully in the silk-covered box. She could see there were many more, years' worth of Julia's love, still to be read. She then prepared to get into the bed.

She realized that she felt a certain titillating excitement about sleeping in Lucas's bed. She lay there for a long time but couldn't shake the sense that she was not alone in the bed. That prompted her into a willing acceptance of her circumstances, and her next decision.

She was quiet leaving the room, quiet walking down the steps. The lights were out, but she'd come to know the layout of the house, its corners and crevices, very well. Rachel could detect Lucas's outline stretched out on the sofa that was just a bit too short for his length. Now that she stood over him she felt hesitant. Should she leave well enough alone? Should she force the issue between them, go that extra step?

He said, "I thought you'd be asleep by now."

His voice cut through the darkness to wrap around her. She stepped closer. "I thought the same thing about you."

"So what are you doing down here?"

"There was something I needed to find out," Rachel said.

"It couldn't wait until the morning?"

"No."

There was a slight rustling, and she could discern Lucas rising to prop himself up on an elbow. "What is it?"

Rachel came closer and lowered herself to kneel on the floor at the edge of the sofa, very close to him. Only then was she able to see the outline of his face and the shadows created by its features.

"You said something about, if only you'd done what you started to do I wouldn't have gotten covered under my collapsed ceiling. Done what?"

He took a long time to formulate an answer. "I was coming to your room but I changed my mind."

"Why were you coming to my room?"

"It's not about what you think, Rae. I was actually going to wake you up . . . to talk. I . . . I needed to talk."

She understood instantly. "Is that all?"

"Why do you want to know?"

"I have a better idea."

Rachel put out her hand carefully and touched his face. Lucas immediately took hold of her wrist. Not to stop her, but to touch her. She knew the difference. She found his mouth and rested her fingertips there. Using that as a guide, Rachel leaned forward until she could kiss him. His mouth puckered into a response. It was sweet and tender, and filled with a need Lucas might not have been able to show had the lights been on.

"Let's dance," she whispered against his mouth.

Lucas released her wrist and pressed his hand to the back of her head. That brought their mouths together again, and this time when they kissed there was no teasing, no hesitation, no polite pas de deux, no misunderstanding. The rubbing of his mouth on hers, the force of his tongue tangling with hers, sent off skyrockets. *This is the exciting thing about wanting someone to make love to you,* she thought. She had reached the point when she wanted to rid herself of anything that could keep them apart. Her surrender was a given. Rachel gently broke the kiss and stood up. She calmly and without a word began to retrace her steps back to his room. She knew from the movement behind her that Lucas followed.

She turned off the lights in his room. By the time he appeared in the doorway she'd removed the light robe and gotten into the bed. It felt both erotic and clandestine to be in his bed, and Rachel stretched out her limbs, as if to leave her mark while she waited for him to join her. Rachel didn't wait for him to reach out for her. She turned into his arms and shifted her body to lie against him, fitting herself to his lean lines. She had done her part. Now she let Lucas take the lead and set the pace. He gave them time to adjust to this new intimacy. Then he began foreplay.

Rachel learned the power in his hands. They were warm and knowing as they stroked and caressed her body, familiarizing himself with her skin, her curves, the way she moved. Rachel accommodated him willingly, her breath coming in sharp intakes of desire. When Lucas rolled over her, placing her on her back, she knew the dual sensation of safety and submission.

She closed her eyes and let him surprise her with his expertise and inventiveness, with his strength tempered by tenderness. She let him touch her anywhere, and he touched her everywhere. The slow squeezing of her breasts and rolling of her nipple only enlarged the crests. She knew the sensitive touch on the inside of her thighs, which quivered as he kneaded and massaged between her legs. The heat grew rapidly between them, and in the August heat their bodies grew damp with passion.

Click.

His kiss alone was having a drugging affect on her ability to move, but Rachel needed to satisfy her own senses by touching Lucas. Her hands knew a language of their own. Between the two of them, they elicited the words and poetry and music of lovers. They paused only long enough to protect themselves as the dance picked up in tempo and rhythm. It was perfectly choreographed and syncopated. It was a perfect union of body and soul, hearts and minds. They were in the right place, at the right time.

Click.

The southern night embraced them, welcoming her and Lucas home.

Twelve

Rachel stepped over the frame of her bed, the mattress, and most of her personal things, which she and Lucas had put in the hallway outside her room. She stopped in the doorway and tried to listen to the conversation going on between Lucas and two contractors who'd arrived just moments before to inspect the damage. She'd gotten her first reality check as a home-owner by having to deal with an emergency, and quickly learned that she didn't know how. A collapsed ceiling was significantly different from a clogged sink or your garden-variety noisy-neighbor complaint in her New York apartment.

Rachel handled the task of locating a professional to come in to look at the damaged room, while Lucas dismantled and removed some of the furniture. She first called Harrietta, who gave her the name of another couple, who gave her the name of a reliable company in Annapolis. Thankfully, they were able to send out two men immediately. She helped Lucas to clear and remove the debris in large black garbage bags, leaving them outside the house for sanitation pickup. They'd worked well together with, as Lucas would say to her later, the added benefit of working up an appetite. He was not talking about food.

In lieu of breakfast or a quick morning swim, Rachel had accepted Lucas's proposal that they use their time in a more productive way. In his room she'd gladly entered into the spirit of the moment when they made love again, discovering that the night before had not been an apparition. The experience was even more profound, the aftermath more satisfying, and the conviction that the two of them together seemed perfect was that much more intense. When they heard the heavy vehicle drive up to the house and stop, she even enjoyed the comical speed with which Lucas had pulled on clothes so that he could meet the contractors, discreetly giving her enough time to pull herself together.

Rachel now stood outside her bedroom, gazing in at Lucas and the two men as they discussed the gaping hole in her ceiling.

"It'll take a couple of hours to close this," one man predicted. "I'll have a look at the eave on the side of the house. I think the wood has probably rotted over the years from the weather and water getting in. That has to be fixed, too."

"Is it going to cost a lot?" Rachel asked Lucas as he left the men and joined her in the hall.

"That's what homeowner's insurance is for. I have the policy."

"I want to pay my share, Lucas."

"If it bothers you that much, we need a new sofa downstairs. I found out last night the one we have isn't a pullout, and it's uncomfortable to sleep on."

Rachel gave him a saucy and significant smile. "You didn't sleep on it last night, thanks to me."

He regarded her with more than simple affection. "And I'm eternally grateful. Let's drive into town and get breakfast."

Rachel waited while Lucas left his cell phone number with the workmen. They decided to take his car for the short drive to the nearby strip mall to find a place to eat. Rachel allowed that she was feeling pretty happy, keeping at bay the nagging thought that there was still her life in New York and her design work. There were still her plans to grow her small cottage-industry business and restructure the management of it. It was becoming increasing difficult to be chief cook, and bottle washer. But she didn't have to make that decision at the moment. As she'd been doing since arriving in Highland Beach a week earlier, she'd put off until another day what she didn't want to do today.

She and Lucas rode north until the end of Wayman and the beach, and turned onto Bay Avenue. Rachel spotted Harrietta and a young man. Harrietta was the passenger in a golf cart, seated like a reigning ancient queen out to inspect her domain. It was Lucas who had learned that the golf cart was the accepted mode of transportation for getting around the small beach community. They had been approved by the homeowner's association to discourage the use of dangerous automobiles, especially during the summer, when the population in children increased fourfold. Rachel asked Lucas to stop so she could greet the older woman through the open car window.

"Good morning," Rachel smiled.

Harrietta was busy craning her neck and squinting past Rachel into the car.

"Who's that? I heard you're weren't alone at Julia's house," she said with heavy meaning.

Lucas got out of his car and walked around the front to personally greet the older woman.

"I've been wanting to meet you," Lucas said with sincere but practiced charm. He extended his hand to her and, clearly impressed by his good manners and good sense, Harrietta laid hers, limp and bejeweled, in his palm.

"This is my grandson," she said, indicating the young man next to her.

"I know Rachel has spoken to you about me. Lucas Monroe Scott. Julia Winters was my mother."

Rachel suppressed the urge to giggle as Harrietta gaped at Lucas, her mouth again forming her habitual circle of surprise.

"Who's Monroe Scott?" Harrietta questioned.

Rachel listened attentively. She hadn't gotten around to asking that question, although she knew half the answer.

"I guess you didn't know that Monroe was Julia's real last name. She changed it legally to Winters when she began her stage career. I'm told she thought Winters read better on a billboard. Scott is my father's name."

"Oh, I see," Harrietta chirped.

But Rachel was sure that some of the nuances had escaped her.

"I understand that you were a good friend to my mother. She was very lucky to know someone like you on Highland Beach. Thank you for being kind to her," Lucas added.

Rachel watched the interplay. Judging from the broad smile from Harrietta, Lucas had managed to ingratiate himself to her for life.

"Why, aren't you nice? It's good to have you take over Julia's house. That is . . . er . . . you and . . . I don't really understand this arrangement you have with Rachel," Harrietta complained.

Lucas soothingly patted her hand. "I don't want to keep you out here in the sun. It's going to get hot. But I promise to explain it all to you some other time."

"I look forward to that. Now, are you and Rachel coming tomorrow afternoon to the beachfest?"

Rachel and Lucas exchanged a glance. "I don't think we know anything about it," she said.

"It's the annual end-of-summer celebration. We hold it before Labor Day because everybody leaves early. They have to get the children ready to return to school. We have a clambake, and contests for the kids, and entertainment. It ends in the evening with a dance for the grown-ups.

"I heard someone say you play an instrument," Harrietta addressed Lucas.

"Saxophone."

"Good. You can join right in."

When they finally were able to leave, Rachel was aware that Lucas had fallen silent. "You don't have to go tomorrow. I mean, we didn't even know about it until she told us. If it's going to make you uncomfortable to be interrogated—"

"I'm a lawyer. I know how to deflect any questions I find too personal."

"So, does that mean you want to go?"

"Do you want to go?"

"I asked you first."

"Sure, why not? We're going to have to face them all sooner or later. Let's give them something to talk about."

"Man, I can't remember the last time I had pancakes," Lucas mused as the waitress set a plate before him. Melted butter ran down the sides and she indicated the dispenser of maple syrup already on the table. "There go my arteries," he chuckled, winking at Rachel.

"Are you telling me you have no vices? You eat healthy all the time, take all your vitamins, and get eight hours of sleep a night?" she teased.

Lucas enthusiastically began cutting into the stack and then poured liberal amounts of syrup over it. "Do I have to remind you that I got no sleep at all last night? I'm a weakened man." He lifted a forkful of pancakes into his mouth with obvious enjoyment.

"Not my fault," she said righteously, digging into her bowl of yogurt covered with walnuts and blueberries. "I don't recall having to twist your arm and take you to the mat. I didn't hear any complaints this morning."

"And you won't, Rachel," he said quietly.

Lucas chewed thoughtfully and regarded Rachel closely. Suddenly, everything he'd experienced in the past two months came into sharp focus. She was pretty and appealing. Only more so. She was good company, often very funny, only more so. She'd shown herself to be nobody's fool and no pushover. A good sport and an unforeseen wonderful lover. And more so.

With her spoon halfway to her mouth, Rachel paused to take in what he'd just said. It made him feel good that she seemed really pleased and surprised by his confession. As if she wouldn't have held it against him if he did have morning-after regrets. Lucas took her reaction to mean that she didn't have any, either.

"Besides, I didn't feel that anything needed explaining," Rachel admitted. "Sometimes you can talk a thing to death."

"I agree."

"And then this morning when we—"

A cell phone began to ring. They both began searching for their units, but it was Lucas's call.

"Sorry," he said at the interruption, reaching to squeeze her arm as he answered.

"Lucas. It's Jen."

"Hey," he said in surprise. "How've you been?" He glanced casually at Rachel, but she'd returned to eating her breakfast.

"You didn't return my calls."

Lucas frowned at the accusatory tone. "You're absolutely right. I'm really sorry about that. Was it anything important?"

"Lucas, you're my friend. Does it have to be important? Okay, yes. I haven't seen or talked to you in more than a week and I . . . was worried."

"Again, I apologize," he said patiently.

"Where are you?"

"I'm not in DC right now," he answered carefully. "I've been really tied up." Lucas caught Rachel's gaze just briefly enough to see her quizzical expression. She wasn't eaves-dropping, but even he knew that his explanation came across as evasive. "Is something wrong? Another case?"

"No, it's nothing like that. It's personal. And I don't want to talk about it over the phone. When are you coming back to DC?"

Her directive preempted his attempt to find out right then what was happening. But her question had more of an effect in the most simple way. Returning to DC meant leaving Highland Beach, and Rachel. He knew it would come to that sooner or later. He wasn't expecting sooner. He wasn't ready.

"I don't know," he said. Rachel was pointing to his plate, indicating that the breakfast he was so much looking forward to was getting cold. "Look, I'm in the middle of something right now. Let me call you back, okay?"

"Will you?" Jen asked.

The question annoyed Lucas. "Of course. I said I would."

"When?"

That annoyed him even more. "In about an hour. How's that?"

"Okay. I'll be waiting."

Lucas hung up. The waitress suddenly appeared and reached to take his plate.

"I'm not finished," he said, confused by her action.

Rachel smiled. "She knows. I asked her to nuke it for a minute to heat up the pancakes. I don't think they'd taste good cold. Not like day-old pizza."

"Thanks," he chuckled.

He watched her sweep a lock of hair back behind her ears. She never fussed with it or worried about whether it was set. Somehow, Rachel always managed to look as if it was all effortless. She never wore much makeup and had none on this morning. Her sunglasses were being used as a headband to hold her hair back from her forehead. Her unexpected action the night before, seeking him with an offer he couldn't refuse, had blown his mind. It was erotic, but it was also caring. How did she know that he really needed the comfort of someone's arms? When did she know that someone had to be her?

"I wasn't really eavesdropping but that sounded like contact from the outside world," Rachel surmised.

Lucas thanked the waitress for returning his plate, once again wafting the aromatic smell of pancakes and syrup. "Unfortunately, yes."

"It's been hard to think of anything being more important than being here, hasn't it?"

He nodded. "I hadn't expected to become so . . . so comfortable here. Highland Beach is a tiny little community. There's nothing here, and yet it's hard to think about leaving."

"I disagree with you. The nothing that you're referring to is the very reason you like it here. No pressure, no crowds, no rush, no deadline. But I know what you're talking about. It's not the real world where you have a job and responsibilities and you're expected to act normal and fall in line."

"That's exactly what I mean. You know, I just remembered I have a club date this weekend. I wonder if I would have forgotten if that call hadn't jogged my memory. I could do the weekend and then drive back down."

"I have orders to fill and designs to execute for new samples. I can't just drive back down anytime I want. I'm in New York."

Lucas finished his breakfast and reached across the table to take her hand. "We've just gotten together and already we're talking about going our separate ways." He could feel the pressure of her fingers as she gazed openly at him.

"Seems that way, doesn't it?"

"I don't much like it, Rae. It's too soon," he said with real feeling. "We're just starting to get the hang of your fifty-fifty split."

"It is what it is, Lucas. It's too early for anything else."

He nodded, reluctantly. "You're probably right."

Lucas was pensive and introspective on the short drive back. He felt like his entire life had changed in the course of two months. He was still a lawyer and a musician. But he'd also become more aware, more peaceful, and more forgiving. It was so strange that he might have Julia to thank for that. But Rachel had also played an important role. How was he going to thank her?

At the house the workmen had finished with the sealing of the hole in her room and had replastered, and they were starting work on replacing the eaves.

"Let the ceiling dry about another day before painting it," one of the contractors advised.

"That's a project for my next visit here." Lucas said.

"Yeah, that's the downside of owning a big old house like this. There's always a honeydew list," the man laughed.

"A what?"

"You know. Honey, do this, and honey, do that."

"I think of it as a labor of love," Lucas grinned.

"My labor of love is my boat, and my ole lady. In that order."

Lucas continued to talk to the men as they loaded equipment into their truck. He had questions to ask, and they seemed willing to give him pointers and advice. And they reminded him that they were available for hire to do work on the house if he wanted.

"I can't make any changes without the agreement of the co-owner, but I'll keep you guys in mind. Thanks for coming out so quickly."

They moved her things into his room, never considering using the fourth guest room across the hallway. Lucas suggested they spend the rest of the day on the beach. But, in between Rachel getting out of her shorts and tank top and into a swimsuit, he got her into bed. They eventually made it to the beach with a blanket, lemonade, and a bag of red grapes. At one point Lucas had the peculiar feeling that this was where he belonged. On the beach. Hedonism started to seem like a perfectly reasonable way of life. The past no longer seemed a heavy burden fraught with bad memories. The future held an unknown and provocative allure.

He was happy.

They returned to the house late, scrounging together another dinner when they decided they didn't feel like driving into town. They didn't want to leave the house.

"I have no place to sleep tonight," Rachel complained. She joined him at the back door where he stood gazing out into the night, as he often did.

Lucas slipped an arm around her waist. "I promise you won't have to sleep on the floor. Or alone."

She sighed. "It was a great day."

"It's not over yet."

"Only ten minutes," she said, glancing at a clock.

"Then let's not waste them. Come on."

He grabbed her hand and started down the steps, pulling a towel from the railing that had been left out to dry earlier. It was absolutely silent up and down the beach. The moon was high in the sky but only half full, casting a light that was subtle and low. Lucas kept walking until they were standing in the sand, close to one of the manmade jetties. The pilings created a shadow that trailed out into the water.

"There's no music tonight. Are you going to ask me to dance again?" she teased.

"Something better."

He let go of her hand and spread out the towel.

"Lucas," Rachel began, her voice filled with skepticism.

He turned to her again, taking both her hands and drawing her close. "Ever make love on the beach?"

"No."

"Ever wanted to?"

"For about twenty seconds once, when I was a teenager. I didn't like the idea of getting sand in—"

"You won't," Lucas said as he began gently removing her clothing.

"Lucas! You've got to be kidding." But he wasn't as he continued to remove her top. He stepped closer and began to kiss her. "That's not fair," she whined when her body betrayed her, responding of its own accord. Not just to the stimulus of his kiss, but to the idea of doing something so scandalous, so . . . tempting. She kissed Lucas back, encouraging him. She was suddenly naked, feeling a wanton freedom that was exciting. The sultry August air caressing her skin in a different way than Lucas's hands.

She sank to the towel and lay watching as he removed his clothing as well. They were like Adam and Eve in the Garden of Eden, without the apple or snake. Lucas joined her on the towel, gathering her into his arms. Under the stars and the moon their lovemaking was a homage to Aphrodite and Venus, and to Julia, who'd made it possible for them to be together.

They partnered for another dance, moving smoothly and rhythmically to music of their own making. Rachel had to admit she wasn't sure it could get much better than this.

The midnight tryst kept Lucas in bed late the next morning, something he almost never did. Not even after playing in some club or, in his previous life, when he was preparing to try a case. He knew when Rachel got up because she ran her hand gently down his chest and left a warm kiss on the skin. When he finally got up, he found Rachel in her room attempting to put the bed together on her own.

"Let me do that," he said, taking over and replacing the box spring and mattress.

"I'm not helpless, you know."

"Yeah, I've noticed."

"Now you'll expect some sort of favor in return, I suppose."

Lucas stood aside and watched as Rachel remade the bed in fresh linens and redid the personal little flourishes that made the room cozy and her own, and wondering after the last two days why she bothered. "Last night suited me just fine."

"Me, too," she softly confessed.

"So, how do you feel about—"

"No. If we're going to the festival and you're going to play, *like you promised Harrietta . . .*" He groaned. "Then we have to get moving. It's almost noon."

"Do you think we should bring something?" he asked.

"I think there's an unopened bottle of Harvey's Bristol Creme in the pantry. I happen to know that Harrietta likes a little nip of something in the evening. She says it helps her arthritis."

Lucas hooted with laughter. "I think I have something to hold over the redoubtable Harrietta."

"If you *dare* to even hint that I told you that, I will have to kill you," Rachel threatened.

Lucas pulled her into his arms and kissed her soundly. He encountered no resistance, and the fact that he didn't increased his ardor.

"We can't," she sighed softly. "We have to go."

He kissed her again before letting her go, with a tender promise and more than a little regret. "Can I take the first shower? It's the least you can do for turning me down."

She smiled. "Sure, if you think a cold shower will help." She called out after him. "Lucas? Have you forgiven Julia?"

He stopped in the bathroom doorway and thought about it. "I think it's fair to say I'm less angry. That box from my grandparents helped a lot, I admit it. But it doesn't tell the whole story."

"Don't you think that maybe it's time to just let it go?"

He shook his head. "No, it isn't," he said honestly.

Rachel considered that reply and had to be satisfied with it. After all, it was not she who had to come to an answer that she could live with. She didn't know if Lucas was at all aware of how far he'd come since Julia's death, though perhaps it wasn't far enough.

In the middle of selecting a short white skirt and a tangerine sleeveless knit top to wear to the beach party, she heard a phone ring. Rachel rushed for the staircase to the first floor, but then realized the ringing was not downstairs but from Lucas's room. It was his cell phone again. Knowing it would record a message he would get later, she went back to her own room.

She could hear the live music and lots of voices and chatter even before they arrived at the site of the celebration. It was a short but broad stretch of sand along a narrow inlet of water separating Highland Beach from Bay Ridge. Everything was in full swing, and everyone seemed to be having a good time. Rachel was aware of the stares and looks of curiosity from many of those in attendance, whom Rachel could only assume were Highland Beach residents. They'd no doubt gotten word about Julia Winters' son and a woman sharing the house on the beach. If Lucas was aware or concerned by any such gossip, he didn't show it.

She spotted Harrietta sitting well back from the beach under the shade of a tree, comfortably ensconced in a chair from which she could see what was going on. Rachel presented her with the sherry and could see that the older woman was genuinely surprised and pleased by the gesture.

She and Lucas endured a confusing round of introductions, although everyone was really more interested in him. She didn't care. Lucas had a more intriguing history and connection to Highland Beach than she ever could. Julia had made her an added-on member of her family, part of her entourage, but Rachel understood and accepted now that she was in on a pass. This was definitely the Lucas Monroe Scott show.

Rachel was also surprised by how many people remembered her as a child and the unusual relationship she enjoyed with their neighbor, Julia. Surprisingly, there was more than one voice with complaints about Julia. It seemed very inappropriate to speak ill of the dead, as far as she was concerned. She was glad that she heard the remarks, rather than Lucas. She couldn't guarantee how he would have responded.

Someone found her a chair and offered a plate of food. She got separated from Lucas and occasionally spotted him in conversation with the musicians or with other visitors who were, almost invariably, women. But at one point she finally made eye contact, and that was enough for her to be assured that he had not forgotten about her.

There was a microphone set up, which kept booming with the sound of the wind catching in the sensitive instrument. It allowed one of the town officials to introduce the group performing and the musicians. Then he announced the addition of Lucas Monroe Scott. First there was the necessary mention that he was the son of the recently deceased "famed" actress and singer, Julia Winters, and then there was also a brief and knowledgeable mention of some of the groups that Lucas had performed with over the past three years. It came out that Lucas had studied with Grover Washington, Jr., the great sax impresario, and that Sonny Rollins was a friend of the family. Rachel knew that some of those at the party had quickly figured out that it was his horn that serenaded them in the evening, the sound of music traveling up and down the beach. It was interesting to her that Lucas's stature grew even more when it was learned he was a member in good standing with the DC Bar Association as a civil-rights lawyer.

With that, Lucas joined the quartet already positioned on the beach, and they began to play.

Rachel watched those around her to see their response to him. It was a mixed bag, ranging from rapt attention to obvious enjoyment, indicated by tapping feet and heads nodding in time to the music. She herself was enthralled, remembering her first introduction to Lucas's ability with his memorable appearance at the service for his mother. He had a fluid, natural movement and gait as he played his horn. He was completely in tune with the instrument and at home with the music. He was clearly at his best during the solos, when he could riff and interpret on the score.

"Excuse me."

Someone tapped her on the shoulder. Rachel turned to find a very attractive young woman standing next to her, huge dark glasses hiding most of her face, which was fair and freckled in a very becoming way. "Yes?"

"I know this is going to seem like a silly question, but Mrs. Cousins said I should ask you because you're a friend of the sax player."

Rachel sensed the question was neither silly, nor the young woman shy. "You mean Lucas. Yes, I know him. What's the question?"

"Well, can you tell me if he's, you know, available?"

Rachel stared at the woman, studying her and the incredible confidence that would allow her to ask such a question without any sense of embarrassment. Rachel smiled sympathetically.

"I'm sorry but, no, he's not available. It sounds a little old-fashioned, but he's spoken for."

For the rest of the afternoon, until all the food had been consumed and the beer and lemonade were gone, and until people started to drift away, Rachel could not forget the brass with which anyone would ask such a question. But the episode was informative in that, if she hadn't thought about it before, she now knew that Lucas was a desirable and highly prized eligible bachelor. She had his attention for the moment for what had been an incredible experience. But he could have anyone he wanted.

It was almost twilight when Rachel saw him make his way up from the beach to rejoin her. She didn't mind in the least that he'd been the center of attention and curiosity. But she felt a secret vindication when he made it obvious that they had come together, and they were going to leave the same way.

Harrietta had long since gone home, but Rachel was sure that the older matriarch would hear about everything that had happened after she left.

"Did you have a chance to get anything to eat?" Rachel asked him when they were in the car with his saxophone and headed back home.

"A little. I don't like eating before I have to perform. It throws off my breathing control," Lucas said.

"I'll remember that."

"That was nice, don't you think?"

"Not exactly what you're used to, I bet."

"No, it isn't. But that's what was so nice about it," he said. He surprised her when he reached to take her hand and held it as he drove. "I had a good time. One of the other musicians wanted to know who you were."

"And you said?"

"I said you were an artist and designer, with business all over Europe. That your designs are worn by the rich and famous and even those who wished they were—"

Rachel laughed. "I don't believe you. You never said all of that."

"I swear." He glanced briefly. "It made me feel really good that you were noticed."

She made a face at him. "Why? Because it made you look good?"

"No. Because it proved the guy had good taste, which meant that I have good taste."

Rachel smiled to herself. "Good answer."

She went to turn on the lights in the living room.

"Leave them off," Lucas said from behind her. "At least for now."

"Why?" Rachel asked, turning to face him. She could just make him out in the approaching darkness.

"Because it's nicer like this. I like when it's quiet and we don't have to talk."

"Did you have something else in mind?" she asked.

"I seemed to remember getting interrupted in the middle of something we started earlier. Come here."

She didn't have to see his face to understand the sultry quality of his voice, which seemed to have dropped an octave. He wanted to make love. That moment. It was thrilling to hear someone wanted her that much. No, not someone. Lucas, to be exact. He held open his arms, and she walked into them. His body felt so strong and protective. He found her lips in the dark, and the kiss they began and shared was excruciatingly slow and thorough. It was debilitating, her mind quickly taken over with one thought. How to get upstairs, undressed, and into bed with him. Fortunately, he seemed to have had the same thoughts.

Rachel didn't want to go to her room. She wanted his room. That's where it had begun the night before, and that's where she'd conditioned herself to think of as the place where magical things happened.

Lucas began kissing her again as soon as they were in his room. He held her captive just with his lips while he peeled her clothing off, and she did the same for him. They were on the bed tangled in each other's arms, legs entwined, their breathing hurried and hushed. Suddenly, the ringing of the telephone startled them both and shattered the mood. Lucas lay collapsed on Rachel's body, their chests heaving and their limbs quivering.

"I have to take that," he said.

He rolled away and sat up searching for the annoying unit. As he answered he maneuvered into his shorts. Rachel stroked his back. When he turned to her, she leaned forward to kiss his chest.

"Hurry back," she whispered.

He stroked her cheek. Then he left the room and headed to the first floor, which struck her as odd. Was the call that private? Was it someone she was not meant to know about? Did the call have anything to do with her?

After ten minutes, it became clear to Rachel that the call was important enough to Lucas that he was not returning soon. Her ardor faded and her heated body began to cool. She gathered her clothing and went to her own room. There, she pulled on her robe and had the sudden thought that it was time to begin thinking about returning to New York.

She could tell by the rhythm of his footsteps on the stairs and the slow walk down the corridor they would not be making love again that night. Had the call been bad news, after all? Lucas appeared in the doorway and leaned against the frame.

"I have to get back to DC."

"I have to get back to New York," she said, deliberately misunderstanding. "Day after tomorrow?"

He sighed, stepping into the room and sitting on the side of her bed. He looked right into her eyes and Rachel knew he was looking for understanding. "I don't think I can delay that long, Rae."

"What's wrong?"

"That was Jennifer Cameron. You met her."

"I remember who she is. What happened?"

"I honestly don't know, but she seems pretty upset and she has to see me."

"*Has* to see you? If it's not an emergency—"

"I can't explain right now," he said, getting up abruptly.

She took a deep breath. "I think I can."

"I don't think so," he chortled.

The sound grated on her nerves, as if she'd just said something completely foolish. "I don't think you should dismiss what I have to say until I at least say it."

"Jennifer is my best friend. I think I know her pretty well. If I'm not sure what this is all about, how could you possibly know? I'm not ready to leave. You believe that, don't you?"

"Yes," she said softly.

"So if I do it's because I feel it's *that* important."

"Lucas, you keep saying she's your best friend. You may not think so, but of course you have *some* idea what's going on with Jennifer. Otherwise you wouldn't be so . . . so tense about telling me, or about leaving. Do what you have to do, but I just want to say one thing."

"What?"

His tone was suspicious, short, and impatient. But she wasn't going to let him get away with using her to ease his frustration.

"I promised myself I wouldn't do this, but—"

"Then don't. I was counting on you not to make this hard."

"Don't blame me. You're free to leave if you have to."

"But you think I'm making a mistake. Especially now that we've—"

"We've made no promises to each other, and I'm not talking about us. I'm talking about you and Jennifer."

That stopped him cold and she had his full, but confused, attention.

"What?"

"I can't believe you don't know that she's in love with you," she said, incredulous.

"What?" he repeated.

Rachel sighed. "You *do* know."

"Where did you get an idea like that?"

"From Jennifer. Body language, how she talks to you. Touches you."

"What is that? Woman's intuition?"

"Whatever. Yes."

"That doesn't make sense, and it doesn't hold up."

"So now you're the lawyer again. What about the demanding phone calls and Jennifer's personal crises that make you feel you're the only one in the universe who can solve what's wrong? From the moment I first saw you two together at the service for your mother I could see it, and I hadn't even met you yet."

"You don't even know her."

"That's true. But that's exactly why I can see clearly what's going on. Look, I'm not going to try to stop you. If you feel you have to go to her, then go. I think whatever her story is can wait until tomorrow at least, or even the day after . . . or even next week if you *tell* her that's the way it is."

"Sometimes we have to do things that need to be done, even when we don't want to," he said.

"I know that. But sometimes you have to say no. You feel you have to go to Jennifer because she says she needs you. I feel I have to tell you she's being a little hysterical, and I risk that you'll be angry with me for saying so. Or worse," she admitted.

He approached her where she sat in the middle of her bed with an open box of designs she'd been working on for several days. He took hold of her hand. "Rachel, I'll say this again. I don't want to go. I'm hoping that what you'll keep in mind is everything we've said to each other in the past few days, everything we've done together and have been to each other. That covers a lot of ground. That will tell you everything you need to know and believe about me. I'm a man of my word."

"I know."

"I'm nothing if I can't be true to that."

"I know."

Rachel stared long and hard at Lucas. She was up against more than he realized, but she wasn't going to bring up another white woman that he also felt committed to. Maybe it was unfair, but she believed that leaving her for a friend having a PMS attack and hissy fit was unfair as well. The odds seemed stacked against her.

"I have to go. I have to," he said earnestly.

"I know. It's your call. Whatever the consequences."

Thirteen

Lucas was haunted by the conversation he'd had with Rachel just two hours earlier. It was all the more ominous and disturbing because she hadn't been outwardly angry with him. They hadn't yelled and screamed and pointed the finger of blame at each other. In her own way, she'd been understanding and level-headed about his leaving. That in itself was amazing when he considered past relationships with some pretty vitriolic exchanges. Perversely, he still secretly wished that Rachel had lobbed a few insults or threats at him. In a bizarre twist of reason, he'd rather have left her feeling like they'd had a lover's quarrel.

During the entire drive to DC, a drive he wasn't looking forward to, he could hear Rachel's argument. With a wry smile, Lucas thought what a great lawyer she would have made. But he liked the person she was. Strong and self-assured, but not cunning or argumentative. Sensitive and caring, but not selfless. The bottom line was, he'd rather face her across the bed than in a courtroom. That realization had also been planted in his brain during the drive, along with the nagging conviction that he might now be making a huge mistake.

He was not in the best of moods when he finally reached Jen's building and parked his car. He hadn't even bothered going to his own place first. He wanted to get this over with so he could turn to whatever damage he'd caused his relationship with Rachel. He knew enough at that moment, and since leaving her, to be sure he didn't want to lose her.

Lucas entered the lobby of the elegant high rise on the banks of the Potomac. Jen's seventeenth-floor unit had been made possible by a successful and lucrative case she'd handled several years ago, a case on which he'd advised her. He never came to visit and he didn't remember being puzzled by the purchase, made just months before she was to have been married, especially given that her soon-to-be husband was an entertainment attorney in LA and it had been decided Jen would relocate. But she'd called the wedding off.

"Evening, Mr. Scott," the doorman greeted him. "I'll ring Ms. Cameron, let her know you're here."

"Thanks," Lucas nodded and headed toward the elevators.

Jen had been upset when she'd called. He hoped that since he'd agreed to drive back to see her she wouldn't still be emotional and inarticulate. Or, as Rachel had so well stated, hysterical. He stepped off the elevator and headed for her apartment, mentally preparing himself. Lucas rang the bell and heard the familiar chimes. He could also hear music from her CD player. He took this as a good sign.

The door opened quickly.

"Jen, are you—" Lucas started, and then stopped.

"Hi. Come on in," Jen smiled warmly at him, holding the door open.

Lucas obeyed. He gaze studied and followed her movements. He was bewildered when she approached, throwing her arms lightly about his neck, then kissing him on the corner of his mouth. Instinctively he placed his hands on her waist, not to hold her close but to hold her back. She stepped away with another bright smile.

"I'm so glad you're here. I've been in such a bad mood."

Lucas stood dumbfounded as she sashayed into the living room where two glasses and an opened bottle of wine were set on a tray on her coffee table. She was dressed in long bright red knit dress that hugged her well-maintained figure, and she was barefoot.

"I got your favorite Merlot."

"Jen—"

"And I know you love prime rib so I got a great cut. Want a glass of wine now, or shall we wait until dinner is ready?"

"Jen, what the hell is going on?"

She stopped, tossing back her blond hair and giving him a smile like he'd never seen before. "I'm just so glad you're here, Lucas. I knew you'd come once you understood how important it was to me. Oh, let's have a glass of wine now. This is like a celebration, isn't it?" She poured a glass and extended it to him.

He merely stared at the offering as if she might also have poisoned it. He finally accepted the wine reluctantly.

"Cheers," she grinned, taping her glass rim gently against his. He stood, disapproving and uncooperative.

"Exactly what are we toasting?" he asked, his annoyance growing with every intimate social convention she offered.

"You being here, if you like. Us having a nice dinner, and spending the evening together. Do you realize we haven't seen or spoken to each other in almost two weeks?"

With a deep sigh of frustration, Lucas finally moved. He walked with long, impatient strides to the nearest table and put the wineglass down. When he faced her again it was with a concerted effort to remain calm.

"Jen, I know you understood the question. I'm asking you to tell me in plain English and without the romantic props, what's going on. When I spoke with you less than two hours ago you were . . ." *Go on. Say it.* " . . . nearly hysterical. You scared me. I thought something had happened to you. Maybe you'd gotten fired, or been threatened by a client, or even gotten sick. I left Highland Beach like a bat out of hell, and you're greeting me with mood music and wine. Did I miss something? *Where's the emergency?*"

Even as he talked, he could see her attempt to be cheerful

and engaging fading from her countenance. It was replaced with a play of emotions that was difficult for him to witness. It came to him that he'd only seen this kind of pain once in all the years he'd known Jen. It was when her younger brother had died in a car accident. It had been a terrible loss for her.

Lucas walked slowly toward her and repeated his question. "Where's the emergency?"

She turned away quickly as the tears fell. Her crying was silent and heartfelt but he made no attempt to comfort her.

"I just . . . wanted you here, Lucas." Her voice was barely a whisper.

"I'm here. I came right away because you said you needed to see me. You're my best friend, and that should show you how important you are to me. Now it's your turn. I need you to be honest with me. Because if this is some kind of staged performance—"

"Can't you tell?" she asked.

His heart sank. In that instant, what came to mind was a clear image of Rachel sitting on her bed, patiently trying to warn him. Already knowing. How did she know?

"Why don't *you* tell me?"

She turned to face him, her face streaked with tears, her nose turning red. "It's so . . . humiliating, Lucas, that you have no idea how much I love you," she sobbed. "How much I've always loved you."

He was stunned to have her actually say it. And yet, Rachel had been right about something else; he shouldn't have been. The signs had been there all along. He'd chosen to ignore them.

"I'm sorry," he said sincerely. It sounded so inadequate.

"I've been hoping for years that sooner or later you would look at me . . . and see . . . and feel . . . feel the same way I do about you."

"Jen, I *never* led you to think—"

"You did nothing. That's what's so damned frustrating," she chuckled bitterly. "You were always just my dear, dear friend.

I couldn't get you to see me as anything else but a friend." She walked toward him. "I wanted more, and you couldn't even see that. Why?"

"You already know the answer to that. If I didn't see it, it's because I never felt the same way. God knows I never wanted to hurt you, but I'm not in love with you the way you want me to be. It's not going to happen."

"Is it because I'm . . . white?"

"Jen," he said, incredulous. "You'll have to explain to me how that's relevant. Have you forgotten that I was married to a white woman? It didn't work out, but that was *not* because she was white."

She nodded firmly, sniffling and wiping the tears from her face childishly with the heel of her hand. "I saw you with that other woman. The one on the train after you did the program at John Jay in New York."

"I don't follow you," he said. "What's the connection?"

"Oh, Lucas," she scoffed impatiently. "You really are blind sometimes. First I can't get you to see I love you, and then you can't see how attracted you are to that woman—"

"Her name is Rachel."

"See! You do know who I'm talking about. Well, she's black and pretty. And I . . . I could tell you liked her," her voice broke again.

"Look, I know you're really upset right now. Maybe under different circumstances you wouldn't be talking like this about my business. You don't have a right, and we're not attached at the hip. So do us both a favor and let it drop."

"But you do like her."

"What's that got to do with anything?" he confessed, cautiously.

"You're being evasive. How? Why? You've only known her, what? Two months?"

"Maybe that's all the time I needed. It's either going to click or it's not. You either know . . . or you don't."

* * *

Rachel made an effort to stay out of the way as her mother said goodnight to her guest, the gentleman caller named Bill whom she'd been quietly seeing for more than a year.

There was a sudden silence at the front door, and Rachel knew that Bill, smart man that he was, was saying goodnight to Lydia in the time-honored tradition of kissing her under the porch light. Rachel was envious, remembering Lucas kissing her under moonlight. Must run in the family genes.

"Bill's talking about coming up to New York with me," Lydia said, returning to the living room where Rachel was waiting for her. "Is that offer to use your apartment still open?"

Rachel looked scandalized. "I can't believe my own mother is talking about a rendezvous in *my* home with someone she's not married to."

"Oh, please," Lydia said dryly. She sat in one of the two Queen Anne chairs and picked up her knitting. She was working on something new. "Bill is a lovely man, and I like him. I might even feel more than that, but just because he helps with the dishes doesn't mean we're engaged."

Rachel laughed, which drew a companionable smile from her mother. Rachel asked, "How old is he?"

"He's two years my junior. I tell my friends I'm dating a younger man. I know you're going to ask, so here's the lowdown. He's divorced, too, with a grown son who's a career officer in the Navy. He has three grandkids, all girls. He owns two franchises and his own home, and here's something that might interest you. He sometimes spends a few weeks during the summer or fall with friends who own a house on Arundel On The Bay. He says it's right next to Highland Beach. I happened to mention Julia Winters to him, but the name wasn't familiar and he didn't think he'd ever met her."

"I have to say, on paper, he looks good."

"I could do worse."

"But he's not Daddy," Rachel observed.

"Of course he's not like your father. I'm not looking for someone to replace Simon. Bill is a different man. I'm comfortable with him. There's no drama. We're both too old for that," Lydia chuckled.

"Then you have my blessing." Her mother made a face at her. "What are you making now?" Rachel asked.

"Beanies for the preemies. The neonatal unit at the hospital always has a need for them. Isn't that cute?"

Lydia held it up, and Rachel was startled to see that it was only big enough to cover something the size of a tennis ball.

Rachel said, "The next time I come to visit I'm bringing a business plan for you to look at. I've been visiting some of the craft stores and galleries in New York and around Annapolis. I'm convinced we can find you an outlet for your work. You're so good, you should be getting noticed and making money."

"You proposing to be my business manager?"

"Why not? Maybe I can come up with an idea for a mother-daughter business. You know, I bet I got my artistic genes from you."

Lydia smiled at the idea. "So, are you finally leaving Maryland to go home?"

"Yeah. I've been neglecting too many things," Rachel responded pensively.

"Must have been something really interesting to have kept you on Highland Beach all this time."

"I told you I love it there. I wish I could stay permanently."

"Maybe you can. You said Julia left you that house. All you gotta do is have a plan."

"Technically I own only half the house. Her son, Lucas, owns the other half."

"That must be cozy," Lydia murmured.

Not, Rachel thought caustically.

"What's he like?"

Rachel cast a suspicious glance at her mother. The question seemed innocent enough. But she knew that just thinking about him left her feeling dispirited and lonely.

"Very smart, very intelligent. He's an attorney. Civil-rights law, I think."

"Nice."

"And he plays the saxophone. I think he's actually performing more than practicing law right now."

"How old is he?"

"About Ross's age."

"Good looking?"

"Oh, yes. I would say so," Rachel chortled.

"Married or ever been?"

"Divorced years ago. No children."

"As far as you know," Lydia smirked. Rachel looked shocked at the suggestion. "You know how men are."

"I seriously doubt that Lucas would do something so irresponsible. He even remembers to . . ."

"What were you going to say?" Lydia pushed.

"I've heard him talk many times about the need for more personal responsibility."

"So he's not necessarily opposed to having children?"

"I don't think so. You know, he was raised by his grandparents, so I think the whole package deal is important to him." Rachel stared at her mother. "Why all the questions?"

"Just curious. You know a lot about him."

"Enough. Okay, fair's fair. Can I ask you a personal question?"

Lydia put her knitting down and peered sharply at her daughter. "How personal?"

"About you and Daddy."

"What's the question?" Lydia asked.

"Did you ever regret the divorce? Did you still love him even after he moved out?"

Lydia began knitting again. "That's two questions. The answer is yes to both."

"Then why did you do it? Couldn't you two make up and get over it? Couldn't you forgive him?"

"Rachel," Lydia began patiently. "Despite what the reverend says in church every Sunday about forgiveness, it's harder than you think. I was hurt. And I was bitterly disappointed that your father risked everything for a summer affair. You just got through telling me about Lucas and his personal responsibility. Same thing. Then there was the matter of his disrespect. And I was always wondering, what did Julia Winters have that I didn't have? Why couldn't I hold on to my man?

"I think it's funny that now you're down on Highland Beach, in *her* house, with *her* son, carrying on. Turn around is fair play."

"Excuse me? How can you suggest—"

"Rae," Lydia stopped her. "This is your mother you're talking to. Why do kids always think their parents are stupid and don't know anything about love? Or sex?"

"Mom, look . . . okay, I like him. But it's way too early for the L word. I don't want to jump the gun. And he's got issues."

"So do you, my dear."

"Well, how do you know?"

"You have a successful business. You travel and you do interesting things. Things I always wanted to do and never did. If anything, I need to thank Julia for making sure you did all of that. Am I hearing that the excitement of life in the fast lane is wearing thin? You've been down there with her son off and on most of the summer, Rae. Highland Beach is the perfect incubator for cultivating a romance. But when you showed up here last night I knew you had your first, or maybe second and third, run-in with reality. Does it feel right? What do you have in common? Is he the one? Can you make it work?"

"You should hire yourself out as a therapist," Rachel said dryly.

"I know what's going on with you because you're my daughter. I want you to be happy."

"He left Highland Beach yesterday to go running off after this woman who's a long-time friend. She called with a sob story about needing to see him."

"It worked," Lydia pointed out.

"It sure did. I know the real reason, but he's got to figure it out for himself."

"Well, you could look at it another way. He was willing to stick by his friend."

"I know. To be honest, I don't know how he could have handled it differently."

"Sure you do. You wanted him to make a choice."

"Well, he did. But that's okay. I have my own plan, thanks to Julia."

"Does this mean that after everything I've been through because of that woman I'm going to end up being grateful to her?"

"Not you, Mom. Me."

Lucas was never aware of the audience sitting before him when he played his saxophone. That was originally the idea. If they enjoyed his playing and welcomed it with applause, then that was a by-product of his performing. From the beginning, when he'd picked up his first horn, music was something to get lost in, covering up the deficiencies in other areas of his life. He knew this to be particularly true when he was growing up and he suffered a sense of displacement in his family. Just recently, however, he'd come to find out that music was a poor substitute for living, for getting in there down and dirty, and doing the hard work. So this evening, he played because it helped ease the self-recrimination and regret that he may have made one of the worst mistakes of his life.

Lucas released his lips from around the mouthpiece of his instrument, coordinated a quick intake of air deep into his lungs, and blew out the final phase of his number. The pianist seated behind him added a rapid-fire tickling of the keys, and then the drummer finished. When the audience applauded, he came back down to earth.

Lucas opened his eyes, stepped back, and mouthed a thank-you before leaving the stage. He never bowed but would raise his hand briefly to acknowledge the audience's response. He placed his instrument on its rack and left for his break.

"Lucas, you got a minute?"

Lucas turned to the young black woman who handled reservations, seating, and customer complaints at the club. "Sure, what's up?"

"There's someone here who's asking about you."

He was instantly interested but maintained a cool demeanor. "Who is it?"

"He said you probably wouldn't know who he is, but I can get his name."

He'd already lost interest. "Do that. I'm going in the back to make a call."

Lucas headed to the quiet of the club's greenroom, a former office which had been converted into a place where performers could spend downtime. He took a folded sheet of paper from his wallet and read off the phone number. He punched it into his cell phone and waited for the ring. There was no answer, and when the voice-mail message began to play, he ended the call. There was no point in leaving a message, since his earlier ones had all gone unanswered. The only number he had for Rachel was her cell phone and her business line in New York. He'd been told that her personal number was unlisted at her request.

There was a soft knock on the door.

"Lucas, you in there?"

"Yeah, what is it?" He opened the door.

He found the female manager in the hall standing with a man.

"I know this is your break, but this is the man who wanted to have a word with you. Mr —"

The man stepped forward, holding out his hand. "Ross Givens."

Lucas took the hand and immediately looked for a family resemblance. Ross was a little stocky but was, of course, much taller than Rachel. "You're Rachel's older brother."

"Nice to meet you," Ross said. "Hope you don't mind me insisting on seeing you. My wife and I were in the audience."

"Thanks for coming," Lucas said, polite but curious. "Sit down."

"Thanks. I can't stay but a minute. My wife is waiting out front. We have kids at home."

"Right."

"First of all, I'm sorry to hear about your mother's death. I was the one who called to tell Rae after I saw the obit in a DC paper. I'm sure you know she lives in New York."

"I suppose that's where she is now?" he casually questioned.

Ross shrugged. "I'm not sure. She could be traveling. She does that a lot for her business."

"I know."

"She's very enterprising. Smart."

"Yes, I know that, too," Lucas confirmed quietly.

"Rachel told me about you being a sax player. She said you're very good."

"Did she?"

Ross nodded. "I don't know a lot about jazz, but my wife and I enjoyed the set."

Lucas checked the time. He had to return to the stage. The second set was going to start in fifteen minutes. "She's heard me perform a few times, but not in a club setting. I was hoping she'd come one night when there's a regular audience."

"You know, your mother really made a big impression on my sister. They were tight."

"So I've heard. It came as quite a shock when Rae found out I was Julia's son."

"It was, but I already knew," Ross said. "Look, I don't want to open up any—"

"It's okay. I've found all the skeletons in the closet. I can handle my mother's secrets and my family history."

"Your mother was having a bad day when I found out. I remember she was pretty hard on herself about you. So whatever the story is, I hope it had a good ending. I think she suffered a lot."

"Thanks for letting me know. Look, I've got to get ready," Lucas said, standing.

"Oh, right. Didn't mean to use up your entire break. Listen, one of the other reasons I wanted to see you is I have an offer and an invitation for you," Ross said.

"Really?" Lucas said, trying to keep his eagerness in check.

"I'm with the national office of the NAACP in DC. We'd like to ask if you and your group would perform at our annual gala next February."

"I'll certainly pass that along to the band members. We all bring in offers to play, so I'll have to see how that fits in with the calendar."

"Good enough. The other thing is, I know Rachel said you don't do much lawyering these days, but I checked out your record, and we could really use your experience on a couple of national issues. Any chance you'd consider being a paid consultant for us?"

"I'll at least listen to what you have to say."

"Great. That's a start," Ross said, standing as Lucas opened the door. He pulled a business-card case from the inside pocket of his suit. "Here's my card with my office, home, and cell numbers. Call me when you're ready and I'll set up the appointment."

Lucas accepted the card and read the information with interest. "You're an attorney also," he said with genuine surprise.

"Yep. My younger brother, Gordon, is in law school now. He said he's going to specialize in entertainment law. That's where the money is."

"Not a bad choice, but the serious money is in corporate law. Entertainment is more fun," Lucas said. "Tell him to have a backup plan." He held out his hand, and Ross shook it again. "Thanks for stopping in."

"So how do I reach you?" Ross asked.

Lucas obligingly wrote down his cell and home phone numbers, as well as the office number for the band's business agent. As he was about to hand the information over to Ross Givens, he had a thought.

"I'd appreciate it if you could pass this along to Rachel, in case she needs to reach me. I suppose you know we share equal ownership of my mother's house in Highland Beach."

Ross nodded. "I'd heard about that. Do you know why your mother made that arrangement?"

"It's starting to make some sense. Can I get Rachel's numbers from you? Just in case."

"Absolutely." Ross took out another of his business cards and wrote on the reverse side. "I take it you've been trying unsuccessfully to reach her?"

"That's right," Lucas confessed.

"Well, don't give up. If it's important, that is. Rae sometimes goes into hiding when she'd trying to work out a problem, or she'll bury herself in her work."

"Did she know you were coming to the show tonight?" Lucas asked.

"I did mention it and invited her to come along. She said she had things to do."

"Then she's probably traveling again. She said she had a lot of catching up to do."

"She said she had to drive back down to Highland Beach. There was something she'd left unfinished. She wanted to take care of it before it was too late."

Lucas kept his reaction to himself as he walked Ross out of the room. They said goodnight, and Ross assured him they'd be in touch.

"Keep trying to reach her. She'll surface eventually."

"There could be another explanation," Lucas said. "Maybe she's trying to make a point by staying invisible and not returning my calls."

"Even if she is, don't let her get away with it. You're a lawyer. Serve her with papers," Ross joked.

Lucas took Ross's suggestion to heart. But it wasn't Rachel that he needed to have a face-off with.

He realized that if he was to make sense of the past and learn to live with what it was and was not, then he needed to deal with more than Julia's story. He'd come to see that there was a lot a blame to go around in the forces that had shaped his life. He had a feeling that his mother was simply the red herring.

When he pulled into his grandparents' driveway, Lucas was very aware that on his last visit he was met with disturbing news. It had begun a two-month journey which, he now believed, rescued him from a life filled with anger and had put him on the path to healing. He stepped from the car carrying an overnight bag. And the pink box.

He wasn't surprised when neither Nick nor Kay met him at the door. He could have used his own key to enter, but he rang the bell and waited on the welcome mat, like a visiting guest. Kay answered. There was a smile on her face, and warm hugs and kisses that she'd never denied him. But Lucas saw immediately that her eyes were filled with a plaintive sadness and fear. When she spotted the pink box, she clasped her hands tightly together.

"Oh, Lucas," she murmured.

"Let's go inside, Gram," Lucas said.

Nick was standing just as anxiously in the foyer. One of the things that struck Lucas was how frail and vulnerable his grandparents looked. He put out his hand to his grandfather.

"How's it going, old man?"

Nick uttered something between a cough and a laugh, shaking his grandson's hand. "I've been better. I think age is finally catching up with both of us."

Kay took up position next to her husband, who put his arm around her narrow shoulders. Lucas noticed that they both stood, like a unified front, regarding him as if he were about to condemn them to death.

"Do you mind if I stay the night?" he asked.

Kay frowned. "What kind of question is that? Of course you can stay, Lucas. This is your home. You can come and go anytime."

"We weren't sure if you'd want to stay," Nick added tentatively.

Lucas placed his hand on the older man's shoulder. "No matter what happens, I know this will always be my home, okay?" He glanced at Kay. "Aren't you going to offer me something to eat?"

"We were just going to have some lunch. Now, put that

stuff down. Go wash your hands and come sit at the table."
She headed to the kitchen.

Lucas was left alone with Nick. He studied his grandfather's troubled face, with his pale and moistened gray
eyes. "I guess you both know why I called to say I wanted
to stop by."

Nick nodded, staring at the floor. "We've been waiting."

"I wasn't totally sure that I was going to do this, but I
have to. Does Gram understand that?"

"Oh, yes. We both do, Lucas," Nick said with a heavy sigh.
Then he reached out to grab his arm. "We want you to know
that—"

"We'll talk about it, Nick. Let's go have lunch. I have a lot
to tell you, too."

He did what he could, by his behavior and his voice, to assure his grandparents as they sat and eat lunch. Lucas talked
about his last several performances. He talked about Rachel
Givens and the arrangement by which they both shared the
house on Highland Beach. Nick and Kay had a lot of questions about Rachel and about what he proposed to do with the
house. But there was no mention of the pink box, the letters,
or Julia. Lucas tried to help his grandmother with the cleanup,
as he'd always done growing up. She shooed him away, telling
him she'd just be another minute.

Soon, there was no more reason to delay. They remained
seated at the dining table while he retrieved not only the pink
box, but also the two albums Rachel had found and given to
him from Julia's room. When he returned to the table, Kay
and Nick were holding hands. He hated seeing them so anxious, but he had to know. Otherwise Julia would remain a
ghost instead of a flesh-and-blood person who, even in her
absence and death, was an integral part of his life.

"You remember this, don't you?" he said to Kay. She
silently nodded. "There are more than one hundred letters and
cards in this box, all addressed to me. There are dozens of

photograghs." He opened one of the albums. "And all were removed from these. They were mailed to me from Julia all the years you were raising me. I need to know why you didn't think I should see them."

Kay looked at him, helpless. She tried to speak, but started sobbing instead, covering her face with a shaking hand. Nick immediately leaned to comfort her, trying to gather her into his arms. She clutched at his sweater sleeve, mumbling incoherently.

Lucas forced himself to stay seated. He forced himself not to let his desire to comfort his grandmother derail his efforts to get at the truth. His jaw flexed with his own tension. His eyes burned with sympathy. He caught his grandfather's gaze, which seemed to be begging him to stop. He looked at his grandmother's hunched body, remembering instead that his own mother had lived on the periphery of his life, and she'd never blamed anyone for that circumstance but herself.

"I'm sorry . . . Oh, Lucas, I'm sorry," Kay cried.

He knew this was going to be hard. He hadn't anticipated feeling like he was crushing his grandparents' hearts, and his own. But one thing Lucas had determined: he owed it to himself and Julia to find out what really happened.

"Just tell me why. I promise I'll try to understand."

It was still a few minutes before Kay could pull herself together, and only then because her husband gently withdrew his arms and quietly insisted that she speak.

"I . . . I thought that hearing from Julia when she'd been away from you for so many years would only confuse you."

"Didn't you think it was important that she at least made some attempt to get in touch, keep in touch with me? Didn't you think it was maybe her only way of letting me know that she did think of me, whatever her reasons were for walking out of my life?"

Kay's chin and lips trembled, but she kept her control. "I wanted you to be happy, Lucas. That was my only concern. I didn't think, nor did I care, what those letters meant to Julia. I was only afraid that they would upset you."

"How did you feel they would upset me?" Lucas persisted.

Nick stepped in. "Lucas, when we accepted the responsibility to raise you, we had to decide how to create a stable environment, one in which you felt safe and where you knew you belonged. If we'd allowed Julia to contact you whenever she felt like it, we thought it would be too confusing. You'd asked questions that frankly we weren't sure we could or should answer. Our whole objective was just to give you a loving home. Haven't we done that? Did you ever lack for anything that we couldn't provide, or your father couldn't provide?"

"Yes. My mother," Lucas said calmly.

When Kay began to cry again, he wasn't sure he should go on. Her heart was breaking, but his had already been broken.

"But we are your family," Nick said, his voice becoming as emotional as his wife's. "We were always there for you. And it was sometimes very hard. We *never* let the difficulties sway us from loving you."

"You mean, because I was half black."

"I don't think I have to persuade you that that was not an issue for your grandmother and me," Nick said, defensively.

"Of course I know that," Lucas said gently.

"What was I supposed to do?" Kay asked in a wobbly voice.

"Like you said, you did what you thought was best," Lucas said. "But I can't help but wonder how things might have been different had I been given the chance to read those letters, and see the photographs of me with my parents. We were a family."

"But she left you!" Kay said angrily. "If you're going to be mad with anyone, be angry with Julia."

"Why did she leave?"

Kay gasped. She glanced pleadingly at Nick. Now that it had begun, it would all have to come out in the open.

"To pursue her career," Nick said simply.

"She was so determined to become a star," Kay added.

"Are you saying that her career was more important than her family?"

Neither Nick nor Kay responded, holding on to each other for support. Lucas finally realized what they were waiting for. He reached across the table and took his grandmother's hand. She clutched it and lifted mournful eyes to him.

"Gram, don't you know how much I love you? I know that whatever happened, that you and Nick did what you believed in your hearts was for my own good. How could I fault you for loving me that much?"

Kay succumbed again. Lucas held on to her hand, but again it was Nick who comforted her.

"Your mother was a very talented singer, and a pretty good actress. Your father first met her at a little club performance somewhere down in the Village in New York. He was struggling with his first restaurant at the time, and he wasn't involved with anyone. He said he loved her almost at first sight. We weren't really happy about the match," Nick confessed. "It had nothing to do with Julia personally. She was a lovely girl. But interracial relationships were still not common, and we thought they'd have big problems."

It was the first time Lucas had ever heard that from his grandparents. Certainly his father had never suggested that there had been problems early on. "Did they?"

"No," Nick said, still astonished himself. "They loved each other and seemed to do fine. Julia continued getting work as a singer and actress, and Brad's restaurant began getting good notices and a following. They were living in a terrible apartment in the Village, but they didn't seem to care. It looked for a time like the gods were on their side and they were going to have a wonderful life together. Kay and I were relieved . . . and we liked Julia."

Kay accepted her husband's handkerchief and dried her tears. "Brad and Julia were married about two years when she got pregnant. She continued to perform almost until you were born. They were both so happy with you. You were a beautiful baby."

"So far, it sounds like a nice love story," Lucas murmured.

"I think it was," Nick agreed.

"When did it fall apart?"

"When you were about two, almost three," Kay recalled. "Brad was spending a lot of time at the restaurant. It was successful, but a lot of work and long hours. Julia wasn't being asked to sing as often because she was being a mother to you."

"But we knew she was restless," Nick added. "She was anxious to get back to performing. Finally she got a month-long engagement at a club in midtown Manhattan. She opened for another group but quickly became popular. That's when we began baby-sitting you on a regular basis. You stayed with your grandmother and me on the weekends, and went back home on Sunday afternoon.

"Then Julia got a really big break. She was asked to be in the Broadway production of *Timbuktu*. She was part of the cast for almost the entire run. That led to another play, and an invitation to Paris. That's when things began to change."

"Brad wanted her to cut back a little," Kay said. "He wanted her home more, and he felt she was away from you too often. But he didn't insist. He left the choice up to her, hoping that her family would be more important."

"But he probably knew he couldn't force her to give up her dream," Lucas guessed.

"Exactly," Nick nodded.

"So your grandfather and I made her an offer. We said we'd bring you to live with us temporarily. At least she and Brad knew you were in a safe place and would be taken care of," Kay said.

"Okay. That sounds like a good compromise," Lucas began. "So what happened?"

Kay sighed, shaking her head. "We meant well, but everything got out of hand. When Julia accepted the invitation to perform with a troupe in Paris, she was away almost a year. She'd come back to the States whenever she could, but it was expensive, and she was afraid she'd be cut from the show."

"And what was I doing all this time? What about Dad?"

"Well, your father wasn't very happy about it, but he was glad that Julia was getting some attention and the chance to fulfill her dream. He figured that after a year or so they could work out a better arrangement. She'd find something in New York again, and you would come back home."

"What began to happen was, whenever you visited when she was back, you wanted to come back to us. By the time Julia was prepared to return to the States, you didn't want to go with her," Nick told him.

Lucas' gaze went back and forth between them. Kay was holding tightly to her control, tears threatening to fall again at any minute.

"Why?"

"She was away so often, Lucas, that after a while you lost the connection. You were almost six. You didn't remember who she was," Kay said sorrowfully.

"Kids get separated from their parents all the time. They get back together and start over again," Lucas said.

"Julia decided to keep working. I think she thought there would be time to make it up to you, to become part of your life again."

"What about her and my father?"

"Brad finally asked for a divorce," Kay told him. "He didn't want to continue to live the way they had—apart. He wanted a wife and family, and Julia wasn't ready to give up her fledgling career to do that. There was no animosity. They just let one another go."

"And me?"

"You stayed with us. After a while, there didn't seem to be any question about you returning to Julia. Brad was here and involved in your life. To a great extent, your mother wasn't."

Lucas rested his elbows on the table. Clasping his hands together, he rested his chin against them trying to absorb and process the details of his family history. It wasn't at all what he'd expected. But the revelations didn't make him feel any better. He was still restless with a sense that something was missing.

"Did I ever express the desire to return to my mother?"

Kay shook her head. "You never asked about her. I assumed you eventually forgot all about Julia. Now that I think about it, maybe you just didn't know what to ask."

"Make no mistake about it, Julia would try to regain custody of you now and then, Lucas. But she was caught between wanting to take you and make a home for you, and trying to keep her career alive. It was her decision, but we knew it was hard for her," Nick said.

"Well, it was not completely her decision," Kay murmured. "At one point I told her she'd have to stop getting in touch. I told her it was only making you unhappy."

"You forced her even more to make a decision against taking responsibility for me?" Lucas asked for clarification.

"You were happy with us," Kay defended. "You never asked about her, never indicated you wanted to see her or go to her."

"She agreed?" Lucas asked.

His grandfather nodded. "Yes, she agreed. She felt that that was probably best for everyone, especially you. She could see you were doing well living with us. Your life was stable, you had friends, you were doing well in school—"

"And I never asked about her," Lucas finished. "But then she wrote those letters and sent the photographs."

"We knew she wanted to make sure you didn't forget who she was. But your grandmother saw no point in that. She kept the letters and photographs from you."

"Why didn't you just throw them out? If I'd never known about them, I could have just written Julia off."

"I don't know, but when she died, I didn't want her going to her grave with you believing she didn't care," Kay said, quietly crying once more. "I didn't want that on my conscience for the rest of my life. You needed to know because . . . because I needed you to forgive me for what I did."

Lucas finally got out of his chair and reached for his grandmother. He knelt next to her chair and pulled her into his arms. She held on to him with a stranglehold filled with her love for him. He comforted her as best he could, feeling drained and sad, with forgiveness.

Lucas entered the house, which was quiet and still. He'd held out hope that Rachel might be inside waiting, even though there was no car parked in the driveway and little evidence that she was around. The outdoor lights were on, as well as ones in the kitchen and living room. But those were set on timers so the house didn't appear deserted.

He was disappointed. He went upstairs to check things out. He found all the rooms neat and empty. He found no notes, phone messages, or clues. He was disappointed a second time. Frustrated, Lucas wondered if he'd perhaps misunderstood Ross Givens when he'd not-so-casually mentioned that Rachel was coming down to the house. He should have asked more questions. He'd acted impulsively, overanxious to make amends.

He brought his things into the house and took them up to his room. As was his habit, he walked to the end of the hall and switched on the light in what had been Rachel's room. All her things were back in place. That had to mean that she intended to return at some point. The question was, when?

Lucas slowly returned to the first floor, not sure what he was going to do with himself for the rest of the night. He went to see what was in the kitchen to eat. He was surprised to find fresh food in the refrigerator. There was even ice cream in the freezer. He returned to the living room to turn on the CD player. He spotted the white envelope on the coffee table and snatched it up. It had his name on the outside. When he opened it, there was yet another envelope inside. Attached to the envelope was a note. Recognizing Rachel's handwriting, he read it, expecting the worst.

"Lucas, this is for you from Julia. I found it in the box she left me, asking that I make sure you get it. So here it is. I haven't read it, but I hope you will. This could be her last letter to you. I hope you find what you are looking for. If you do, you'll know where to find me."

Lucas had to read the note twice and he still wasn't sure he understood Rachel's cryptic message. The most important thing, in any case was that she had been there, she was waiting, and she was offering him a last chance.

Fourteen

My Dearest Son:

I have always longed to call you that in person. I have lived for many years hoping for the chance, but it's too late. I am out of time. Where do I begin to set straight a lifetime of mistakes and wishing for a second chance? I will start by simply saying I'm sorry. It is not adequate, not repentant enough, but I've said it a thousand times every day since we've been apart. I'm sorry I have shared so little of my life with you. I'm sorry that I didn't perform as a mother, think as a mother, or make decisions with your best interests instead of my own, like a mother. I am selfish and a coward. I'd rather have you remember me, if you do at all, the way I was when I was whole. Photographs are all I have to give you since you were denied the real thing. I have sent you hundreds to choose from. Have you seen them all?

Lucas, you were a beautiful baby when I was still your mother. We were still a family, and I had not bartered away your life. I did not mean it to be forever. I only wanted time to follow a dream which, as it turns out, burned short and glorious, leaving me with only a few memories. I gave up so much for so little. I failed. You had a family anyway who, with the best of intentions, raised you with the love they did not believe I could ever provide. Your grandparents are wonderful people. I believe with all my heart that they always thought of you first ahead of all else, including me or your father. You were lucky to have them.

Life is a tricky parlor game, and filled with terrible rules and choices. The ones I made turned out to be permanent, but I did not act alone. I did not give you away, Lucas. I loaned you. I was willing to share you. I wanted you to have as much love as people were willing to give. I did not mean for it to exclude my own. The rules of the game were switched when my back was turned. Now that you are grown, you will probably already have learned how this can be. Things are not always fair. People make up their own rules as they go along. The strongest survive. The weak live to regret, over and over. Please forgive me.

This is the last letter I will write to you. I can't remember what I've already told you in all the letters I've sent over the years. What is still left to be said? Have I told you that I love you? Do you know that you're the greatest achievement of my life? Will you believe me? I want a second chance. I want your forgiveness more than anything, even though I have not earned it. My heart has already been broken. Please forgive me.

Dearest, dearest, I have lived ashamed for so long for my part in denying you, but I will leave soon so very proud of you and the wonderful man you've grown into. Nick and Kay and your father are responsible for that. I can make no claim. You have grown to be the kind of person I would want you to be had I been there to guide you. I do take credit for that. You are my son, after all. You will always be my son. Even after I am gone I will not be dismissed from your life. Please remember me. Find a way not to forget me.

I must tell you about Rachel. I call her Honey Child, in the same way I call you My Dearest, son. Rachel saved my life, although she has no awareness of that. She was sent for me to meet one summer, and from Rachel I was able to learn how to be kind and loving and patient; how to laugh and how to get going every day. I borrowed Rachel from her family every summer she came to Highland Beach. In another moment of weakness and with another selfish choice, she too was taken away from me. I only have one more chance to make amends.

If my will has been executed as I instructed, you have both come together at the house in Highland Beach. If you are the people I know you both to be, you will each find what you are looking for and meant to have in each other. I have only provided the setting. The rest is up to you, Lucas, and up to Rachel. With almost my last breath I believe this is as it should be. I have taken a lot from both of you. Now, I can give it all back.

I cannot take the chance that you may never see this letter, so I am leaving it for Rachel to find. I know that she will make sure you get it. I pray that you will read it. I pray for you to forgive me. I hope you will do both. It has always been up to you.

With all my heart always,
Your mother, Julia

Fifteen

"Why Rachel, these are beautiful. Did you really make them yourself?"

"Yes, I did. My next plan is to see if it'll be profitable for me to have my own store."

"My goodness," Harrietta gushed, adjusting her glasses and bending over the tray of samples that Rachel had placed on her lap. "You're a real CEO. I'm so impressed. Are you sure I can have these?"

"Yes, please."

"I'm going to wear them to church on Sunday. I know Flo is going to ask me where I got them from. I don't know if I want to tell her. That woman always has to make sure she has the same things I have. And she's such a gossip."

"Maybe she admires that you have such good taste, Harrietta."

"You know, you're absolutely right. That's probably exactly what it is."

The doorbell rang loudly, the sound adjusted for Harrietta's poor hearing. Startled, Rachel dropped the earrings she was about to place into Harrietta's hand.

"Was that the door?" Harrietta asked, glancing up.

"Would you like me to answer?" Rachel offered.

"No, let my grandson get it."

Rachel remained seated and tried to compose herself into a study of calm and nonchalance. She had already rearranged the tray of jewelry twice after having removed several pieces. She began needlessly shifting them around again. Her fingers seemed clumsy and uncoordinated. She heard a familiar male voice, and nearly upset the entire tray.

"Let me move this to the table," Rachel said. She lifted the black felt-lined flat and got up.

"Nana, there's someone here to see you," the grandson announced. "Lucas Scott." He gestured for Lucas to enter the parlor, and disappeared.

"Mrs. Cousins, I'm sorry to bother you this late."

Harrietta tittered when Lucas bent down to take her hand and give it a warm squeeze. "It's so nice to see you, Lucas. Sit down, please. When did you arrive?"

As yet unnoticed, Rachel watched as Lucas did as he was told, but saw he sat forward on the edge of his chair, as if he didn't intend to stay long. She studied him for any giveaway signs as to what he might be thinking. She couldn't tell anything by either his voice or expression. Was it possible he hadn't noticed her yet? Was it a deliberate oversight? Was he trying to torture her?

"Not too long ago. It was a last-minute decision to drive down."

"You know I'm always glad to see you. I was just asking Rachel about you earlier. She said you had to return to DC to take care of some kind of business deal. If I'd known you were coming, you could have joined us for dinner."

Finally, Lucas looked at Rachel, which promptly caused a spasm in her stomach.

"Hello, Lucas. Welcome back."

"Rachel."

"Will you be staying long?"

"It depends," he said smoothly.

Rachel met his gaze head-on, trying not to give any indication that she was nervous, trying not to tip her hand and let him see what she was really thinking.

She said nothing, as well. The fact that he had shown up was not proof positive that he was going to follow the script to its logical end. Lucas pointed to her display box.

"Miss Harrietta, is Rachel hustling you with her wares?"

Harrietta got a huge laugh out of that, but Rachel suspected it had more to do with the fact that Lucas was being attentive and charming by teasing her. Rachel had to give him points for that. There had never been any question that he was capable of seduction, regardless of age, race, or country of origin.

"No, not at all. Rachel offered to show me her things after I mentioned seeing this article in one of my granddaughter's magazines. Why, our Rachel is almost famous. Did you know that?"

Lucas slowly turned his attention again to her, and Rachel mustered enough poise to smile serenely. "I know that and much more," he murmured.

Rachel inclined her head. "Thank you. I hope it's all complimentary."

"It is," Lucas said.

He said the words with such intensity that it finally dawned on Rachel that he was waiting for her. "You know, it's probably close to your bedtime, Harritta. I think I'm going to say goodnight and head back to the house," Rachel said, standing and assembling her sample case, reattaching the removable lid and closing it.

"Lucas arrived just in time to escort you back," Harrietta said.

"Yes, he did."

Without asking, Lucas stood again and took the case from her hands. Then he spoke directly to Harrietta. "Miss Harrietta, would you do me the honor of being my guest at dinner some evening? Perhaps after Labor Day, when the vacation crowd has thinned out from Annapolis."

Harrietta made her habitual O and then melted right before

Rachel's eyes at the invitation. "Young man, are you asking me on a date?"

Lucas, surprised by the retort, burst out laughing. Rachel, hearing the rich deep sound that again evoked his mother's laugh, began to relax.

"Yes, I am. But I have to warn you I have an ulterior motive. I wonder if you would be willing to talk to me about my mother."

"Yes, I understand, I understand," Harrietta nodded sagely. "Are you planning on being around a few days?"

Rachel merely raised her eyebrows when he looked at her.

"Yes, I do."

"Why don't you come over in the morning? You and I can get started. Now I have a stipulation of my own. When we go to dinner, I'd like Rachel to join us."

Rachel hid a smile at the adroit manipulation. She had to remember to throw in a necklace and a box of candy for Harrietta.

"Fine with me. I may be tied up in the morning. Could I stop over around noon?" Lucas asked.

"One-thirty, after my nap. I don't want to fall asleep during our conversation."

Saying goodnight seemed to take forever, at least as far as Rachel was concerned. But Lucas was nothing if not patient and accommodating with Harrietta, and Rachel gladly waited until all the pleasantries and departing rituals were done. Harrietta herself walked them to her door, peering out as they stepped out into the night.

"I'm so glad you both are here on the beach. Your mother was a smart woman, Lucas. Don't you agree?"

She closed the door.

Rachel looked at Lucas to see if his reaction was the same as hers. She had this dawning suspicion that they'd both been royally played. First by one woman, who only feigned fragility when it suited her, and by another who was deceased.

But there was another look she was really searching for. When he took her hand and held it tightly, she fell into step next to him as they headed together back to the house.

Rachel was glad that they didn't say anything right away. *It's nice to walk like this, like lovers,* she thought. It felt companionable and right. The silence wrapped around them, protective and very still.

"I didn't see your car when I got here," Lucas said to her.

"I pulled it into the garage. I didn't want you to know right away that I was here."

She felt a certain tension start to rise, however, once they reached the house. The minute she and Lucas were inside with the door closed they turned to face one another. He put the case down and then slowly bent to kiss her. They didn't touch except for their mouths. She was glad that the kiss was not blatant or complex, but gentle and sweet. Only after that introduction did she open her arms and invite Lucas to her. Like the kiss, it was an embrace of warmth and solemnity.

They moved to let their bodies settle together at the chest, groin, and thigh. His cheek rubbed against hers.

"I found the letter," Lucas whispered.

"Was it hard?"

"Not as much as I thought. I read it over and over. Right now, I don't want to talk about it. I just want to take you to bed and make love. I want you close enough that I'll believe we're really here together and I haven't almost thrown everything away."

His confession released a rush of heat in her. It softened her tension and made her more aware of those touch points: chest, groin, and thigh.

"Where?" she asked.

"My room. And then yours. Then the sofa . . ." She laughed. "Maybe the floor in the solarium. The beach if it wasn't so damp . . ."

She put her hand lightly over his mouth to stop the rush of outrageous suggestions. "You'll never last."

"Don't you want me to try?" he asked, kissing her hand.

Rachel took the lead up the stairs into his room. There things got serious, fast. Lucas maneuvered her to the bed. With his arms wound around her and her arms about his neck he lowered them to the mattress with a force that made them bounce. They began kissing again but this time there wasn't time nor need for niceties. Rachel felt an urgent need as she undulated beneath him. Lucas felt it too, and he tried to remove only as much clothing as they needed to make skin-to-skin contact.

She shimmied and he wiggled and with his helping hands they struggled their way out of shorts and jeans and underwear. Lucas worked a hand under her top and found her breasts conveniently bare. He massaged them slowly, playing with the nipples to her satisfaction, as was evident by the quiet little moans and hissing intake of breaths. The union was accomplished with efficiency and a respect for time. They did not rush.

Then they took off the rest of their clothing and did it again.

She was the first to awaken the next morning, a little before dawn, to find herself using his arm for a pillow and pressed into his side. She lay for a long time, watching the rise and fall of his chest as he slept. Light began to slowly fill the room when she eased herself from the bed. She found Lucas's henley shirt on the floor. She put it on, and the hem fell to her thighs. Feeling sufficiently covered, Rachel quietly left the room.

In the kitchen, Rachel started the coffeemaker up. She turned on the living-room radio for low background music broken by occasional local news and weather reports. Birds were already chirping and flying off on reconnaissance missions. She opened the back door to a vision of the sun, its bottom rim just pulling above the horizon. A Coast Guard cutter ran silently and smoothly on the Chesapeake. All was right in her world. Rachel closed her eyes and inhaled deeply.

"Thank you, Julia," she whispered.

Lucas quietly joined her twenty minutes later when the morning was in full swing and Rachel could see someone jogging along the beach. He came to join her as she sat on those back steps, squeezing in next to her. He hooked an arm around her neck, pulling her to him and nuzzling near her ear.

"You're naked," she said, incredulous.

"Is that a complaint?"

"Do you want to be arrested for public exposure?

He chuckled. "Good morning."

She responded by relaxing against his chest. She was feeling wicked and carefree, but she loved this playfulness between them.

"Can I say it, now?" she asked.

"Go ahead."

"I told you so."

"I know."

"Having gotten that off my chest, I do know why you had to go, Lucas. Next time, you should be sure of your priorities."

"Yes, ma'am," he growled in amusement, kissing her shoulder. "I almost blew it, didn't I?"

"I don't see it that way. We're here, aren't we? Maybe it was our first real test to see how much we trusted each other and what we're starting to feel."

"I've set some limits for Jen. I hope she's smart enough and values our friendship enough to back off and take a break. I told her she needs to get her own life. She can't live anymore through me."

"You think she heard you?"

"I don't know. We'll see." He rested back against the side of the house.

"We have our own problems," she reminded him quietly.

"Those aren't problems, Rae. I think it's called a relationship. We'll work them out."

"I guess that means that you want to go ahead, see what we have between us?"

"Don't you?"

"Yes. That's what I want. I'm sure that's what Julia intended, don't you think?"

"Yes, but . . . I'm not sure if I understand how she knew that."

Rachel chortled. "Haven't you learned anything this week? Woman's intuition. Better, it was probably mother's intuition."

"Sorry. That doesn't work for me."

She craned her neck to frown at him. "Don't question it. Let's just roll with it for a while."

"Rae? I want to forgive my mother."

"You're getting there."

"From what I read in her letter it wasn't easy on her, either. There was plenty of blame to go around, and no one to blame. I think she got a raw deal. I think my grandparents know that."

"You're not going to be angry with them, are you?"

"What if I am?"

"Just remember that they loved you and raised you and you turned out to be a pretty decent human being. Okay, so now we come to the house."

"What about the house?" he asked.

"I want it."

"So do I."

"I was here first."

"Julia is my mother."

"I could see myself living here year round."

Lucas was slower to answer. "Okay. I think I could do that."

"There's a lot of work to be done on the house."

"We'll do what we can ourselves and contract out for the

rest. We'll share expenses. We can set up an escrow account of some kind, deposit equally into it."

"I'll talk to my lawyer," Rachel smiled at him.

"Yeah, I think I know a good one, too."

"What else?"

"My mother's old bedroom is bigger than either of the other two. I think it makes sense to move in there."

"Together?"

"If that's okay with you."

"Just checking. I'll need a studio space."

"How about one of the other rooms?"

"No. We'll need those for guest rooms. And maybe later on . . ."

"Right, right. Third floor, then."

"I forgot all about that space. I never went back up there."

"I did," he said.

"Really? What's in the corner?"

"Old toys. A tricycle, plastic dump trucks, a kid's rocking chair—"

"Your mother kept your things?"

"Dad said she had them in storage for years. That's something, don't you think?"

"I'm so glad. Don't you throw them out. They can be used later."

"That's what I thought."

"Do you think we're falling in love?" she asked quietly.

"Feels like it."

"Do you think that's what Julia wanted all along?"

"Well, she seems to have believed that we would be a good match."

"Yeah, but what do you think?"

"I'm hungry."

"Lucas . . ."

He laughed. "I didn't know we were going to have a major referendum this early in the morning."

"Answer the question."

"My mother didn't give birth to any fool. Who am I to question her?"

"Lucas . . ."

"I think so. I know that when I got to DC the other night I was sure I'd made the wrong decision and I'd lost you."

"Good. I hope you were miserable."

"I can make it up to you."

"How?"

"Let's go inside."

He discreetly and gracefully got up, butt naked, and retreated into the house. Rachel followed.

"You want breakfast?"

"I want you."

He pulled her into his arms and began to kiss her. Just the way she liked, where the gentle manipulation of his lips against hers stoked fires within. He relieved her of his shirt and tossed it aside, making Rachel giggle at the careless gesture.

"Here?" she asked, backing toward the sofa.

"I hate that sofa," he groused. "Upstairs. Last one there is a rotten egg."

"No way are you getting even," Rachel said, sprinting off to the staircase.

Lucas smiled and took his time following. Rotten egg or not, he'd already won.

Dear Reader,

My idea of adventure is to do something I've never done before, especially if it's scary. But there was nothing but warmth and friendliness when I visited Highland Beach, Maryland, while writing *Southern Comfort*. The residents of the community were entertaining and generous in sharing wonderful memories of summer vacations spent at the beach. Like my herione, Rachel Givens, I can imagine myself owning a home there.

I hope that *Southern Comfort* inspires all of you to be explorers. Seek out adventure and romance in your lives every day.

Enjoy!

Sandra Kitt

Note: In conjunction with the release of *Southern Comfort*, I am sponsoring a reader contest. It will run from July 15 until Labor Day, September 6, 2004. Answer all ten questions posted on my Web site based on my novel, and you could win a lovely handcrafted necklace from Italy! For details, visit www.sandrakitt.com.

Sandra Kitt, one of the foremost African American writers of romance fiction, was the first black writer to ever publish with Harlequin. In 1994 she launched the successful Arabesque line with *SERENADE*. She received a Waldenbooks Award for the second Arabesque novel, *SINCERELY*, in 1996. Twice nominated for the Best Contemporary Novel of the Year from *Romantic Times*, Sandra is the recipient of its Romance Writer of America.

A native of New York, Sandra holds bachelors and masters degrees in fine arts and has studied and lived in Mexico. A onetime graphic designer and freelance illustrator, she has exhibited across the U.S. and is in several corporate art collections, as well as the Muesum of African Amerian Art in L.A. She has designed cards for UNICEF and illustrated two books for the late science writer Dr. Isaac Asimov. Sandra has lectured at NYU, Penn State, Sarah Lawrence, and Columbia and teaches courses on publishing and fiction writing. She has appeared on NBC's *Today,* Black Entertainment Television, and *Good Morning, America*. E-mail her at: *sandikitt@hotmail.com* or *author@sandrakitt.com*.